After the Dragon Raid

Vanessa Ricci-Thode

IGUANA

Copyright © 2014 Vanessa Ricci-Thode

Published by Iguana Books

720 Bathurst Street, Suite 303

Toronto, Ontario, Canada

M5V 2R4

All rights reserved. No part of this publication may be reproduced, stored in a retrieval system or transmitted, in any form or by any means, electronic, mechanical, recording or otherwise (except brief passages for purposes of review) without the prior permission of the author or a licence from The Canadian Copyright Licensing Agency (Access Copyright). For an Access Copyright licence, visit www.accesscopyright.ca or call toll free to 1-800-893-5777.

Publisher: Greg Ioannou
Editor: Kathryn Willms
Front cover image: courtesy of Shutterstock.com
Front cover design: Kate Unrau
Book layout design: Kathryn Willms

Library and Archives Canada Cataloguing in Publication

Ricci-Thode, Vanessa, 1981-, author
    After the dragon raid / Vanessa Ricci-Thode.

Issued in print and electronic formats.
ISBN 978-1-77180-082-2 (pbk.).--ISBN 978-1-77180-084-6 (epub).--ISBN 978-1-77180-085-3 (kindle).

    I. Title.

| PS8635.I229A47 2014 | C813'.6 | C2014-906480-2 |
| | | C2014-906481-0 |

This is an original print edition of *After the Dragon Raid*.

To my husband,

Mike,

for sticking with me through the worst of it

and making me laugh.

CHAPTER 1

Tassia stood to the right of and slightly behind the commander and his top men, peeking around them to get a better idea of what they faced. They had marched to the head of a crumbling staircase, and from behind her friend Butch's wide frame, she could see down to where the staircase ended at a tunnel jutting from the hillside. Rows of grim, grey-faced Doomsayers stood shoulder to shoulder in the tunnel's mouth, stretching back into the gloom.

Tassia looked across the line at her fellow soldiers. They were tall and broad-shouldered, while she barely came up to the commander's chest, which was why she was always relegated to the second line — at least at the start. In their dark brown leathers and shining armour, the soldiers stood patiently, swords drawn. The gold and blue banners of the Wheat Sky empire rippled gently in the breeze while the commander dutifully shouted terms to their enemies, giving them the opportunity to surrender. Everyone knew they wouldn't — their mad leader, Hetia, had absolute control over them — but the commander was required by the queen to offer the option. Once the killing started, some would surrender, but not many and not now. As the commander finished and silence fell, Tassia took a fighting stance, holding her sword with both hands, every muscle taut in anticipation. She took slow, controlled breaths.

Finally, on command, the top men charged down the stairs toward the Doomsayers who had braced themselves, readying to defend their compound. Tassia was right behind the first line, already slightly ahead of the rest of her line, moving her blade with the efficiency of years of training, injuring her foes just as much as she needed to continue a swift advance. As cracks began to appear in the wall of Doomsayers, Tassia plunged forward, passing between Butch and Max and slipping through enemy ranks and into the tunnel. The sound of metal clashing filled the air, and already the floor of the cave was slick with blood. In this wide entry of the tunnel, the fiercest fighting would occur. But the Doomsayers' clubs and inferior swords were no match for the queen's army. The enemy didn't even have proper armour, just boards and metal garbage strategically strapped to their bodies.

The commander shouted at Tassia to hold rank. She didn't know why he bothered. She always got ahead because, despite what he thought, her small stature was an advantage. She slipped past her enemies, the thin but strong blade of her sword nothing but a steely blur, and penetrated deep into their ranks, killing anyone she encountered. She was not too short to slit throats and pierce hearts, and often remained at the periphery, unnoticed until it was too late. The commander's voice faded into the background as she surged forward.

After her last reprimand for breaking rank in battle, she had taken her case directly to the queen, but that hadn't turned out as she had hoped. Queen Nalea had trained with Tassia before the revolution — the pair had been friends since — and she had acknowledged Tassia's talents, but was quick to point out that she had chosen her commanders for a reason and they must be obeyed. Tassia pushed that from her mind. She was confident that her skills were too valuable to be released from the army for breaking rank. Reprimands had always been little more than formalities, like offering an enemy the chance to surrender.

Earlier that morning, in the pre-dawn light, the commander had laid bare the situation. The colony had become a threat to the queen and all of her subjects. The orders had been simple: kill anyone who didn't surrender. Most would rather die than surrender. But once the army had cleared the tunnel and entered the labyrinth of the underground compound, their enemies would be less eager to fight to the death. This would make the work go quickly, but Tassia hadn't enlisted for an easy job. She was disappointed when her rank finally caught up to her — it meant this part of the fight was almost over and the slaughter would begin. In the heart of the compound, battle would intensify again to protect the mistress, but she was surrounded by enchanters and that was no place for a soldier. The queen's enchanters would have to clear through the spells of their enemies. As the mistress was an enchantress herself, it was unlikely any regular soldiers would see the inside of her chambers.

The commander scowled at Tassia as he went by, but she met his gaze calmly, refusing to feel ashamed for doing what she felt was right.

"He's going to skewer you one of these days."

Tassia turned to find her friend Livia beside her. She barely reached the woman's broad shoulders. Livia was heavily muscled, but femininely so, and her glacial blue eyes now twinkled with mischief.

"If that were true, he would have by now," Tassia replied with a shrug.

"Your skills won't last forever."

"And when the day comes that my confidence falters, then I'll hold rank. Or maybe quit altogether and become a strategist."

Livia shook her head, her braided red hair swinging between her shoulder blades. "Or you'll just end up dead."

"That's just something I'll have to deal with." Tassia smiled wryly and turned her attention back to the battle. The sooner they were done and out of here, the better. It was a dark place, despite the regularly spaced lamps, and the musty air was cold, seeping through Tassia's armour to elicit a prickling wave of goosebumps down her arms.

The deeper into the compound they fought, the more scattered they became, and the lines divided and divided again until finally, not far from the mistress's chambers, Tassia and Livia found themselves alone. Livia kicked in a door off the long stone hallway they'd fought their way down, and Tassia charged into a large common room, rounded like the rest and made of the same drab grey-white stone. She heard the crackling energy of a spell before she saw the enchantress. She ducked the spell and flicked out the thin blade of her sword, slashing the woman's throat. The enchantress appeared to be the only defence for the handful of Doomsayers left in the room. Tassia tried to take proper count, but the room, like most of the cavernous compound, was lit by dim, grimy lanterns hung on the walls, casting long, deep shadows. She was also confounded by a large window that looked out into the underground blackness.

"Tassia?"

"I've got it," Tassia replied, gaining confidence in the enemy's numbers as they moved toward her.

Livia disappeared back into the hall to continue further into enemy territory.

Tassia assessed her situation. Of the six Doomsayers in the room, only three were closing in on her. She rushed forward, driving her sword through the heart of the first. As she tried to get a good line at the neck or chest of the man she was battling, another circled behind her, clubbing her on the back. The attack had little effect against her thick armour, but drove her forward, giving her a clear line at her enemy, and she slashed his throat. She spun to the right, swinging her sword as she went. In her peripheral vision, she noted that the man with the club was too tall for her to get a clean slash at his throat, so she readjusted her stance mid-spin and thrust forward, piercing his heart before he had the chance to attack her again.

Then she felt the agonizing sting of a spell. Screaming through gritted teeth, she fell forward, but managed to roll, landing on her back to get a clear view of who had attacked her. The enchantress whose throat she had cut was still alive, crouched back on a rickety barnboard bench against the far wall, sputtering blood and clutching at her throat with one hand while she flung attack spells at Tassia with the other. The pain of the first spell had already begun to recede, and Tassia rolled left just in time to avoid the next attack. She sprung to her feet, roaring as she lunged forward for the kill. This time, she took the enchantress's head clean off her shoulders.

The last three Doomsayers in the room cried out in terror as the head splattered onto the gritty stone floor. Tassia turned to face them and caught one of them trying to rush her. It was a woman, even smaller than Tassia, and she hadn't any weapons or armour at all. None of them had armour deeper in the compound. Tassia drove the blade down and through her heart, leaving only a man and woman left in the room. The man was crouched in a corner, partially hidden behind a shoddy wooden chair. The woman, tall and lean, stood defiantly before Tassia.

"What will it be?" Tassia called to her.

She paused, lips pursed and eyes ablaze. She wanted to fight, Tassia could see it.

"Heart," the woman said at last, the fire going out of her eyes.

Tassia approached her carefully and rested the tip of her blade against the woman's breast.

"You're sure?" Tassia asked.

"Just make it clean. Quick."

Tassia nodded and took a good stance, holding the hilt firmly to be sure to give her enemy the quick death she asked for. She plunged hard, driving the blade deep, and she admired that the woman didn't make a sound — simply crumpled straight down, almost dragging Tassia with her. She yanked the blade out and turned to the man in the corner.

"How do you want it?" she asked, getting tired of this already.

"What? Want what?"

He looked confused and terrified as he cautiously stood and stepped around the rickety furniture to approach her. He was on the tall side of average height, broad yet lean, with short, dark hair that offered a hint of curl. Tassia quickly noted he was not nearly as pale as the others, meaning he hadn't been with them long. His eyes were grey storm clouds as his nervous gaze darted around the room, searching out more danger. He'd spoken in the common tongue with an accent she couldn't place, so he must be a foreigner. It was clear he wasn't ready for battle and didn't know the customs.

"Look, slashing your throat would be easiest for me," Tassia explained. "Your comrade there chose the heart. It's a harder blow, but ensures you lose consciousness quickly and has none of the distressing pain and coldness of bleeding to death. I can take off your head if that will suit you. I think that's the quickest, though few people have the stomach for it."

"You're giving me a choice?" He was incredulous.

"Why wouldn't I?"

"You didn't give them a choice," he protested, nodding toward his fallen comrades.

"There's always a choice," she insisted, standing more at ease but keeping her sword ready. "They had the choice to surrender and not attack me. Attack means death in whatever manner I can manage. You wish to surrender?"

He hesitated, glancing at the dead woman at his feet as Tassia's words sank in.

"I don't want to die," he said at last.

"Then you have to surrender."

"What will that mean?"

"Depends on your crimes," she said with a shrug. "The queen may have you put to death anyway. The lightest punishment for prisoners is slavery — the length and severity of which also depends on your crimes."

"I'm merely trying to survive." He was growing defiant. "What does your queen consider a crime?"

"You've obviously lived in these lands long enough to make an informed decision about joining this clan, so I'm sure you have a good enough idea of what our queen deems appropriate." Tassia glanced around nervously, searching the doorway and dim hallway beyond. She couldn't just kill the man and move on because he wasn't attacking her, but his refusal to decide his fate was frustrating — and dangerous.

"Look, why don't you just follow—" she began, turning to face him again. He had moved closer to her, and his expression had softened, startling her into silence.

"You're really waiting for an answer from me, aren't you?"

"It's your right," she replied, surprised he would expect anything less. His steely gaze was intense and holding her in place even though she knew she needed to keep moving. He took another cautious step forward, fixated on her.

"You're so full of life — so much colour and warmth," he said almost absently.

He moved in closer, eyes on hers, lips parted, and she gasped, bringing her sword up between his face and hers when she realized his intent. It broke the spell, and he straightened, taking a hesitant step back.

"Are you an enchantress, too?" he asked, alertness returning to his expression.

"Not on purpose," she whispered. She shook her head to clear it and rested the tip of her sword on his chest. "I'm going now. You can follow me or stay here and risk being discovered by one of my ill-mannered comrades who will be more than happy to make this decision for you. You can weigh your odds while we go, and if you wish death, I will bring it to you in whatever manner you choose. The queen's executioner won't be so kind — he'll behead you."

She turned to leave.

"Can I touch you?" he said.

She whirled around, half in a fighting stance now, to see that same entranced expression back on his face. This time he shook it off on his own.

"Just a hand on your shoulder in the hallways," he clarified. "So you don't lose me in the chaos."

She tersely removed bindings from the back pouch on her belt. "Hands out, wrists together," she instructed, relieved he was making some kind of decision. She bound his wrists in front of him, a tether attached, and led him out of the room. The halls were desolate now, reeking of death, and she began to shiver, but not from the cold. She had not looked forward to this mission and was starting to realize that many of the rumours they'd heard had been true. The silence was far too unnerving, and her voice issued forth before she realized what she was saying.

"Is it true," she began, "that the mistress is entitled to every man in the colony?"

She felt him stumble, but he didn't reply.

"Plenty of perks for her, then. Not such a good lot for the rest of you though, is it? Have you got a wife? Does she mind sharing you with the mistress?"

"I'm alone here," he replied quietly.

"I don't understand the appeal," Tassia continued. "Being kept like a slave and living underground — never seeing the sun, never being able to give yourself to only one person. And the smell!" She wrinkled her nose and realized she'd largely been breathing through her mouth since reaching the deeper portions of the compound. Even over the pungent smells of battle — sweat and coppery blood — the stench was growing unbearable. The smell of smoke from the lamps couldn't quite mask the mould, rotting food, and fluids best left unconsidered.

"We miss the sun," he admitted. "Some of them like the communal spirit of sharing everything. A lot of them don't care much for monogamy."

"Some of them? But not you."

"I guess not."

"All right, so let's say you don't like the sun and don't enjoy keeping anything as your own — is this place really the best option?"

"I don't know. But how is your queen any better? You live in a society beset with rules and bureaucracy. You give up your freedom and for what? Your queen can't always keep you safe either."

"Maybe not, but she keeps us trained and protected, educated, healthy, and fed, and we get to choose to share or keep what we like so long as we don't harm others in doing so. It's a poor comparison, really. There are rules here, and they are enforced with violence."

"Maybe you're right," he said thoughtfully.

She stopped. The hallway was completely empty except for the corpses of Doomsayers, with the sounds of battle muffled in the distance. She turned around to face him.

"What are you doing here? You haven't even been here long — too much colour left in you."

"Looking for answers."

"Did you find them?" She noticed her long braid had slid out of her helmet, and she tucked it back under and glanced around, looking for new threats.

"No, I guess not, or I'd have chosen heart instead of surrender. Are you content with your lot?"

"I wish they'd put me in the front line, but otherwise I can't complain. I wish the people we fight, like your comrades, would stop lying down — stop choosing heart, head or throat

— and earn their deaths with a sword, club or spear. I enlisted for the glory of battle, not to slaughter lambs."

"I like a challenge, too," he said. He kept trying to gesture with his hands, forgetting they were bound. He frowned down at them now, pulling at the bindings a little.

She checked to make sure they weren't too tight. "What are you doing here, then?" she asked, keeping a close eye on him in case it was some kind of ruse.

"Bit of wanderlust. I'm bad at making good decisions." He paused, a sardonic smirk pulling at the corners of his mouth. "And then there's those answers I'm looking for."

"To what questions?"

"All of them." He shrugged with one shoulder and looked down at his hands again, no longer trying to move them.

Tassia shook her head and turned to lead them further into the darkness, glancing back at him now and then. "Your home is far from here, then?"

"Not so far. I've been farther. I think I was working my way back there. I don't think I'd have stayed here much longer, even if your queen hadn't sent the raid. I never stay put for long." He paused. "But maybe going home would have been all right. Or maybe I'd hate it just as much as the day I left."

There was a bitterness to his laugh.

"Why's that?" Tassia asked.

"I don't like being ruled. Doesn't matter if it's by my parents, the mistress, your queen, or the emperor of Glasctinea."

"Glasctinea?" Tassia asked, astounded. She turned to face him. "You must be joking. I suppose you've been to one of the moons. Or both of them!"

"That would be something — to go to the moons. Don't you think? I'd find some answers there."

"Glasctinea?" she persisted, arching her eyebrow.

"I told you — wanderlust."

She thought about it for a moment and realized she believed him. "You must have been young when they turned you out, then."

He nodded. "Fifteen. You would think places like this would put my parents' rules into perspective."

"They can't have been as bad as the mistress!"

"No, Hetia is a pure tyrant, and I've been tyrant-ed by worse than her, but I still can't bring myself to accept what my family wants and return home."

"Start a new family, then."

He looked at her thoughtfully.

"You're not a boy anymore," Tassia pointed out. "Make your own rules. Find a woman with the same wanderlust and start a wandering family, and you can all look for answers together."

He tilted his head back and laughed, fully amused. "Is that what you did? Forged your own path?"

She gave him an oblique look, but didn't like the way he was watching her so expectantly. She turned without a word.

Sounds of battle echoed down the hall toward them. There were bodies — all Doomsayers — littering the hallway. As they passed them, she glanced back at her prisoner, but he seemed unconcerned. They reached a three-pronged fork in the hall, and Tassia stopped, listening for the shouts of soldiers to get an idea of which way to go. She knew she should take her prisoner out to the wagons, but couldn't resist the call of battle; any minute now, the enchanters would take over. She turned to the left, rounded a bend and ran straight into her commander.

"Nothin' for it here, Tass. Hetia is powerful, and swords won't do us any good," he said. "Take your prisoner out and wait with the others."

"Sir, can't I just watch?"

"Take him to the wagons. I won't tell you again."

She stiffened and turned back the way she had come.

"Tass?" the prisoner said when they reached the fork again. She turned to face him. "Your name is Tass?"

"Tassia."

He smiled. "I'm Sam." He extended his hands, palms up, in greeting. Not willing to relinquish her sword, she only half-returned the gesture, taking one of his hands instead of both. She bowed a slight greeting, returning his smile, but kept her sword ready. She realized she was at ease with Sam, though she couldn't explain why. It concerned her how easily she trusted him. She started to turn right, to head back outside, when the tether went taut. She turned to see that Sam had stopped.

"I can get you into Hetia's chambers," he said. "There are several secret ways in, and I know one of them."

"Is that how she brings men into her chambers? Through secret tunnels?" She hadn't meant to be so forward and felt bad when something dark passed behind Sam's expression.

"I can bring you," he said, brushing aside her question. "Would battling an enchantress be enough of a challenge?"

"It would be suicide."

"Her attention will be on the main doors. I can bring you in behind her."

Tassia considered it, but she knew she shouldn't accept the offer.

"Tell the commander," she said flatly as she started moving again. "He can send—"

Sam held his ground, and Tassia had no choice but to stop. She could yank on the tether and pull him over, but dragging him out would be dangerous and difficult.

"Hetia would be able to detect another enchanter," he explained.

"I should at least get another soldier to come with us. Maybe more than one."

"That's not what you want."

"I want this battle to be over," she admitted.

"Let's go end it, then."

Tassia loosened the slack on the tether and let Sam guide her down the hallway to his right and through a twisting maze of tunnels. He pushed back a panel of stone, revealing a black tunnel beyond. She lit the small lantern on her belt and continued into the darkness until Sam stopped her again.

"What is it now?" she asked, taking a half step toward him to ease the tension on the tether. She didn't want him to be able to use it against her.

"Will you put your sword away?" he asked, approaching her cautiously. "There's no one but us in here."

"There's you, and I don't know you."

"Yes, you do. And you trust me or else you never would have followed me here. Please. I won't hurt you," he insisted.

She let her sword hang at her side, but refused to sheath the weapon. She gripped the hilt as he approached her.

"It's a terrible place where we're going — it's awful. I just — you're full of life, and I need that as a shield against her. Please."

Tassia stood still as he pressed against her, leaning the side of his face against her head and one of his shoulders against her chest. If his hands hadn't been bound, she suspected he would have embraced her, and she slid her left arm around him to hold him loosely. He inhaled deeply, breathing the soapy smell of her dark hair and the sweat and adrenaline of battle, drinking her warmth and absorbing her courage.

"This isn't a good place," he finally admitted, stepping back. "Whatever fate your queen has for me, I'll be glad to see the outside of this hill again."

They picked their way down the tunnel until it stopped dead at a wall. She could hear screams and the sizzle of spellcraft coming from the other side.

"There's a vent," Sam whispered, barely audible. "We're behind the hearth."

"What is this place?"

"It's for watching," he said and shuddered.

"She likes to be watched?"

Sam shook his head but wouldn't clarify. "You can unlatch the opening there," he said, pointing to her left, "and watch through the vent until you see an opportunity. We'll have to be quick though."

"We? You're staying right here." She unlatched his tether and draped it over one of his shoulders.

"Don't be ridiculous."

She shook her head to indicate that this was no time to argue and peered through the vent. The drab, filthy room was dominated by a large bed on the left; it had an ebony frame and was heaped with grey, tousled sheets. Everything was dirty and cluttered, a soiled, lifeless tomb. Hetia lumbered into view, fully nude. She was terrifying to see — not remarkably tall, but thin and angular with pale grey skin and white and black hair standing out in all directions. The only colour was her blood red lips, raked back into a snarl over yellowing teeth that had been filed to points. Most enchantresses looked like anyone else, but this one had long ago gone mad, making her even more dangerous. She would be completely unpredictable.

She paced right past the vent where they hid. Over the sooty, charred wood of old fires, Tassia could smell something musty mixed with rancid body odour. She cringed.

"She doesn't bathe," Sam commented once Hetia had passed by. "Ever."

Tassia ignored him and watched the madwoman, waiting for her to turn her full attention back to the queen's enchanters who were holed up in the antechamber to Hetia's bedroom. Through the open doors on the other side of the room, Tassia could see them moving now and then behind pieces of old furniture as they tried to get better positions. The wards shone translucently across the doorway. Hissing and gnashing her teeth like a beast, Mistress Hetia turned to the open doors and rained spells of death on anyone not wise enough to jump clear.

Tassia unlatched the wall panel and gave it a shove. She sprang forward, not waiting to see if Sam would follow. She ran softly, slightly crouched to create the smallest target possible, but still caught Hetia's attention before she could get close enough to strike. The enchantress slung a spell at her, and she dropped under it, rolling forward. Before she got to her feet, Hetia threw another at her. Tassia braced for the impact. But now Sam lunged ahead, catching the spell and shielding Tassia. He wailed in agony, but Tassia knew they would both be killed if she hesitated now.

She jumped over Sam and made a diving charge at Hetia. It was a desperate and sloppy attack. Her sword caught Hetia high in the abdomen, not in the heart as she had intended. At the moment of contact, Tassia felt a jolt, like electricity, as she became vulnerable to the woman's personal wards. Through the pain, Tassia held on to her sword. She had to keep Hetia's attention until the queen's enchanters could do their job.

Even as she began to collapse, Tassia held the hilt in a vice grip, dragging a long, diagonal gash across Hetia's abdomen, finally eviscerating her before losing consciousness and the grip on her sword.

"What were you thinking?" the commander shouted.

Tassia sat up quickly, adrenaline jolting her awake as she realized she wasn't dead but possibly still in danger. The commander was kneeling in front of her, and Sam was sitting to her right, badly dazed, with his hands still bound and hanging between his knees, the tether coiled at his feet. A glance to her left gave her a view of Hetia's headless corpse. Tassia saw for the first time that she had collapsed at the edge of a pool of Hetia's blood, and the left side of her uniform was soaked with it. In fact, the whole room was splattered in blood. Tassia's move had distracted Hetia long enough for the other enchanters to bring down the wards and move in to attack.

"It's over," Tassia said, shocked and delighted.

"You nearly got yourself killed."

"I'm okay."

"Twice in the span of an afternoon you've actively disobeyed my orders," the commander growled. "This time you nearly got yourself killed. You're going to hold rank from now on, is that clear? You're going to leave enchanter's work to the enchanters. Now, for the last time, take your damned prisoner to the wagons!"

He thrust the tether back into Tassia's hands and stood without a word, rejoining the enchanters and his top command. Tassia received a few curious glances from the others, but no one spoke to her.

She picked her sword out of the blood on the floor and futilely tried to wipe it clean on the filthy bedsheets. She only succeeded in smearing it around and finally gave up, realizing she'd have the miserable task of cleaning everything back in her room that evening.

"Come on," she said to Sam.

They wound their way through the tunnels and back outside, slowly ascending the crumbling staircase to the fields beyond. The sun was low on the horizon, casting long shadows across the field where the army had assembled and the wagons now waited to take soldiers and prisoners back to the city. It was a two-day ride back to the capital, and they would lodge in a nearby village tonight.

"Tass! By the moons, what's happened to you?" Livia called as she caught sight of Tassia covered in blood.

"It's not mine," Tassia replied quietly.

"Of course, it's not," Livia said. "Whose is it?"

"Hetia's," Tassia said, barely audible. She looked up at Livia cautiously.

"Have you gone mad?" Livia blurted.

Tassia gave her friend a dark look and shook her head to silence her. "We'll talk about it tonight," she insisted, and turned away from Livia, heading for the wagons.

"I'm sorry if I got you into trouble," Sam said.

"I'm the one who listened to you."

"I just wanted to help."

"Don't apologize. It was the right thing to do, even if I'm the only one who sees that. Now we can all start the journey home while there's still sunlight left to enjoy."

Sam smiled at her. "After the endless dark of that hell, even twilight would be welcome."

Tassia looked around at the long afternoon shadows gathering around the wagons and her comrades, who were cleaning weapons and preparing for the long journey home. Twilight wasn't far off now, so Sam was likely to get his wish.

"What were you doing in that place?" she asked him. "You clearly didn't belong there."

"I don't know where I belong."

"So you just crawl into the darkest hole, hoping for the best?"

"Not *only* dark holes."

They reached the prisoners' wagon, and Tassia was half tempted to cut Sam's bonds and let him flee. She suspected he would receive a light punishment, given his help defeating Hetia and the likelihood that he wasn't a lifelong criminal, but she would have rather spared him the rigours of a formal trial.

"Who've you got here?" the guard asked.

"His name is Sam." Tassia looked to him for the last name.

"Sam Ta Nalertan," he said.

"Ta Nalertan?" the guard asked suspiciously. "What kind of name is that?"

"From Sletrini, near the Western Sea," Sam explained.

"Long way from home," the guard commented. "All right, Sam, in you go."

Tassia watched as the guard helped Sam into the prisoners' wagon, which was caged on top and all sides. It wasn't very full — only Sam and some women and children. Tassia was surprised. On a raid this size, they often filled a second prisoners' wagon, but this time Sam was likely to be the last Doomsayer brought out of the tunnels alive. Hetia must have been treacherous to convince so many people that death was the better option. Once the barred door of the cage had clanged shut, Tassia approached the guard again.

"He helped in there," Tassia said. "Will you make note of it?" She gestured to the leather-bound ledger where he kept track of names and circumstances of capture. "He surrendered without incident and then helped me ambush Hetia. Make sure the court knows." She watched to be sure he jotted it down.

"Very well, but I'll need your name too, then. Sometimes they need witnesses for special circumstances like this."

"Tassia Raven. You think the court will need me?"

"Not likely, but I have to keep track of it anyway."

As she turned to go, she glanced up at the wagon and saw that Sam was huddled with his back against the bars, watching her. When he saw she was looking, he gave her a small wave. She smiled, but didn't return the gesture. She was in enough trouble as it was.

Tassia sat on the edge of her cot in the tiny room she was sharing with Livia and scrubbed at the tacky, drying blood on her uniform while she tried to ignore Livia berating her for her stupidity. The top-ranking soldiers were housed in the village's inns, while the rest had pitched tents on the outskirts. The prisoners were still in the wagons but had been provided blankets, and the cages had been covered in tarp to offer them some comfort. Tassia found it easy to ignore Livia as she concentrated on cleaning her gear and focused the rest of her energy on resisting the urge to go out to the prisoners' wagon.

"So, who was that guy then?" Livia demanded, cutting through Tassia's focus.

"Some wanderer," Tassia said with a shrug, trying to be disinterested. "Seems to have wandered down the wrong hole."

"You just let some stranger lead you into Hetia's lair? What if it had been a trap?" She was incredulous.

"It wasn't."

"You couldn't be certain."

"I was." Tassia scrubbed harder at the blood, hoping Livia would stop.

"But how? You'd known him five minutes!"

"He's obviously a stranger to these lands. He wasn't pale enough to have been there long and didn't even know any of our customs. He was infuriating, actually."

"And that was a good reason to trust him?"

"I talked to him a little. He was just some lost fool, and I could tell he realized how much a mistake joining Hetia's lot was. He shuddered when I asked him about her practices and — he was terrified in the passage to her chamber," Tassia explained, biting her lip as she realized she'd almost told Livia about Sam hugging her in that awful darkness. She dipped the rag to rinse it in the bucket and brought up a fresh piece of armour to scrub.

"You're blushing," Livia said, waiting for more.

"I felt bad for him — a grown man afraid of the dark, like some motherless child. He was pathetic and yet useful," she said thoughtfully. "He came with me into her chamber, you know. Probably saved our lives — he took a spell for me."

"He fancies you."

"Yes," she replied without looking up. She felt her cheeks flush as she furiously wiped at the blood. "That might be why he helped. What matters is that he did."

"Tass, why aren't you telling me everything?" Livia said, quiet and concerned now, finally dropping her accusatory tones.

Tassia cast her a dark, warning glance, hoping her friend would know better than to make her explain any further.

"Ah, I see."

Tassia shook her head, still embarrassed and not sure why.

"It's just been a long day. And a long time since a man has noticed me for anything other than my skills with a blade," Tassia finally said.

"Aye," Livia agreed, sighing, and sat on the edge of the cot beside Tassia. She picked up a bloody shin pad and an extra rag out of the darkening water in Tassia's bucket and began to scrub at the blood, too.

"I keep thinking that maybe it's time to quit this and find something different," Livia said. "Something where men will see me as more than a comrade. Or won't be afraid of me."

"Yes, but what?"

Livia shrugged and fell silent, pursing her lips in concentration as she scrubbed. Eventually, their rags came out of the water almost as dirty as when they went in, and Livia offered to refill the bucket. Tassia welcomed the moment of solitude and thought over what Livia had said. Tassia seldom thought about leaving the army. She was beginning to wonder if she never thought about it because her options seemed so dull. The only possibility she had given any consideration to was becoming part of the military council in Queen Nalea's court. It would be hard work, but less work than starting something completely new, and it would still be interesting enough.

"Face it, you're just not ready to walk away from battle yet," Livia said from the doorway. She sloshed the bucket down in front of Tassia and sat across from her on her cot. The room was so small that it was like they were sitting across a table from each other.

"You're ready," Tassia pointed out.

"Not quite. I still keep hoping that one market day, some fine gentleman will see past the sword to my charms and give me a real reason to walk away from battle."

Tassia chuckled over her friend's longstanding daydream. "You ever going to get tired of that one?"

"Soon, I think. Another summer without a lover ought to cure me of this foolishness."

Tassia smiled wryly but said nothing, and plunged the rag back into the water. She shrugged her long braid, black as midnight, out of her way as it threatened to dip into the murky water as she leaned forward.

"You're never going to get it clean with just water," Livia said.

"The more I can get out now, the easier it will be to get rid of the rest once we're home with better supplies."

"You'll be up half the night," Livia commented, kicking her boots off into the pile with the rest of her armour. She rolled onto her back on her cot, pulling the sparse blankets around her. Away from battle, she wore her medium-length hair loosely, and she fanned it out over her pillow now as she got comfortable.

"I'd rather sleep through tomorrow," Tassia said. "Wouldn't have to deal with the commander that way."

"He'll have your head this time," Livia agreed.

Tassia didn't want to think about what the commander would have to say in the following days. She had only done what any soldier would have done in her situation, she thought furiously. And she knew she wasn't the only one who had disobeyed the commander's orders — many of the soldiers thought he was too cautious — but she was the highest ranking of the dissenters and he would want to make an example of her. She'd happily risk aching joints to sleep most of the day in a wagon if it meant avoiding that confrontation. Yet again, she was tempted to bring her concerns to the queen, but perhaps now was not the time. She didn't need to cause any more waves until he had time to get over this latest stunt.

Long after Livia began to snore softly from her cot, Tassia finally dumped the bloody water down the drain at the end of the hall and changed into her bedclothes. Even the moons had turned in for the evening by the time sleep found Tassia.

CHAPTER 2

The sun was low in the sky as the towers of Queen Nalea's court appeared on the prairie horizon against the backdrop of the mountains, and Tassia knew it would be well after dark by the time they made it into the city and to the barracks. Everyone was road-weary, but Tassia was stiff and sore — partly from the after-effects of Hetia's spell, but also from sleeping in the wagons to avoid the commander — and Sam. Every time she caught a glimpse of him, he was watching her.

Tassia wanted nothing more than to drop into bed the instant she was back in the hut she shared with Livia, but her uniform was still bloodstained and they had a lot of gear to put away. Some of it was strewn over the table beside the woodstove, and the rest was dropped beside the bunk bed or in front of the wardrobe in the corner where they kept most of their supplies. They still needed to get fresh water from the pumps in the central courtyard and see if there was anything worth eating at the evening market, which was run by prisoners and kept open late when the soldiers were returning.

Livia was already pondering where they'd be sent next as Tassia put the last of their fresh water in the kettle and started a fire.

"I heard there's another colony of these crazies — revolutionists, they call themselves, and why, I don't know — we just got over a revolution! Anyway, they're south by the river, and apparently they're gathering arms and starting to train. Why can't they just keep on their little farms and live quietly and not bother trying to overthrow the queen? She's good to us and to them, whether they deserve it or not. And they're by the river, so it's not like they don't have resources or comforts. Just stay put and quiet, and nobody needs to get cut up."

"Then we'd be out of a job," Tassia commented.

"Good riddance to it then! I'd rather be a farmer."

Tassia laughed. "Don't be ridiculous! You barely help me with the garden."

"Sometimes I get tired of coming home covered in blood."

"Ha! Try falling into a pool of entrails sometime!"

"Have it your way." Livia shrugged. "Oh! And Butch mentioned that he's heard talk of a skirmish in the foothills. One of our prospectors found a silver deposit near the border, and the Krunleks are insisting it's on their side."

"That could get interesting."

"We'll probably head to the river next, unless things really escalate with the Krunleks. But then there's—"

Livia stopped abruptly. The commander stood in the doorway, unannounced. His expression was grim, and his face flushed crimson.

"Tassia, give me your sword," he said, his words clipped.

"Sir? What do you need with my sword?"

"What do you think?"

Tassia felt the blood drain from her face. "Am I being discharged?"

"Not yet, but you'll be on probation for a long time after this one. You're off for the next three deployments, and you're not to train with your platoon or the rest of the brigade for a fortnight."

"Sir! I don't think—"

"This isn't a negotiation, Tassia. Give me your sword and be thankful. Don't bother trying to appeal this one either. I just came from the queen's chambers, and she's the one who insisted you be reprimanded properly this time. If you want to call your own shots, then take the strategist training. Otherwise remember your place from now on because you won't get any more warnings."

"My *place*!" Anger sparked in Tassia's dark eyes as she moved toward the commander. She couldn't believe the extent of her punishment after all she had done to secure victory.

Livia grabbed her shoulder and shoved her into an old wooden chair.

"Sir, why don't you put her on the front line where she belongs?" Livia suggested carefully.

"I said this isn't a negotiation. I'm not rewarding her disobedience by moving her where she wants to go."

"Then why don't you reward her skills by putting her where she belongs?"

"When Tassia learns to accept my command, I may be willing to revisit which line she belongs on. But she nearly got herself killed this time. My decision is final."

Tassia watched the commander leave with her sword. She fought to keep her rage in check and to push back the thought of being out of battle for so long — it could be winter before she was deployed again. But as soon as he was gone, she could contain herself no longer, swiping her arm furiously over the tabletop and dumping their supplies on the floor. She stood and paced the length of their hut, her boots tromping a rapid beat against the floorboards, cursing. Livia remained silent until she could see most of the rage had gone out of Tassia.

"Three battles will be over before long," Livia said, beginning to replace the supplies on the table. "And if war breaks out with the Krunleks before then, they'll have you back early."

"Why doesn't Nalea see what a brute he is? There's *never* been a woman on his front line, not even one taller than me and better with a sword."

"Then take the strategist training and forget about him."

"I might. And get Nalea to put me in charge of his brigade. I'll put him on the final wave and see how he likes the view from the back."

"Spite and revenge won't do you any good," Livia replied. "Play his stupid game and obey every last stupid command he gives you. Become the perfect soldier he wants, and if that doesn't get you on the front line, then bring your claims of bias to Nalea. But as long as you continue to defy him, he can use that as an excuse for not putting you up front."

Tassia shook her head in frustration. She knew Livia was right, but that didn't make the situation any easier. Still seething, she started to pick up the rest of the supplies she'd scattered on the floor, letting Livia finish lighting the fire. The two women unpacked as the water boiled. Outside, the neighbouring barracks were alive with murmurs and muffled laughter, but their hut was silent but for the hiss of the water in the kettle and the clattering of cupboard and wardrobe doors as Tassia shelved their clothes and Livia retrieved mugs and tea.

The huts were all the same inside; each contained a bunk bed, a wardrobe, a cupboard and a table with two chairs. Some had rickety shelves for books. There was one window and two doors: one leading outside and one to the adjacent latrine that contained a simple toilet, large bath pail, and a counter for the washbasin and water jug. Lined up in dozens of rows, the huts formed a square around the central courtyard where much of the soldiers' training occurred. The queen's city was surrounded by similar squares of barracks for each brigade — eight of them situated along the compass points around the city — and the outermost line of huts on each square backed onto fields that some of the soldiers chose to farm in their spare time. Tassia and Livia's hut was one of these, and Tassia had cultivated a garden over the years. She grew flowers against the side of their hut and tended to a berry patch out back. Rows and rows of vegetables stretched out into the prairie. In the spring, she divided her time between training and the garden, but through the summer months, when not deployed, she spent her time away from training out back, sometimes receiving help from her comrades with weeding and maintenance.

As Tassia put the last of the clothes away, she sighed. She would need to find a way to keep herself busy in lieu of training with her comrades. Her suspension would give her plenty of time to spend in the garden, whether she liked it or not. It wasn't too late to plant more, and the sustenance would be welcome over the winter. In the autumn, she and Livia always spent a frenzied week canning, storing as much as they could in their tiny hut, and taking the rest to market.

"Teatime," Livia said, finally breaking Tassia from her reverie.

The spring evening had turned chilly; Tassia wrapped her fingers around the warm mug and was glad to sit near the fire and relax.

"He's wrong," Livia said suddenly. "You were stupid, but this is an overreaction. I wonder why Nalea is supporting him."

"She's only been queen for five years, and she needs the support of her commanders."

"Well, then maybe we should both take the strategist training and give her some commanders she doesn't have to coddle," Livia said. "Maybe in Nalea's court we'll find some men who aren't intimidated by female soldiers."

"You'd prefer being a counsellor over a commander," Tassia commented. "Surrounded by plenty of lords and you'd never see the inside of a battle again."

"There is that," Livia replied, raising her mug appreciatively.

"I never thought I'd look forward to war with the Krunleks," Tassia said.

"Anything to get your suspension lifted faster. I just can't believe they won't even let you train with us! That won't go over well with the others. Butch will be furious."

"He should take the commander test. He's done the training and I'm sure he'd pass."

"I think he's too attached to our brigade, and it's unlikely Nalea would put him here when there are so many other groups with ailing commanders."

Tassia shrugged, resigned to the defeat, and sipped at her tea. Her thoughts wandered to Sam and how he was making out in the court jail. She shook her head, annoyed. She would have to keep herself busy to keep him from her thoughts. Tomorrow she would start cultivating more field.

Tassia rose at dawn with Livia and geared up after they'd had a quick meal. Livia didn't comment when she noticed Tassia in her armour, ready to train, but wasn't surprised when Tassia didn't follow her to the courtyard for morning exercises. Tassia watched with a sour look on her face until Livia was out of sight, and then rounded the side of their hut to the back where she kept her gardening supplies. She found a sturdy garden stake that was roughly the length of her sword and went through her opening stretches in the field where no one could see her. The commander had only said she couldn't train with her comrades, and Tassia doubted she would be reprimanded for keeping her skills sharp. Still, she didn't want any more trouble for the time being.

Tassia moved slowly at first, working out the stiffness from the long journey, but was soon spinning, flipping and jabbing — attacking the tall weeds beyond her garden. She continued the drill from memory and hoped nothing new would be taught while she was suspended. Livia would do her best to impart any new techniques, but while still mastering them herself, she would be unlikely to be able to correct poor form.

There were only so many weeds to spar with, and in the absence of a proper training partner, Tassia finally returned the stake to its place behind the hut and went inside to change. She had a thick pair of trousers, sturdy for kneeling on the rough ground, and a light shirt to keep her cool in the blazing sun. It was too early in the season for her to roll the sleeves up; in the summer, she'd have them right up to her shoulders.

Despite the cool spring breeze, she worked up a sweat and was covered in dirt by the time Livia returned at noontime.

"You going to cultivate it straight out to the horizon?" Livia called out, standing at the back of the hut.

Tassia looked back at the sound of her voice and was surprised to see how much land she had weeded and turned. Lost in the loamy smell of earth baking in the sun, she had cleared a square of land almost half the size of her existing garden.

"Beats thinking about everything," Tassia said with a shrug.

Livia held up a basket filled with bread, cheese and fresh fruit.

"I stopped by the market," she called out to Tassia. "You're probably hungrier than I am. Wash up and I'll make you a sandwich."

Livia was still in her armour, slicing up a loaf of bread and some cheese, when Tassia entered the hut. Some cured meat had been left in the pantry from before the raid on Hetia's, and Livia piled it high onto the bread. Both women were famished. They ate hastily and silently, washing their meal down with wine, since Livia wouldn't be returning to training that day. After such long days of travel and battle, the soldiers only had morning exercises scheduled for the rest of the week. Most of the other soldiers had gone into the city to relax in the markets or take in a midday performance, but Livia had come back to help Tassia with the garden.

"I'll head into the city and fetch another load of fertilizer," Livia offered. "How much land do you expect to clear?"

"Just get one wagonload for now," Tassia said. "We can get more later if we need it."

Livia left Tassia to put away the supplies and clean up from lunch. In the quiet of the hut, she could feel her tiredness sink in. She was still weary from the battle and the journey, let alone all morning working in the heat of the sun. She glanced at her neatly made bunk and then sighed. Her mind was way too busy to sleep. She pulled on her boots and headed back into the garden.

Livia returned late in the afternoon, moving slowly with the weight of the wagon behind her. She stopped at the edge of the field and unloaded the fertilizer in a heap at the back of the hut, sure to pile it opposite their window, and then left again to return the wagon back to the farmer she had rented it from. At the edge of the prairie, deep in her work, Tassia didn't notice her at all. It wasn't until Livia finally returned for good that she awakened from her trance.

"Tassia Raven," Livia called playfully.

Tassia turned, wondering what her friend was up to, and saw that Livia was waving a scroll and grinning. It bore the royal seal and her full name. Tassia's heart skipped. Maybe this was a signal that the queen had finally come to her senses.

Tassia snatched the scroll from Livia and tore it open. She started reading but quickly stopped and had to start again.

"A court summons?" Livia said, reading over her shoulder, also perplexed. "You have to go to court over this? It was only a suspension!"

Understanding finally dawned, and Tassia shook her head, exasperated.

"It's not about my suspension," Tassia explained. "I'm going to have to testify at Sam's trial, it would seem."

"What?"

"I didn't want him to receive too harsh a punishment and told the jailer that he'd helped us with Hetia. He said I probably wouldn't have to testify, but I guess he was wrong." She frowned. "The trial is tomorrow morning."

"They work fast!" Livia commented.

"There weren't many of them to process. The children would have gone to one of the lighter work camps with any mothers who were left — no trials. That would leave a handful at most. I'm sure the ones without witnesses to call upon have been sentenced already."

"It was odd how few surrendered," Livia said. "Did Hetia enchant their very wills? Did she take away their desire to live?"

"I don't know. Sam refused to talk about it, and everyone else chose to die. We knew so little about them, but I will ask Nalea when I see her again."

"She might be there tomorrow."

"If she's not busy," Tassia agreed. She stuffed the summons into her pocket and picked up her spade again. "Let's just get on with this."

They worked into the evening light, Tassia clearing the land and Livia spreading the manure.

Tassia sat on one of the low marble benches outside the door to the court and waited for the guard to call her in. The hallway was brightly lit; full sunshine blazed in through the east-facing windows, lighting up the white marble floors and pale stone walls. She had arrived at first light, dressed in her soldier gear and feeling awkward without her sword. There were other trials slated ahead of Sam's, and Tassia wasn't sure how long the wait would be. She had already been informed that Queen Nalea was presiding over the court that day as two serious murder trials were on the docket; Sam's case appeared to have been squeezed in between them. A parade of witnesses had come and gone from the chamber, and Tassia had heard the queen's voice as the doors had opened and closed.

The queen often chose to preside over trials that were politically charged or had garnered a great deal of attention from the kingdom. Tassia wondered how the queen's presence would affect Sam's punishment and if her testimony would do any good at all.

Another wave of people exited the trial chamber, and a guard finally came to summon her. He ushered her into a circular room with grey marble floors and dark wood-panelled walls, lit by a single, large skylight. Opposite the door where Tassia had entered was the raised judge's throne where the queen now sat, an empty prisoner's box to her left. Tassia was guided to one of the rows of benches near the door to wait until her testimony was requested. She gave the queen a smile and slight bow before she sat, but the queen only nodded in return. They were usually on friendlier terms, and Tassia wondered what the nature of the previous trial had been. She would see if Livia had heard anything if she couldn't get answers directly from Nalea.

The queen did look troubled, though. Her emerald eyes scowled while one pale hand absently smoothed down her ornately plated auburn hair. Nalea tried to dress as simply as her station would allow, but today was wearing a bronze gown of heavy brocade patterned with gold. A bone-white robe was draped over her slender shoulders. The courtroom was cool and crisp on this spring morning, but Tassia was certain the queen's apparel was oppressively warm. Times like these she did not envy her friend at all.

Finally, Sam was brought in through a door hidden in the panelling, his wrists shackled in front of him. He didn't look up at first, but when he did, he saw Tassia immediately — she was the only soul in the gallery. His expression brightened, and he looked ready to call out to her, but composed himself with a quick shake. He took his seat in the prisoner's box and resumed staring at the floor. Tassia suddenly felt exposed sitting alone in the room full of empty benches. She wished she had been able to pull Livia from her morning exercises to come with her.

"Rise," a male guard said tersely. Tassia saw the guard standing in front of Sam instructing him.

Queen Nalea was reading over a scroll held up by an aide. The queen's beauty was understated — she had a wide mouth with thin lips, a milky complexion, and plain features — but she was made striking by her strong air of command and authority. Neither tall nor short, she held herself erect and composed at all times, and when she spoke, her gentle voice rang clear and strong, leaving no room for negotiation.

"Sam Ta Nalertan of Sletrini, you are hereby charged with treason, a crime that carries the punishment of death—"

"Treason?" Sam cried out, alarmed. "Your Grace, I—"

Nalea gave him a warning glance, her head barely tilting, but her annoyance at the interruption was clear. He fell silent immediately.

"You are charged with treason and face death," the queen continued. "How do you respond to these charges?"

"I am unfamiliar with the new queen's laws," Sam admitted. "I have been abroad since long before Your Grace rose to power, and I'm afraid I don't understand how my actions constitute treason."

"You understand that I cannot let you walk free because of ignorance."

"Yes, of course."

"You deny that you were in allegiance with a known enemy of the queen, the throne and this kingdom?"

"I didn't know Mistress Hetia was an enemy of the throne, Your Grace. I thought she was merely a lunatic."

"You may not plead ignorance," Nalea said testily.

Sam sighed wearily. "What may I plead?"

"You are either guilty or not guilty of treason."

"Not guilty," he replied immediately.

"Please clarify why you believe you are not guilty of treason despite being captured in the Doomsayers' compound."

"May I use ignorance now?"

The queen turned to face him, swivelling in her seat, her eyes ablaze. She remained silent.

"My actions were foolish ones," Sam said quickly, dropping any attempt at humour, "but they carried no malicious intent. I was a mere minion, more a slave than a willing follower, and participated in no direct acts against Your Grace. I am guilty of stupidity and poor choices, but not treason."

"Were you brought and held at the compound against your will?"

"Not quite."

"Be clear."

"I went there willingly enough, but leaving was difficult. The doors were guarded and sealed, and anyone trying to leave — particularly during daylight hours — was subject to questioning and often restrained. I longed to leave, but was unsure of how to do so in a safe manner."

"So you felt that you were trapped — a prisoner?"

"Yes, Your Grace."

"How long were you there?"

"Ninety-four days. Enough time to realize my error, but not to devise a safe escape."

"That will be all," Nalea said. She looked out into the room. "Tassia Raven of the southwest brigade, will you come forward for testimony?"

Tassia couldn't remember ever being so nervous to approach her friend and was slow to rise and make her way to the centre of the room. She bowed formally before the queen and stood patiently, waiting to be addressed.

"The register states you claim the prisoner offered you aid," Nalea said.

"Yes. He revealed one of Hetia's secrets. A passage that your council didn't know about."

Nalea gave her a knowing, reproachful look.

"He proved useful then?"

"He was the reason Hetia was ambushed, and he even aided me in the attack."

The queen's eyebrows twitched in surprise, and she nodded at Tassia to continue.

"He brought me through a secret passage to attack Hetia from behind while your enchanters held her attention. When she noticed me anyway, Sam took a spell so I could continue the attack. He risked his life, Your Grace, and I believe neither of us would be alive if he hadn't."

"Very well. Did he resist his initial arrest?"

"No, Your Grace, he didn't. He was initially confused by his options, but was otherwise cooperative, and I didn't see him raise a hand in attack against our soldiers at any point during the raid. I don't believe he was trying to be funny when he pleaded ignorance," she added.

"Thank you, Tassia. That will be all." Nalea turned to Sam. "Your sentence will be delivered this evening," she informed him. She nodded to the guard who led Sam back through the panelled door and out of the room.

"Nalea, may I speak with you privately?" Tassia asked.

"I'm not changing my mind about your suspension," Nalea warned.

"No, I know that. I want to speak to you about Sam."

"You withheld information from the court?" Nalea's tone had a hard edge.

"No. Nothing pertinent to the trial. But it might help you make your decision about his sentence."

"Very well." She nodded to the guard and aides to leave them. "I have some time before the next trial. What is it?"

"I believe what he said to you was true, every word of it. He was confused about our customs, particularly the newer ones you installed when you took power. He was relieved — genuinely relieved — by my presence, that there was someone normal around. He seems uncertain about what to do with his life and says he's been wandering for a decade looking for answers — you know, to life. I think he's looking for somewhere to belong. Obviously, that combined with some poor decision making lands him in some less than favourable places. He's travelled widely — as far as Glasctinea — and seen much." Tassia paused. Nalea's gaze was inscrutable. "I truly believe it would do him good to see the more positive aspects of this kingdom after spending so much time under Hetia's rule."

Nalea nodded seriously. "You don't believe he's a threat?"

"No. He was terrified in there. Nalea, in the dark tunnel leading to that madwoman's chamber, he was so frightened that he needed me to draw strength from — he needed a hug. I think he's just been lacking in positive human affection."

Nalea arched her eyebrows in surprise again. "You let him touch you?"

"He was desperate. I don't know how to explain it. Don't repeat this, please. I wouldn't hear the end of it from Livia, and I fear it would embarrass him terribly."

"Tassia, you're going out of your way for a stranger. Is everything all right? Everything about this battle has been very unlike you."

"Attacking Hetia was stupid, I know. But any of the others would have done the same."

"Yes, but that wouldn't have made it less stupid. And I suspect Sam wouldn't have shared that information with just anyone."

"Someone like the commander might not have even given Sam the chance to surrender, let alone talk."

"You just suddenly got chatty?"

"I was curious about Hetia's practices." Tassia shrugged. "Have you learned anything more than the rumours and glimpses we had beforehand?"

"Not yet. I have a woman working closely with the women and children who surrendered, and I hope to have some answers soon. You tried to do some interviewing of your own?"

"I couldn't help myself, and then he just kept talking, so I listened. The battle was largely over by then anyway."

Nalea studied her for a moment and then nodded. "Thank you, Tassia. I think I know what to do with him."

"You won't put him to death?" she asked, alarmed.

Nalea smiled warmly. "Stupidity isn't punishable by death in these lands — you of all people should know that."

Tassia stuck out her tongue, relieved. She always felt more at ease away from the scrutiny of Nalea's aides and missed the days before Nalea took power when they had been simple comrades and friends. They had met in training before Nalea had any notion of being queen. Back then, she was simply a lady of the court hoping to learn a few skills to defend herself. Her swift rise to power, supported mainly by the friends she had made in the army, had strained those very friendships, but Nalea worked tirelessly not to forget those who had helped her.

"Why didn't you tell Livia he hugged you?" Nalea asked as Tassia turned to go. "She'd keep it a secret if you asked her."

"She'd keep it secret, but that wouldn't stop her from riding me about it. You know how she is, and I've already got to listen to her go on about that whole mess with Hetia. I gave her more than enough of the story to give her fodder for months."

Nalea nodded thoughtfully, giving Tassia the same knowing look as before, but remained silent.

"I'll let you get back to work then," Tassia said. "Unless you want to talk about why that first trial has you so upset?"

Nalea shook her head dismissively. "Some monster killing children. I had to be sure we had the right monster before I ordered him drawn and quartered."

Tassia nodded. "And this afternoon?"

"Attempted murder of a visiting diplomat. That one's going to be tricky."

"Livia bought some very good wine at the market not long ago. You know where to find us if you need to."

Nalea smiled appreciatively. "Thank you, Tass."

Tassia sat on the front steps of her hut, devouring a sandwich. Livia had either come and gone already or had decided not to come home on her break. Tassia had gone through her stretching and drills as soon as she returned from court. Now she was back in her gardening gear. She finished the last bite and picked up the spade again, slinging it over her shoulder as she headed out into her garden.

The day before she had extended the size of the garden by almost a third; now she contemplated whether or not to clear more land. She had to consider the work to harvest it and how much room they had to store what they grew. It would be easy enough to sell any extras at the market, and neither Tassia nor Livia minded the extra money, but they would need extra hands to help with the harvest. Tassia hated the idea of leaving anything to the frost.

Tassia finally settled on working the land she had already cleared. Once the earth had been properly fertilized and turned, she could begin planting. They were going to use the extra space she'd cleared to plant things they could eat straight from the ground or vine — carrots, peas, beans and tomatoes. She would have plenty of time before her suspension was over to extend the garden further if she wished. If she did, they could plant corn.

It was mid-afternoon when Livia finally joined her, picking up a spade to help work the manure into the earth.

"How was court?"

Tassia shrugged. "How were the drills?"

"Nothing new. The others aren't pleased about this, though. It could have just as easily been me or any one of them who captured Sam and learned what he knew. Any of us would have stupidly done the same thing you did." She flipped the dirt off her spade. "Especially if we weren't already in trouble for disobeying orders," she added with a smirk.

"Maybe I should have let you clear that room," Tassia said. "You could have had the punishment to go with the glory."

"I think the commander would have gone easier on someone else. Most of the guys think so, too. It had a lot to do with you breaking rank, but some of the others have noticed he's not fair to you. At all, really."

Tassia smiled, enjoying that small victory, and kept digging.

"Seems ridiculous to punish a soldier for heroics — for doing what we're trained to do," Livia continued, stabbing the spade into the dirt. "If you'd told the commander about the secret passage, he'd probably have been stupid enough to send an enchanter. Hetia would have detected another enchanter immediately and sealed off all of the secret passages to her chambers. That woman was dangerous, and we nearly lost a few to her as it was. Some of the others — especially Butch, he's friends with one of the enchanters — think we definitely would have lost at least one or two if you hadn't barged in when you did."

"I didn't realize Hetia was so powerful!"

"And that only makes going in there stupider," Livia said, looking up and giving her a wink.

Tassia heaved a clump of manure at her, which she easily dodged.

"It's hard to say if she was so powerful or just so unpredictable because of her lunacy," Livia added.

"Nalea still hasn't learned much about her."

"Do you think she ever will?"

"Maybe if she can get Sam talking." Tassia shrugged. "She might learn a bit from the others; they were there longer. But we can only hope the children were sheltered from a lot of what went on."

"You don't think Sam will talk?" Livia stopped to face Tassia. "He spoke to you."

"He didn't, not really. He refused to answer me directly when I asked him. I got the impression he would rather just forget about it."

"You would think that with all the travelling he's done and all that he's seen, that wouldn't have been the most horrifying."

"Probably not, but I doubt he'd want to speak about any of it. We rarely talk about battle — about the things we see at the ends of our blades."

Livia nodded thoughtfully. "Aye. I don't want to hear about the heads that rolled or another word about Hetia's entrails. It was bad enough getting it off your armour."

"Nothing horrifying about dirt," Tassia said, digging in again.

Tassia rose every morning with Livia and went through the standard stretches and drills in solitude while Livia practiced with the rest of the brigade in the square. Sometimes they ate lunch together, but then Livia would head out to spar in the afternoons, leaving Tassia to fill even more time on her own. Mostly she passed her days in silence out in the field. Sometimes she went off to the market to buy supplies, plants and seeds. The days had grown hot, and Tassia was glad to get her exercises out of the way first thing in the morning; training in full armour got tiring quickly, but it kept her muscles from forgetting the feel of a sword and the ceaseless garden work was keeping her strong. Livia was also feeling the effects of the heat and exercise; by the time she came home in the evenings, she was more inclined to sit with a flask of something cold and talk than do any more work in the garden.

Tassia was just finishing her morning drills, slashing at the persistent weeds that threatened her plot, when she saw a man standing beside her hut watching her. She froze in mid-swing and then dropped the garden stake, embarrassed, when she realized it was Sam. He stood with his arms crossed and a half-smirk on his face, not seeming to care that he was still wearing the same travel-worn shirt and dark trousers he'd sported every time she'd seen him. She wondered for a moment if he would get to claim any possessions seized in the raid before she composed herself and walked over.

"What are you doing here?" she called, crossing the field cautiously.

"I came to apologize. I just found out how severely they punished you for that mess with Hetia. It was my fault for putting the idea in your head. I should have let you fetch your commander like you wanted."

Tassia shook her head. "My commander is a fool. He would have sent an enchanter. What I should have done was fetch another soldier or two. It's not your fault that my commander doesn't like my tactics."

"If you insist." He paused as he looked out over the garden. Then his eyes met hers again. "I also wanted to thank you. My tongue gets ahead of me sometimes, and I fear that left to my own devices, I'd have put myself on the gallows with my regrettable performance in Queen Nalea's court. Your testimony saved me."

"Nalea was hot-tempered that day and terser than usual. She usually has a better sense of humour, but she wouldn't have made any decision without properly weighing it."

"Still, I feel like I got away with some terrible crime."

"She often reminds me that stupidity is not punishable by death in Wheat Sky," Tassia said with a smirk. "I think you were safe all along. Did she let you go? How did you find me?"

"Your testimony helped earn me light service under Her Grace. I sleep in the prisoners' quarters, but I'm free to move about the city."

Sam lifted a pant leg to show her the iron clasp around his ankle.

"It's been enchanted," he explained. "I don't know the full extent of its power or my full range across the land, but I've been warned that something very bad will happen if I get too far from the towers."

"It will snap the bones in your leg," Tassia replied. "It's common for low-risk slaves to wear them."

"That's not so bad, considering. I assume someone would follow my screams and toss me back into the dungeons to heal."

"Something like that. Nalea isn't a barbarian — the bone would be properly set before you were tossed into the gaol."

"Do you know how far I can get?" he asked, glancing around at the vast prairie. "These barracks are the outermost region of the city."

"Slaves are commonly used in the fields, so you could get half a league from where we are now and it will give you a warning squeeze to give you the chance to turn back."

"That *is* kind of her!" Sam said with a chuckle. He'd been staring out into the fields, but brought his gaze level with hers again.

"How did you find me?" she asked.

"For the duration of my sentence, I get my orders directly from the queen. She mentioned you may need some help with your garden." Sam glanced out at the land she'd cleared. "I believe she feels badly about your punishment, even if she won't ease it at all."

"People like the commander helped her rise to power, and she hasn't been on the throne long enough to feel comfortable going against them completely."

"Fair enough," he said with a nod, but he was watching her closely and Tassia was sure he still felt guilty.

"What sorts of tasks has she been giving you?"

"Carrying things for her and cleaning. She's giving her aides rotating vacations while I'm in her service, and I'm covering for them. Small tasks, nothing confidential, and I'm to stay out of the court when she sits as judge. I've had to fetch things and people from all over the city and act as a messenger."

"How long will you remain in her service?"

"Ninety-four days in total."

Tassia arched an eyebrow at him. "She's mirroring your time with the Doomsayers?"

"That's her intention. She thought I might learn something from it. At the very least, her aides are happy." He grinned.

"I don't believe she's ever sent an aide to help me in my garden," Tassia commented.

"Have you ever been barred from practicing with your comrades?"

"I suppose not. She and I trained side by side before she became queen, so she understands my motivations and does her best to defend me. She's reluctant but unwavering in her decision on this."

"She's like that, I've noticed."

"Well, you can start weeding if you like," Tassia said, gesturing to her garden. "I'm just going to change out of my armour, and I'll join you." She paused. "You can tell a potato from a weed, right?"

"If I'm not sure, I won't touch it," he promised.

Tassia was slow to change, mulling over Nalea's decision to send Sam to help her. He was being pleasant enough, but she wasn't sure about working side by side with him for the rest of the week. The way he had behaved during the raid and the way he always seemed to be watching her was unnerving. She hoped his time in the court had calmed whatever had drawn him to her in the compound.

When she finally made her way back out to the garden, she found Sam kneeling in the grass, staring at the vegetation and looking perplexed.

"I'm afraid I'm not familiar with the plant life in your kingdom, and I promised not to touch if I wasn't sure," he said. "Looks like I'm going to make a poor field hand."

Tassia laughed. "Just train the beans and the peas around the poles then. You can manage that, yes?"

"I think so."

"Once I've made a dent in the weeds, I'll show you what should and shouldn't be here."

Tassia watched him for a moment, making sure he was adept enough to stick to the narrow paths between rows and not step on any of her crop, before she set to work weeding. She pulled everything, right down to the most minuscule leaf of clover. Getting rid of any weeds before they got very big would save her time later, when she would have less of it, and save more of the soil's nutrients for her crops. She carried a bucket to collect them, dumping it into the prairie when it was full. Along the edge of the garden, she simply tossed the weeds over her shoulder, back into the wilderness they came from.

"I am sorry for all of this," Sam said again. He was crouched in the dirt beside her, watching her work. There was little he could do now that weeding was the only chore left.

"Nothing to be done about it now." Tassia shrugged.

"Still, you'd rather be with the others, I'm sure."

"I like the garden. It's peaceful and gives me a sense of purpose. I get something tangible back in the autumn," she explained. She sat back to face him, wiping sweat from her brow with the back of her wrist, trying not to smear dirt everywhere. "Besides, there's less than a week left before I can at least train with my brigade. Three deployments will be over before long, and I might go visit my parents next time they march without me."

"Is your family far from here?"

"No, no. They live on a farm on the outskirts. In the foothills to the north, a place called Winterberry," Tassia said, waving her hand vaguely in that direction. "It's only a couple of hours' ride from the barracks."

"Is that where you learned to garden?"

"Mamma has a garden well over twice this size. Of course, the farmhouse had enough storage space that we could can everything and keep it the whole winter. Livia and I have to sell what we don't have room for. Mamma always had plenty of help from me and my siblings when it came time to harvest, but I was the only one who helped her all summer long."

"Do you have many siblings?"

She paused to watch him for a moment, wondering where all the questions were coming from and considering how much to tell him. "Less now," she finally said. "Growing up, I had two brothers and three sisters. My oldest brother died in the revolution, and my youngest sister was lost to fever."

"Sorry." He looked passed her toward the mountains in the distance.

"It was a long time ago now. Time has a way of healing those kinds of wounds. What about your family?"

His expression darkened like a cloud over a field. It only lasted a moment, and then he met her gaze and cautiously began, "They were merchants, so the little I know of farming I've learned while earning my keep as I travel. I suppose I could have younger brothers and sisters I don't know about, but I've heard very little about my family, except that my parents are still alive."

"Don't you miss them? It's been so long!" Tassia didn't think she'd ever gone more than a week without at least a letter to someone in her family. Even when at war, she managed monthly correspondence.

"I suppose in some ways I do, but I've been away for so long I wouldn't even know where to begin — if they would even accept me back into their lives." He sighed. "I'm so used to being on my own that sometimes I don't even notice that I am alone. Other times, like in the dark of that compound where there was no one at all I could relate to, the loneliness is unbearable."

"Is that why Nalea sent you here?"

He shrugged. "She said you needed help and company."

"What about you? You were in the dark for an entire season!"

"It's a refreshing change," he said with a smile, turning his face up to the sunshine. "All those weeks in the dark only make the sun shine a little brighter."

"That's still no reason to put yourself in such a bad position."

"I've been in worse." He shrugged and turned away from her again. "And I didn't realize how bad it would be. I never do until it's too late."

"Maybe you just need to stay in one place for a while and get a point of reference. You travel alone and probably don't keep any friends. Having some trusted opinions outside of your own might help you learn to make better decisions."

He nodded. "I think you're right. I was in Glasctinea for a little over a year, mostly because a war on the border kept me from leaving, and while it's not the best place to live, I think I felt the happiest there because I'd managed to make some friends — people I knew longer than a few weeks."

"See? Nalea is fair, and this land is abundant and, I think, rather beautiful with its prairies, forests and mountains. Surely it's enough to keep you from getting bored."

He smiled at her again. "We'll see. I'm here for three months, and then the weather will start to change and I will be less likely to keep moving once the snows start in the mountains. That's the way I was headed."

Tassia nodded. He'd begun to watch her again with that same look from the compound — the mesmerized one that disturbed her so much. She continued to weed, nimbly hooking her fingers into the soil to lift out the roots and filling her bucket. The look had subsided again, so she brought him to a patch of dandelions.

She pulled one out, careful to get the root, and held it up to him. "These are actually fantastic for salads and make a good wine, but they grow abundantly in the wild and will choke out my entire garden if we let them. Easily recognizable, yes?"

"I think I can manage."

"Be sure to get the entire root," she cautioned, pointing the dandelion at him like an accusation. "They grow back in days if you don't get it all — like I failed to do with this one. Grab as close as possible to their base — even if you have to wedge your fingers in the dirt — and pull firmly but gently. Otherwise, you'll have wasted your effort."

His first few attempts were a disaster. He left most of the root still in the ground, but at least he persistently dug them all out until he got the hang of it. She let him fill the bucket and then started pointing out where everything had been planted so he wouldn't get overzealous and pull out something that belonged. Aside from the berry bramble, the pumpkins were all that he recognized.

"They're my favourites," he admitted. "Growing up, we'd store them somewhere cool, and they'd last half the winter. Wherever I go, I always look for vines with heart-shaped leaves."

"I like to add seasoning and roast the seeds," Tassia said.

Sam nodded. "But have you had pumpkin stew?"

"Never," she said, tilting her head curiously.

"If I'm still here in the autumn, I'll treat you," Sam promised.

"I imagine you don't get much time to cook stews while travelling."

"Not good ones," he said with a grin.

"Well, I haven't got stew, but Livia picked up an excellent cheese loaf at the market yesterday, and we've got spiced butter and fresh smoked pork. I could make you some lunch."

Tassia had been concentrating so hard on the work and avoiding his glances that she hadn't noticed lunch hour had come and gone until they started to talk about food.

"Yes please." He smiled. "I'll finish up with some weeds and meet you at the hut."

Sam was sitting on the front step waiting when Tassia came out with two sandwiches and two mugs of mead. She sat beside him, enjoying the company and the pleasant spring day, the heat of the sun mitigated by a gentle breeze out of the mountains.

"Hey, so that's him, is it!" Livia called suddenly, and they both looked up to see her coming from the direction of the square with her gear slung over her shoulder.

"This is Sam," Tassia said. "Are you done already?"

"Just taking a break. I'm Livia, by the way, if Tass hasn't had the chance to mention that yet," she introduced herself to Sam. "I thought I'd come enjoy some of my loaf before you eat it all!"

"It's great with the pork," Sam said, sounding apologetic.

"I could make you one," Tassia offered, holding up her nearly finished sandwich.

"So you can get it full of dirt? By the stars, Tass, don't you ever wash up?"

"It's only soil," Tassia said with a shrug, grinning.

Livia waved her off. "I'd like to get some shade anyway and maybe even catch a nap. Got to get back out there for some dusk training. I think we're doing a night exercise tomorrow; the commander has had us out later and later every day."

Livia disappeared into the hut, and Sam hastily finished off his lunch.

"I should go," he said. "The queen wasn't clear on how long I should stay out here, and it looks like you've got Livia back for a while anyway."

"Thank you for the help. And the apology. Will you be back tomorrow?"

"I'll do my best. It's up to your queen."

CHAPTER 3

Tassia tugged at a large stalk of goldenrod that had managed to nestle against a tomato plant and escape detection long enough to grow almost as tall as she was. It likely had roots all the way to the demons at the earth's core, and she had little hope of getting everything. It was sure to spread.

"How did you miss this?" she asked, playfully accusing.

Sam stopped pruning to join her. He had come to keep her company every couple of days until she had been allowed to go back to normal training, and then he had learned her days off and now came for those instead. Livia had taken to spending more time away from the hut — catching up with other soldiers or enjoying the market and activities in the park.

"You're going to have to burn down the whole garden to get that monster."

"I'll burn down the garden, and this will be the only thing left," she said with a laugh.

"After a dragon raid, the weeds are the first thing to grow back in the scorched fields," he said solemnly. "That's how the farmers know it's safe to plant again."

Tassia only laughed harder. "That old tale isn't going to work on the daughter of farmers! The ashes left behind make excellent fertilizer, and we would plant again as soon as the ground cooled off!"

"Have you weathered many dragon raids?"

"Our farmland is in the heart of the kingdom, between the dragons' mountain routes and the queen's towers." She arched an eyebrow at him. "What do you think?"

"It must be terrifying."

"We hear them coming." Tassia shrugged. "We have shelters. There's always the worry of losing crops and livestock, but they seldom take a whole house and even less often an entire village. The worst we suffered was losing crops just before harvest — when there was no chance of replanting."

"I was a boy the last time I was in a dragon raid. But we were in the heart of the city. Our shelters were sturdier, and we always had more warning than the outlying areas. By the time the dragons reached the city — if they were marauders — they were always more interested in the castle towers than anywhere else. I can't recall ever seeing the red clan. Just the blue because we never had to hide from them."

"You've never been in distant lands during a dragon raid?"

"They stick to the mountains, and I've spent most of my time away from these ranges." Sam cast a cautious glance to the mountains on the western horizon.

"I've never left these lands," Tassia admitted. "I've only been beyond the kingdom's borders in times of war, and that's not exactly the best time to see the most enchanting aspects of other kingdoms."

Sam chuckled. "No, it really isn't. I had almost come to think of Glasctinea as charming when war broke out. Then all I wanted to do was leave."

"What has been your favourite place of all that you've seen?"

"The most enchanting people I've come across so far are the citizens of Elintrin."

"Where's that?" she asked, going back to work on the weed. She knelt in the dirt and started digging around the roots, hoping to expose enough of them to pull it out cleanly.

"It's an island kingdom just off the western shores."

"You've been to the western shores, too?" She paused long enough to give him a skeptical glance.

"I went there first."

"Where haven't you been?"

"Across the seas. But not many people have."

"So what did you like so much about Eltrin?"

"Elintrin," he corrected gently. "The setting was beautiful — warm, lushly forested, with large viny trees unlike any I've seen before — and there were plenty of ocean views. More than the scenery though, it was the people. They were very relaxed and peaceful, full of song, and vibrancy and old wisdom. Their princess — I've forgotten her name now — was stunning. Her complexion was black as midnight — just radiant — and she had a thick cascade of chocolate brown hair that would touch her ankles when not plaited elaborately. And her eyes — shocking grey slate shining from the darkness. She lacked the wisdom of her subjects, though, and it was most unfortunate. She wasn't ill-willed, just lacking. It was too bad, really, because her empty intellect detracted from her overall beauty. Such a contrast to Queen Nalea. Your queen's simple beauty is highlighted by her strong will and intellect — that's what makes her outshine any of the monarchs I've encountered so far."

"She's always had her own beauty," Tassia agreed. "She's unwavering and challenging, and I think the fact that she's so untouchable makes her so desirable. And she's certainly an improvement over the cousin she supplanted."

Sam only smiled. "She's a good queen. And she's lucky to have such wonderful friends."

Tassia flashed him a grin. "Yes, she is lucky. Maybe you ought to mention that to her and get her to put me back into battle."

Sam chuckled. "I'm sure this break is good for you. And you're training with the others again."

"Yes, that's a vast improvement. Anyway, what made you leave Elintrin? It sounds delightful."

"It was. Until I discovered that instead of winter, they have a rainy season. There's absolutely no change in the temperature, but it rains for weeks without end. The air becomes stifling, like trying to breathe soup, and the ground turns to slick muck."

Tassia wrinkled her nose. "So you enjoyed the people, but not the weather?"

"Indeed. And it's not the most memorable place I've been."

"What earns that honour?"

"If you travel far enough south upon reaching the eastern shores, you will eventually reach a vast and stunning desert at the edge of an ancient mountain range. The mountains are so old that they barely seem like mountains anymore — they've been worn down by time. But nestled among them are these treasures — these natural cathedrals."

"Caves?"

"There were some caves — those were stunning, too — but these were above ground and often open on many sides. Massive archways of solid rock, some strong and imposing, some thin and fragile-looking — defying nature by their very existence as they stretched across the sky. And the sky itself was the purest blue I have ever seen and truly seemed endless. At night, every last star in the heavens revealed itself — kind of like it does out on the prairies here, but with a clarity and crispness I can't describe."

"Ha!" Tassia cried triumphantly as she finally uprooted the goldenrod. She turned her full attention to Sam. "The desert? How can you survive?"

"I was there in the winter when they get some rain. There were some natural springs and a massive river coming down out of a farther mountain range. The few people who live there year-round seem to rule themselves. They have astoundingly deep wells and have developed an extensive irrigation system. I was in awe of everything I saw, and if I only get to travel back to one place, it must be that place."

Tassia was amazed. "You've probably seen everything there is to see without crossing the seas, and yet a desert holds you captivated."

"If you could see it, you would understand." Sam had been staring sightlessly at the horizon, but focused on Tassia now. "I'll take you there. We can go this winter. It will give me an excellent reason to go back — to share it with someone would be joy beyond words. I may not need to start a travelling family like you suggested, but I could use a travelling companion or two."

"I can't just leave!" Tassia protested.

"We'll leave after the harvest and be back in time to turn the earth in the spring. The queen would give you a leave if you asked her."

Tassia shook her head. "I don't know. That's a long way to travel when I've never left home."

"All the more reason to do it," he said, shrugging. "It was just a thought. If you change your mind..." He shrugged again as his excitement subsided.

"You'll get back there," she said. "You clearly love the place. You don't need me as an excuse to go back. Why don't you go anyway?"

"I might. Maybe not this winter, but before much longer. I think it's the sort of place that needs to be shared. I'd like to bring someone." He searched her eyes. "I hadn't considered travelling with anyone else until you mentioned it, but it seems so foolish to have been alone all this time."

"You might convince me to go a shorter distance over the winter," Tassia said, trying to be noncommittal. "Unless war breaks out — which seems unlikely for now — I get a full month of vacation in the winter. Have you been somewhere stunning that we could reach in that time? We could make an expedition out of it. Maybe Livia will come, too. And my sisters live in the southern plains of the kingdom; we could visit them if we go that way."

"That's the spirit!" Sam said, brightening. "There are some lovely places we can get to in a week. I'll think it over and pick a good one. There's a lot of time to consider it before winter."

Sam went back to pruning, and Tassia tossed the conquered weed back out into the prairie. She took up the spade and began mixing compost into the earth around the pumpkins and squash, watching Sam carefully. She was not sure why he had been so dejected that she had refused something as rash as travelling to a distant desert. They had quickly become friends, but she often still felt like he was a stranger — there was so much she didn't know about him. Yet the prospect of seeing new lands excited her, and the fact that he hadn't rejected bringing Livia and others along encouraged her. She would certainly be willing to travel with him if she could bring along someone she really did know. There was plenty of time before the winter holiday to give the idea full consideration. It would be an excellent reason to travel to see her sisters as well.

"My sister Varia can't travel," Tassia said, thinking aloud. "She's frail and hasn't seen Mamma and Pa in years."

"What happened to her?"

"She had the same fever as the sister I lost, and it weakened her. She wasn't too bad until after she moved south with her husband. A failed pregnancy nearly killed her and took as much of her spirit as it did her body. Her husband has been taking in strays — cats, dogs, birds, everything — for her to care for, and he's got her talking about perhaps taking in an orphan. It's raising her spirits, but I'm not sure if she'll ever be able to travel again."

"What about your brother and your other sister?"

"My brother, Janso, bought the cabin next to my parents' and still helps them from time to time. He builds furniture, though, and spends most of his time in his workshop. My other sister is in the southern plains as well. She's the youngest and works as a seamstress's apprentice."

"So you seldom see your sisters."

"Mernia, the youngest, divides her holiday time between visiting Varia or coming home, so I see her a bit."

"Your family is close, then?"

"Oh yes. Although I guess we don't see each other much anymore. None of us kids were interested in farming so we followed what we loved and ended up all over the kingdom. We exchange letters regularly, though."

"I've considered sending a letter home, just to say I'm still alive. I did it a couple of times when I was young, but stopped when I decided it was pointless when there was no way for me to receive a reply. My last message home said as much. I didn't want them to think I was dead just because the notes stopped arriving."

"If you think you'll be here over the winter, why not send them a note now? Maybe you'll get a reply."

"Maybe," he said, but she was certain he would do no such thing. Sam had already indicated that it was his intent to make his way back home soon, and given all the years of no contact, she imagined he would send a note only to alert them of his impending arrival — if he bothered sending any message at all.

Sam stopped pruning and began training errant vines up their poles while Tassia finished with the last of the compost. She had just joined Sam in the vines when she heard Livia calling for them.

"You going to stay out there and get rained on?" Livia called.

It had been overcast for most of the afternoon, but now that Livia mentioned the weather, Tassia noticed the temperature had become cooler and the air damper. The clouds to the south were dark bruises, and the land was veiled in grey rain that she could smell on the chilled gusts of wind coming across the plain.

"Guess it's time to head in," Sam said. "I'll see you next week!"

Both women stood quietly and watched as he headed back through the rows of huts, headed for the courtyard to wash up at the pump before he made his way back to the heart of the city and his bunk in the prisoners' quarters. He hadn't explored much of the city yet and tended to spend his time away from Tassia's garden just sitting in the quarters, reading.

"How was the park?" Tassia asked.

"There was a fire-eater putting on a show. It was spectacular! And the fruit trees are all blossoming, so it smells divine."

"I'd love to put an orchard back here!" Tassia commented, looking around at the vast open space.

"Ha! I don't plan on living in this hut long enough to ever see a tree come to bear fruit."

"It would be great if we could just plant them already mature."

"There's the berry patch for sweets, at least. And we've still got your flower garden," Livia said. "The lilies look like they're going to bloom early this year."

"I think they might, if they get enough water and the temperature remains pleasant."

Tassia went in to wash up, and Livia sprawled out on her bunk with a book.

"Did you pick that up in the market today?" Tassia asked, nodding toward the book.

"Aye, we stopped when Butch ran into one of the lords in council he knows — that man knows people all over the kingdom! While they were talking, I took a look over the book tent and found something new."

"That man can be quite the gossip. He should have been a woman," Tassia joked.

Livia chuckled, but didn't look up from the pages. "He was trying to find out more about the Doomsayers."

"Any luck?"

"Didn't seem like it. I wasn't paying attention, but Butch didn't seem surprised by anything he heard. Doesn't seem like any of them are talking. They haven't even been able to get the children to say anything. Nalea's worried that there may have been some extensive enchantments used to keep them silent, but the enchanter Butch knows said no one has been able to figure out how that could even be possible."

"It's probably just the sort of thing that's so awful, you just don't talk about it. Makes it go away faster."

"Has Sam said anything yet?"

"No, but I don't really bring it up." Tassia sat at the table and poured herself a cup of wine, enjoying the break. "I invited him to talk about it once, but he skirted the subject completely — barely even acknowledged what I'd said — and hasn't brought it up since. Maybe he just needs more time, more time in the sun to remind him it's over for good."

"He still being weird?"

"Yes." She put her cup down. "Today was the worst since we sprung him from the compound. He was telling me about this place he's been to — of all the places he's seen, it's his favourite — and he was trying to convince me to go with him. Just pick up and run off with a stranger!" Tassia shook her head and glanced out the window.

"He's not a stranger. You two are friends."

"This place is on the eastern shore!" she said, turning to Livia again. "But south! I can't even fathom how far away that is. He said we'd be gone the entire winter."

Livia sat up, swinging her legs to sit on the edge of the bed, and was silent for a moment, watching Tassia carefully for any trace of exaggeration. Finally she shook her head.

"That's odd. I thought he was getting better — that he was getting over the whole thing."

Tassia sighed. "He still watches me sometimes. Gets that look, the one where he's completely lost. He doesn't really do anything, but still…"

"I wonder if Hetia didn't find some way to mess with everyone's minds. He's been out of her cave for nearly a month now. I know he doesn't really leave the queen's service except to come here, but he does get to the market now and then. You'd think he'd have been able to move on with things and see that there are plenty of other women — how did he put it? —*full of life*?"

Tassia nodded. "The garden is pretty much under control. I can handle it myself for now. Maybe we should bring him to the market with us or to a show in the park."

Livia chuckled again. "Are you so desperate to remove yourself from the centre of his attention that you're willing to set him up with another woman?"

"I'm sure it would do him some good," Tassia replied, rolling her eyes. "And it distracts me still. It would be easier to be proper friends with him if I knew he was over it. Over me."

"What did you say when he asked you to run away with him?"

"What do you think!" Tassia said, looking at Livia squarely.

Livia's eyes glittered with mischief. "So, when are you leaving?"

"Don't be absurd. I told him you'd go."

"What!"

"You don't want to travel?"

"Not with a stranger. A madman!"

"He's not completely mad."

"Mad enough," Livia teased, waving her hand dismissively.

"I did volunteer you for a trip, though. He was so depressed when I said I wouldn't think of travelling that far,

I suggested maybe a shorter trip over the holidays. Maybe in the direction of my sisters."

"How did he take that?" Livia asked, leaning forward and resting her elbows on her knees.

"He's going to think of the places he knows to the south and see if he can find anything."

"He didn't mind me tagging along? Or that you'd stop to see family?"

"He was just pleased that I was seriously considering some kind of travel. It would be nice to see something beyond our borders. I don't know if I'll ever be ready to travel as far as this place in the southeast that he loves, but I'd like to see more."

"Sounds like the man is just lonely, suffering from wanderlust." Livia shook her head.

"I think so. Mostly he seems to be tired of travelling alone."

"Maybe he'll stay put for once. Find someone to travel with him before he goes off again."

"I think that's his new plan. I couldn't imagine spending all of my adult years with no point of reference — no constant except the sky. Could you imagine what that must be like?"

"No, not really. No wonder he's gone mad!" Livia grinned good-naturedly and lay back down on the bunk.

"Oh, hush. He's all right. You should stick around more and you'd see. Why do you always disappear when he's around? You could help us in the garden."

"I just thought I'd give you the chance to — you know. In case you're putting one over me and fancy him back."

Tassia rolled her eyes. "That's a terrible excuse. Stick around next week!"

"I've got plans for next week, but maybe after that."

Tassia had been leaning back in one of the rickety chairs, but now she sat up straight.

"Plans? You've never had plans in your life." Tassia studied her a moment. "Butch?"

Livia turned crimson and buried her focus in the pages of her book.

"Someone finally noticed you as something other than a comrade? Livia! Tell me!"

"Yes!" Livia snapped, still flustered and staring at the book, unseeing.

"Why is that such a horrible thing to share?"

"I don't know. It just is! He's Butch — we've known him forever, and sometimes it just seems a little strange. Sometimes I worry I'm only returning his attention because he's giving it in the first place. You know what I mean."

Tassia nodded. "I'm not worried about that so much anymore. But, yes, I know what you mean. How long has this been going on?"

"Since early the second week of your suspension. Without you there to talk to, I started talking to the others a lot more. I guess Butch has been interested in me for a while, but we never really talked much because I'm always with you."

"That's why you've been leaving me with Sam so much? You could go with Butch any time, but you do it specifically when Sam's around."

"I thought the only way you'd really know if you wanted to return his attention is if I left you to it. I won't make a point of being away all the time when he's here, but our days off are still the best time for me to get together with Butch — you know, privately."

"Have you really been going to the market and the parks all this time?" Tassia asked, smirking deviously.

"Yes," Livia insisted, but blushed again. "Just — sometimes we make detours."

Tassia snickered. "You're going to be out of this army before much longer, aren't you?"

"I don't think so." Livia set the book down and leaned on her elbow to face Tassia. "I mean, maybe if I'd met one of those proper gents in the market I used to fantasize about, but since it's Butch — one of us — it's easier to want to stay. He wouldn't leave, so why should I? If it gets serious enough, the commander would bunk us together. As long as there are no children involved, there's no reason we can't both be here together."

Tassia nodded and smiled, leaning back in her chair. "I'm glad you're sticking around then."

Chapter 4

Sam showed up at first light, just in case the deployment had upset Tassia. The army was being sent to provide disaster relief in the foothills where heavy rains had caused mudslides. Although Tassia was frustrated to not be joining her brigade, she was thankful that Nalea had chosen to include all deployment, not only the battles, in her suspension. This way, she would be joining her comrades again before long, especially if the wet weather in the mountains continued and caused flooding further down the river.

Tassia geared up in her armour and went to the square with Livia and the other soldiers, but stood solemnly to the side of the courtyard with Sam once they began marching out. Comrades who noticed her standing there cast sour expressions toward the commander, giving Tassia a deep sense of satisfaction. Maybe some of them would find the courage to bring their concerns to the commander himself.

"Why don't we follow them to the edge of the city?" Sam suggested. "Looks to be a pleasant day, and I wouldn't mind the walk. We can go until this cursed iron starts squeezing my leg if you want."

Tassia smiled up at him. "Yes, let's. The commander will love that."

The army marched through the main avenue of huts back into the city and directly through to the northern gate. There were gates at each point of the compass, with the imposing main gate facing south. In the fields beyond the city's north entrance waited the ox-drawn wagons that would bring the soldiers and their supplies to the foothills. Tassia and Sam stood with Butch and Livia as they waited their turn to pile into one of the wagons.

"What are you going to do for a week — or more?" Livia asked. "That garden is already overworked."

"I'll work it until I can't anymore, and then I'll probably head home for a few days. Maybe I'll show Sam around the city a bit, if Nalea hasn't got much for him."

"Say hi to your ma if you go," Livia said.

"I will. Be careful."

As the wagons pulled out, Tassia and Sam trailed behind them. They kept a quick pace, walking side by side and chatting idly, and weren't too far behind when the anklet gave Sam its warning. Sam stopped mid-sentence and halted abruptly. Tassia turned to see him take two quick steps backward. A look of relief flooded his expression.

"Looks like this is as far as I can go," he said.

Tassia turned back toward her vanishing brigade and waved for a moment before she turned and joined Sam.

"Back to the city, then. Would you like to go to the market?"

"Maybe another day — when I'm free of servitude and actually have some money."

"You don't have to buy anything. We can just look around."

"I suppose."

"Did you really come out of Hetia's with nothing?"

"Yes," he said with a sigh. "I went in with some clothes, travelling supplies, and a bit of money, but was required to turn everything over when I arrived. I never saw any of it again. I haven't had much since leaving home, but now I have absolutely nothing. Whether I want to or not, I will be here until I'm able to replace what I've lost."

"It still doesn't sound like much."

"No, but it was enough. I don't think it will take long to replace everything once the queen allows me to work for money. I like to have some coins with me when I travel. I try to trade as much as I can — my limited skills for whatever I need — but sometimes that's not possible and I need some gold."

"You're quite the vagrant," she joked.

"Yes. I guess it's not much of a life," he said, shrugging one shoulder.

"You've seen so much, though."

"Not what I'm looking for."

"Are those answers worth all this?" She stopped walking and leaned against a stone wall, facing him as they spoke.

"I'm starting to think maybe they aren't," he admitted. He smiled fondly. "But I'm here until spring, I'm sure. A lot can happen in a year, so I'll see where that takes me. Maybe it won't take me anywhere."

"You want to stay, don't you?"

"I just might. I'll see how the winter goes." He leaned one shoulder against the wall as if to face her, but was looking at his boots. "Maybe this can be the point of reference you talked about. It will take me a long time to get used to the idea of staying put for good. I imagine I'll still wander now and then. But maybe I'll keep coming back here." He finally looked up at her.

"This place has grown on you already, has it?" she said with a grin.

"Your queen is quite possibly the most reasonable leader I've met since my days in Elintrin, and I do prefer this climate to theirs. I can't ask for much more than that, I think. And with all I've learned in your garden, I feel I could make a useful farmhand now. Perhaps find steady work."

There was no trace of jest in his voice, and Tassia could see he was considering these things as he spoke them. She was surprised.

"You're not interested in going home anymore?"

"Maybe not." He paused for a moment, watching carts clatter past them on the wide northern avenue. "I think I'd begun to wander that way because I needed a point of reference. But I realize there's no reason why I can't make a new one — or a new home. I guess that's one answer I've found, even if it's not one of the bigger ones I was looking for."

"That's a good start. I enjoy your company, and it's nice to have someone else around now that I've lost Livia to Butch."

"You really think you've lost her?" he asked, raising his brows in surprise.

"He's had his eye on her for some time, and they've been friends forever. Isn't a solid partnership built first on friendship?"

"I suppose you're right. But if she leaves, you'll get a new bunkmate."

"Yes, there are always new recruits. I won't live on my own for long, but a new girl would be a stranger to me for a very long time."

Tassia pushed off the wall and began to walk again, and Sam fell in stride beside her, thoughtful and silent for a time.

"Does Nalea allow foreigners in the army?" he asked.

"You have to live here two full years to be considered a citizen, and then it doesn't matter where you come from. If you want to defend this kingdom, she lets you. You want to fight?"

"I don't know. It would keep me from getting bored," he remarked, grinning.

"I'm not sure the army holds your answers either. Lots of routine. Lots of training. A bit of killing. That's about it, really. I think people leave the army because they're bored. Either that or they've seen too much death and need something new."

"How do you deal with that — all the death?"

"The garden," Tassia said. "There's so much life in it. After watching so many people die, it's refreshing to see something grow. It feels good to create something."

Sam nodded thoughtfully as they continued into the city, walking up the broad main avenue that split the large northern barracks. The market was on the south side of the city and it was already well past noon, so they detoured into one of the city's many cafe districts for lunch, where Sam reluctantly let Tassia treat him to grilled pheasant.

She led him through the city by a circuitous route, largely avoiding the main north-south avenue they had just taken with the army to the northern gate. She wanted to point out some of the city's landmarks as they went, including Nalea's childhood home and the monument marking where the city's founder had been pyred.

"A tree?" Sam asked, looking up at it.

"The tree was planted in her ashes by her son. When it got older and its health began to fail, enchanters turned it to stone to preserve it for as long as the city remains. The city was sacked about two hundred years ago, and almost everything but this tree was destroyed."

"Why's that?" He turned to her, more interested now.

"The remaining citizens defended it. When they realized the city was lost, they pulled back and formed a massive barricade around this area. Allies finally drove the invaders out, and there's a monument in the cemetery — another tree — with the names of everyone who died specifically to defend this during the invasion."

"Are pyres still common in your kingdom?"

"Not within city walls, but there are some fields surrounding the city that have been designated for pyres. All of the smaller towns and villages still pyre their dead. A lot of the farmers mix their ancestors into the field. How are the dead honoured in Sletrini?"

"Rituals and burial. They still go back to the land; it's just a longer process, much like it is here in the city."

They arrived at the market late in the afternoon, and Tassia led them straight to the information tent to read the scrolls tacked up on its walls.

"I haven't been to the market in ages," she said as she perused the listings of events. She would have to find something to keep her busy until Livia returned. A scroll caught her eye that detailed a week-long festival in the main park to usher in the summer solstice. There were only two days left.

"Why don't you join me?" she said, turning to Sam. "We can go tomorrow and spend the day in the park. Everything is in full bloom by now, and it's absolutely stunning."

"You know I have to check in with the queen first," Sam replied.

"Tell her I insist you come with me."

He smiled. "I'll do what I can."

Sam was at her hut first thing the next morning, not dressed for gardening for the first time in weeks, and he was smiling broadly. It was an overcast but warm morning, and Tassia wondered if they'd see any rain.

"What's got you so excited?" she asked.

"I've been given an allowance," he replied, jingling the coins in his pocket. "The queen said there would be a small market at the festival with seasonal arts and some food. So you're not to buy my lunch today."

Tassia laughed. "Fine, you can treat me instead."

She led him through the barracks into the city and westward to a large park that was awash with music, colour and the smell of food and blossoms. People from every corner of the city were just beginning to trickle in for the day. A pond had been constructed at the centre of the park long ago, and the festival was arranged around it. There was an area for merchants and artists, one for the market where all the delicious smells were coming from, one for games and one for music and dancing. The games were nearest to where Sam and Tassia had entered the park, and they started there, taking in the sights as they made their way around the pond. Tassia made note of the games she wanted to try while Sam enjoyed the park scenery. There were many old trees, tall and stunning, and a few old willows dipping right down into the water. The trees on the festival grounds were full of children trying to out-climb each other.

Tassia and Sam perused the market and the merchant tents, making mental note of what they wanted to come back for later. There were some local dishes Sam had never heard of that he wanted to try, including one that consisted of wild prairie grains and fried locusts.

"It's rather bland," Tassia warned. "And the locusts always seem burned — too crunchy."

He shrugged. "I'll give it a try anyway."

"If you really want to try the wild grains, they're best in stews. And sometimes there's a baker who sells his wares at these festivals, and he bakes the grains into the most delicious pastries."

"If he's here, I'm trying that, too."

"Brought your appetite, did you?"

"Well, the queen was quite generous. I'll feed both of us well for the day."

"You should also buy something from the local merchants, then."

He shrugged. "Maybe next time, if I have a space of my own to keep anything in. For now, I'm focusing on the food."

Sam stopped with Tassia as she glanced through the merchant tents, and she decided she would return for some books to help keep her occupied while the army was gone. She still had to sit out two more deployments after this one, and Livia was right that there was little work in the garden.

They reached the music and dancers, and Tassia gestured for Sam to join her in taking a seat on the pile of square hay bales.

"Wait, I know this ballad," he said excitedly.

"I'm really not much of a dancer," Tassia protested as he grabbed her arm and led her toward the crowd.

"Don't be ridiculous, I've seen how graceful you are. Just follow my lead."

Tassia was not as graceful in dance as she was in battle, but she managed to step on Sam's feet only a couple of times. She quickly bowed out as soon as the song ended and was relieved to see Sam choose someone else to dance with. This new woman was lovely; she had long chestnut hair and was nearly as tall as Sam. She was also infinitely more graceful than Tassia had been. Tassia wasn't sure what she was more relieved about, not having to dance anymore or that Sam wasn't so attached to her that he couldn't have fun on his own. She hoped he'd start seeing his ridiculous infatuation for what it was because she preferred his friendship without any awkwardness.

Sam joined her a short time later without the dark-haired woman he'd been dancing with.

"I don't know these songs," he said sadly.

"And I don't dance, so I can't teach you. Musicians come out here all the time to practice, and they always attract a few dancers. In a more relaxed setting like that, I'm sure you could find someone to teach you more of the local dances."

"Maybe. You could come with me and find some more grace," he joked.

"I've learned that I'm only graceful when there's a sword in my hand. I don't think that makes for safe dancing practices."

Sam only laughed and sat with her a while, soaking up the day, until the band played a jig he knew and he got up to dance once more. A few songs later, they ventured out into the rest of the festival. They stopped at the market for lunch, and Sam agreed with Tassia that the locusts were terrible, but they found the baker she'd mentioned and that certainly made up for it. By then, the weather had turned cooler, and the wind had stirred itself up, signalling rain. Tassia stopped to buy the books she wanted, and then Sam walked her back to her hut. Neither had brought a coat to ward off the cold, and they linked arms, huddled together on the walk back to the southwestern barracks.

Sam stayed long enough to share dinner and warm himself. Tassia enjoyed his presence and didn't even mind when he held both of her hands while he stood at the door to say goodnight.

"I really enjoyed the festival," Sam said. "Perhaps another tour of the city tomorrow?"

"Maybe. If we get much rain this evening, though, I'll want to spend some time in the garden."

"Either way, I'll try to join you." He kissed the knuckles of her left hand and then disappeared into the gathering twilight, leaving Tassia wishing he'd stayed just a little longer.

The dampness from the previous night's rain held in the air despite the heat, and Sam finally took a break from pulling out all the new weeds to wipe away some of the mud plastered to his arms. He pulled off his shirt, which had become uncomfortably damp and stuck to him. As he turned back to his work, Tassia noticed his back was a patchwork of scars.

"What happened? You get on the wrong side of some bad people on your travels?"

At first he didn't understand what she meant. Then he realized she was staring at his back.

"A time or two. The freshest ones are from Hetia," he said. "She thought it was fun. That woman was a pure sadist. The others came from worse tyrants than her, but she was the only one who really enjoyed putting the marks there."

"How did the rest of them get there?" she asked, sitting back to watch him. She tried not to make a show of appreciating how well-muscled he was, keeping her gaze on his scars. She didn't quite succeed, but Sam only grinned. He sat across from her with his forearms resting on his knees.

"I don't always follow orders and I don't like rules — which is part of the reason I left home in the first place and part of the reason Hetia's appealed to me. Last year I was in a small nation to the north — a tiny matriarchy tucked away in an isolated valley — and I'd never in my life been subjected to so many rules before. It made my parents look like anarchists."

"What were some of the rules?"

"Women had more freedom than men, but not by much. There was no public contact between the sexes at all and only chaperoned contact in private, unless the couple was married or otherwise related. There were these much sillier rules, too, and I could never keep them straight. Things like which hand you were to use to hand something to someone — I think it may have been the right hand to give something to a woman and left hand to give it to a man. But that might be backwards. I never got it straight. Everything had some kind of penalty. Most were fines, some were lashings. I was always being fined. Got lashed quite a bit, too."

"How were the restrictions worse for men?" Tassia asked.

"We weren't allowed to expose a single inch of skin in public. We had to wear long sleeves and long pants, gloves on our hands and hoods over our heads. The worst was the masks — there was mesh over the mouth and eyes so we could breathe and see but not be seen. It was the itchiest thing I've ever worn. Once I accidently exposed a bit of neck while readjusting my mask. Apparently, they consider the neck to be a highly erotic area because that lashing was probably the worst."

Tassia grimaced and ran her hand along the back of her neck in an unconscious gesture. "Why on earth did you go there?"

"Travel in was quite simple, and I made the mistake of assuming it would be just as easy to travel out. As soon as I realized how severe things were, I packed up and tried to leave, only to be seized at the border for not having the proper paperwork. That was a lashing."

"What did it take to get out of there?" Her eyes widened in disbelief. She half wanted to believe he was making it all up.

"I ended up leaving a lot of my possessions behind. I took only what I could carry in my pockets or would fit into a small shoulder bag. I left in the summer so that I could leave my blankets and wore an extra set of clothes under my uniform. I had very little food with me, and only a tin small enough to brew some tea in. But when I got to the border and said I was going to visit a friend in the next village, they believed me. That was another time I was glad to carry some gold. I was able to buy some new supplies — mostly cooking gear — as soon as I reached the next village."

"You have no real possessions, then? Nothing of sentiment or value?"

"Just one thing," he said, undoing the clasp of the chain he wore at his neck. She realized that instead of a pendant, there was a ring hanging from it. "I keep it hidden, usually under my clothes when I travel or stashed in some hiding place when I'm stuck in places like Hetia's."

He handed her the ring. It was a wide gold band set with a flat blue stone that had a crest carved into it; the carved spaces were white, contrasting the faded royal blue of the exterior.

"It's my family crest," he explained. "It's the only thing of meaning that I've kept all these years."

"How did you manage to keep it from Hetia?"

"She just assumed everyone coming in was being honest about giving up possessions. Not everyone was — I wasn't the only one who kept something of personal value — and some of them were discovered and others weren't. It was a sound lashing for being discovered though."

"What did you do to deserve lashings from Hetia?"

"I caught her eye," he said with a little shake of revulsion. "I had been there over two months and thought it was just a rumour that she could have whoever she wanted whether they liked it or not. There was a lot of sharing, and I had no doubt that she got plenty from willing participants. At any given time, you could enter a room and walk in on a couple, or even a group. They didn't care if anyone or everyone saw, and very little of it took place in bedchambers. Most of us slept in dorms anyway, not that it was easy to sleep over the never-ending frenzy. It wasn't just the sex, either. There was all manner of drugs and potions and ale to quench any appetite."

Tassia realized it was the most he'd ever said about his time with the Doomsayers, and she held very still, not wanting to discourage him. She nodded faintly and let him continue.

"I participated little, especially at first, and chose to observe — not out of any perverse voyeuristic needs — but just to try to get an idea of what the big deal was. There was so much decadence and gluttony in that place, and I have no idea where it all came from — the food and the drink."

"Hetia had some wealthy comrades," Tassia commented. "Very wealthy. Some were farmers who turned over their farms to her. Those were worked by slaves to benefit the big party she had going."

"Yes, it seemed like a big, never-ending festival. I think that's what attracted so many of them. I think if it had stayed at that, I may have tolerated my stay. But Hetia was a very sick woman, very sadistic, and her appetite for physical pleasure was insatiable. Even with an endless supply of willing partners, she wanted a taste of every man and even a few of the women in there."

"So that part was true," Tassia said quietly.

"More than you know. I escaped her attention for two months, but I started hearing rumours about other things that happened, not just about Hetia's preference for unwilling partners. By that time, I had learned that you weren't as free to leave as you were to join and had begun to despair and drink ale almost constantly. I let my guard down, and she finally noticed me and realized my face was one she wasn't familiar with."

"I didn't realize a man could even be an unwilling sexual partner," Tassia said, mystified. "I thought you'd need to be willing to be aroused."

"The body has its urges, whether the mind likes it or not." He shrugged, trying to get the story out without reliving too much. "But Hetia had plenty of enchantments and potions to help things along. And she liked pain — not her own, but others. Hence, the new scars." He shivered despite the heat of the day.

Tassia wished she hadn't brought it up. She moved to his side, touching his shoulder softly, and he turned to face her and pressed tightly against her, clinging to her like he had in the tunnels outside Hetia's chambers. His head rested against her shoulder and neck, and she could smell the soap of his hair mingling with sweat and dirt from the garden. It made her head swim, and her skin tingled where it made contact with his.

"She liked an audience, too," he continued, releasing the embrace, "and I'm thankful at least that I never had to bear that — neither watching nor being watched. But she would make some of the children watch and would make older ones participate. I never saw any of this directly, but I heard accounts of how she'd take a boy and several girls into her chambers and would make the girls watch while she *initiated* the boy, and then make them watch while he took turns *initiating* each of the girls. Initiate — that's what she called it."

Tassia gasped. "No wonder those children we rescued won't talk."

"I don't think I have it in me to repeat this again, but you should probably let Nalea know what she's up against with those children — so she can find a way to help them."

She nodded, but was still confused. "How was Hetia not the worst tyrant you encountered?"

"Except for those occasions, and the fact we couldn't leave, she actually had no rules at all. She wasn't much of a tyrant, but my time in the compound was certainly the most disturbing thing I've been through since the wars in Glasctinea. The rebels there did unspeakable things."

"You almost expect that sort of insanity in a war — especially in some places. But to find it in a simple compound in a kingdom like this — I'm so sorry for you."

"It's over," Sam insisted. "I'm grateful for the service Nalea has *punished* me with because the time I spend under her rule and in your company — the same amount of time I spent in Hetia's nightmare — is helping me reclaim what was taken."

"I suspected it might. I spoke with Nalea after your trial to help persuade her that you needed some help, not a heavy hand."

Sam's face washed over with gratitude, and he leaned forward, cupping her face in his hands and kissing her quickly but intensely. It was over so fast that Tassia barely realized it had happened, save for his muddy handprints on her cheeks and the salty taste of his lips on hers. She was relieved when he spoke again right away so she didn't have to respond, but in the close heat between the rows of corn, she almost wished he hadn't stopped.

"Tassia, you've helped me gain my life back. I hope you realize that. I almost chose death when you offered it to me, and I can see why so many others did. Hetia placated everyone with whatever pleasures they desired and provided enough decadence to bury any misery that came with it. I'm sure many chose death because they just couldn't see how they would ever put their lives back together and gain any sense of normalcy, if they even had any to begin with.

"But the way you spoke and the way you gave me a chance made me reconsider, and to hear you talk about your homeland with such conviction — I had to at least see the other side of it. I had been afraid of being turned back out into the world — alone, and scarred by Hetia. Of having to wander again with no purpose after what I had endured. Your friendship is giving me the opportunity to heal."

Tassia sat up on her knees and leaned forward, pushing his muddy hair away from his face and kissing his forehead.

"This garden is good for both of us, I think," she replied.

Sam hugged her once again and then sat back, finally composed, though Tassia could see the dark memories lingering under the surface.

"I didn't realize how damaging all the years of solitude have been until now. Having people to talk to — trustworthy ones — is more healing than I realized. I think — I don't want to wander anymore. If I don't stay here, then I'll just go home and face whatever my parents have in store for me there. I can still travel, but no more wandering. I need somewhere — something — to keep coming back to."

"I don't know how you've managed all this time — with all that's happened."

Sam looked at her with a half-happy, half-sad smile.

"Look at me," he replied, waving a hand at his tattered clothing and abundance of scars. "I haven't managed very well at all. It hasn't all been bad, but I haven't found my answers wandering. I'm happiest when I'm somewhere stable and safe."

"You can at least recognize what's safe, can't you?"

"Yes, I've always known on some level when I was headed somewhere bad — somewhere like Hetia's. It's always a feeling — the kind you ignore — and it takes my brain too long to catch up with what my heart knows. But I always know when it's bad. There's a part of me — a little voice — that begs me to turn back. I think that's a voice I need to listen to now."

"I think you're right. What does it say about being here?"

"It's quite pleased with your garden and your company. In fact, that little voice doesn't really want to be anywhere else. It has no objections to your kingdom, either. It might not be the best nation in this world, but it's a reasonable place and that makes it better than most."

"You understand what is and isn't reasonable, but plunge into darkness anyway."

"My parents' demands of me could be considered perfectly reasonable by many. I sought a lot of extremes and everything in between, hoping to go back to them — if not with answers — then at least better armed to counter their demands. I guess I still find them unreasonable — not dangerous or unsafe — just not acceptable to me."

"You're older now, and that in itself makes a difference. You'll be going back to them as a grown man with worldly experience. Maybe that hard-earned wisdom and perspective are the only answers you'll ever get."

"I hope not," he said gravely. "I don't think that alone would be enough to sway them."

"What can possibly be so bad that it's worth all this?" she demanded.

"No one likes to be told how to live their life," Sam said. "With my parents, I had no freedom and no room to be the kind of man I wanted to be."

"This is what you wanted to be?"

"Not entirely. I wasn't completely sure of what I wanted when I left. I hoped I'd know when I found it. I have a better idea now — now the question is whether I'll ever achieve what I want."

"What do you want?"

"Normalcy. I don't think my parents would allow that if I were to return."

"Then don't go back. You said yourself that it's the only home you've ever known but that it doesn't have to be that way."

He nodded. "So you agree? Good! It's done then — this city is my new home." He slapped his hand against his knee for emphasis.

She smiled. "I'm glad I wasn't wrong about convincing Nalea to help you. I think she'd be pleased to hear that you're thinking of staying." She picked up her bucket and waded back into the rows of corn to weed, but called back. "Have you put any more thought into where we'll travel this winter? Livia rather liked the idea."

Sam looked up surprised, as if he had thought she had merely been placating him during their last discussion.

"Livia will get the same vacation time as you?"

"And our entire brigade. There are eight brigades in total, and two get a full month at the same time. That way, the majority of the army is always available if needed. Usually, our time is in the winter so we can celebrate winter solstice and the new year with family or travel to warmer places. I wouldn't mind the opportunity to do both. Maybe I can get my parents to meet us at my sister's for the holiday. Have you picked a spot?"

"I have a few ideas, but nothing solid yet. Let me know exactly where your sisters are, and I'll pick something that would put them directly in our path."

"Varia and her husband have a farm on the outskirts of Baelorn. Do you know it?"

"I haven't heard of it before. You'll have to show me on a map."

"I'm not sure I've got a map..." she replied thoughtfully. "Nalea will if you ask her."

Sam wore a big smile as he got up again, picking up the weeding bucket.

"I'll find something special, and we'll get you to your sisters, too. It will be a fantastic winter."

Tassia laughed. "I rather dislike the cold. I don't think I've ever thought of the winter as fantastic."

"This one will be — we'll find you some warmth. Does battle ever take you anywhere warm in the winter months?"

"Sometimes, but I don't really get the opportunity to enjoy it. It's difficult to be surrounded by death and enjoy much of anything. We saw very little battle when things initially settled down after the revolution, but now the malcontents are starting to get organized and arm themselves. Livia has said the commanders are expecting a battle to the south before much longer. I hope things simmer long enough for this suspension to be over. The battle is likely to be on the river not far from my sisters, and I'm sure I can get a brief leave to visit them."

"How do you centre yourself again after battle when you don't have your garden to come home to?"

"Drink," she said slyly. "A lot of it. And sometimes men." She paused, embarrassed. "Although I try to go home after battle if I can. It's easy enough to get a leave after a battle, particularly a long or terribly bloody one. It's even easier when I only need a day or two because my family is so close. Livia's family is much farther away, in the forests to the east, and she seldom sees them outside of her holiday leave."

"Will she really be willing to take that time to come visit your family, then?"

"I think she might. She'll just request extra time, and as long as there are no major battles going on, she'll get her request."

Sam nodded, pleased.

"See? Nalea is reasonable."

"She really is," he agreed. "These weeds are not."

Tassia knelt beside him with the weed bucket between them and began digging into the patch he'd started working on. They were all new weeds, small, damp and extraordinarily green. Their tiny size made them difficult to grasp and the work was tedious, but Tassia welcomed the peaceful solitude that settled between her and Sam after such a heavy conversation.

Seeing the change in him — that he was unburdening himself and trying to apply some order to the chaos that had been his life for so long — gave her the same sense of peace that her garden work did. The day's revelations made her feel drawn to him in a way she never had before. When his arm brushed against her as they worked, she grinned at him, not minding.

Sam watched her a moment as he sat back and wiped some of the dirt from his hands onto his pants. He seemed more content than she'd ever seen him, and it pleased her inexplicably. After hearing what he'd been through, she wanted to keep holding him until the last of the darkness disappeared from his countenance.

He leaned forward again, setting the bucket aside so that it was no longer between them, and brushed his fingertips across her cheek, sweeping stray wisps of hair from her face. Even though she knew what was coming, she remained still and watched him. When he slid his hand around her head and pulled her forward, she came willingly, reaching a hand out to touch his chest, her palm resting beside the ring.

When his lips met hers for the second time that day, she welcomed it, realizing just how long it had been since she'd had a man. Her breathing quickened, and every part of her ached for him. He leaned farther forward, bracing a hand in the dirt next to her, and stealing more greedy kisses. The angle was far too awkward though, and she found herself pulling him down across her as she lay in the baking earth.

It was only when he reached his hand up her shirt, squeezing her breast in such a way that she felt she would explode if she didn't tear off her clothes that instant and pull him inside her, that she began to realize their error. Sam seemed to feel it at the same moment, and they each let out an embarrassed laugh and pulled away from each other again to resume weeding without a word.

They passed the afternoon quietly after that, and Sam finally went back to his quarters as the sun began to sink. Tassia went inside to wash up and roast the pheasant she'd bought at the market earlier that day. She lit the lantern hanging in the latrine and was leaning over the basin to scrub the dirt from under her nails when she noticed her reflection in the mirror. The mud still on her face, dried now and lighter, clearly showed Sam's handprints.

Tassia froze, her hands hovering above the fresh water, as the memory of his kiss came rushing back. She finally pulled her hands away from the basin, bracing them against the countertop and bending her head so that her braid nearly dipped into the water. She'd nearly pushed that first kiss from her mind; it had been overwhelmed by Sam's revelations.

Sam was still clearly emotional, still recovering, and was likely to be prone to such outbursts for quite some time. Part of her longed for his gesture to be sincere — her heat rose just at the thought of his touch — but part of her wanted to stick to safer things — to simple friendship. As she finally forced herself to look into the mirror, she realized she wasn't sure of her motivations for either desire.

Tassia was relieved as she passed through the southern gate and entered her brigade's barracks to see that everyone had returned from deployment in the north. The day after Sam's revelations in her garden, she had decided to go home to visit her parents for a few days. Nalea had told her when to expect the brigade to return, but since the soldiers would be recuperating for a few days before delving back into training, Tassia hadn't been concerned about getting back when they did.

She pushed open the door of the hut, expecting to find it empty, and was surprised to find Livia in there napping. She went in and began to put her things away, pushing clothes back into the wardrobe and storing all the vegetables from her mother in the tiny cold cellar beneath the hut. Her rustling finally woke Livia.

"Hey! How long was I out?" Livia said sleepily. She pushed herself up onto one elbow. "How were your parents?"

"Good. Mamma put in extra pumpkins this year and gave up on corn entirely."

"Really? Why would she do that?"

"She's letting Janso handle the corn this year, so he's growing it at the edge of their properties so they can share. She wanted to put in something that takes up space but doesn't require much maintenance. I told her that she'll have to learn one of Sam's stew recipes if she hopes to eat all those pumpkins. She said she'll just bake pies for all the neighbours."

"And she probably will, too!" Livia chuckled. "What did she think about Sam?"

Tassia shrugged. "I didn't say much. Not much to say."

"I guess she *is* your mother. It's not like you'd have to say much — she'll fill in the blanks."

"There really isn't much to say. Nothing that would interest her. He helps in the garden and fancies me, even still. I don't think there's much else unless I repeat some of the tales he's shared, but I don't know how much foreign lands would interest my parents."

Livia sat up and regarded Tassia squarely. "Did he talk?"

"He did."

"About Hetia's?"

"Yes. But I had to repeat it once already for Nalea, and I don't think I can bear to do it again," Tassia said, turning away to finish the last of her unpacking.

"That bad?"

"Everything we heard was true," Tassia said carefully. "But there was more, and it was worse. It's just as bad to hear about as it is to talk about."

Livia shrugged, giving in.

"I thought you'd be with Butch," Tassia commented. She sat at the table with a cup of water, leaning back in her chair to face Livia.

"I was — earlier. We got back late yesterday, and he stayed here. I — um — cleaned up, don't worry."

Tassia grinned. "I suppose my absence served its purpose then."

"He's trying to convince his bunkmate to request a leave to give us some more convenient privacy."

"I suppose it won't be long before that's a permanent arrangement," Tassia said, all jest gone from her voice now.

"I suppose," Livia replied with a one-shoulder shrug. She turned away for a moment. "It's exciting and terrifying. I've fantasized about something like this, but now that it's here, it feels like it will spell the end of adventure. Everyone calls it settling down, and it seems so irrevocably adult and boring, like it demands me to become someone different."

"Maybe it would be if you'd found one of those mystery gents of yours, but Butch won't expect you to change. He probably fancies you better the way you are."

"Probably, but there'll be babies before you know it. Will he fancy me then?" Livia shifted uncomfortably. "I'll have no choice but to find a cottage somewhere, to give up this grand adventure."

"I can't claim to know that man's mind," Tassia said with a shrug. "You're going to have to talk to him about that one, and probably soon."

Livia nodded, solemn for a moment as she reluctantly considered the serious side of her relationship. She climbed down from her bunk and dug out a fresh flask of wine.

"So, what got Sam talking?" she asked, pouring a cup for Tassia.

"It's a long story."

"And I've got nothing but time." Livia winked.

Tassia took a generous gulp, trying to consider where to begin. She recounted the days she had spent with Sam, starting with how they had seen the rest of the brigade off and the day they had spent at the solstice festival. Livia seemed pleased to hear that Sam had taken to another woman, no matter how briefly. Tassia chose her words carefully as she told Livia about the afternoon in the garden when she had learned so much, not wanting to say anything that might embarrass Sam or give Livia any ideas. She didn't mention the kiss at all.

"Sounds like he's getting over it," Livia said. "Especially if he's finally talking about settling somewhere — even if it doesn't end up being here, at least he's finally considering it. But why would a man who so clearly despises his family go to such lengths to keep one heirloom?"

Tassia was relieved that Livia had fixated on the ring and not any of the more awkward parts of the tale.

Tassia shrugged. "I didn't ask who he got the ring from, or how. Maybe it was given to him by a grandfather or uncle who he thought more highly of than his parents."

"Could be. I guess just because he dislikes his parents doesn't mean he dislikes the whole lot of them."

They began to prepare dinner with the items Tassia had brought back and some that Livia had picked up in the market that day. While they worked, Livia told Tassia a little about the deployment, but so many had been killed and so many more had lost everything that she quickly changed the topic.

"It was nice to get back home where it's dry and clean and get out into the garden and pull a couple of the weeds you left me. Also, I got to enjoy the first of the pea crop."

"We've got peas already?"

"Uh, we *had* peas. I finished the ripe strawberries, too. Sorry."

"You ate them *all?*"

Livia nodded sheepishly. "There weren't that many to begin with. But there are plenty of pods that should be fattened enough to eat in a few more days. And the berry plants are covered in blossoms."

Tassia stuck her tongue out at her. "See if I leave you alone with my garden again!"

CHAPTER 5

Sam knelt in the middle of the modest throne room, relieved by the cool marble after the blazing summer sun of Tassia's garden. His hands were caked with soil; he hadn't been given the opportunity to wash up. He remained kneeling with his head down, waiting for Queen Nalea to address him. The room was bustling as advisors came and went, and he patiently waited while she finished with the last of them.

"Sam," she finally said.

He glanced up and cautiously stood.

"Approach."

He carefully made his way to the base of the elevated throne where she sat watching him intently. After so much time in her presence, he knew it would be dangerous to go any further without her permission. She was well-guarded, and Sam could clearly see the dagger she wore at her hip and had no doubts she was proficient in its use.

"I understand you have a ring with you."

"It's just a family heirloom," he replied, trying to remain calm. He hoped the ring wasn't the reason she'd called on him.

"Is it a ring of power?"

"No, Your Grace. It's just a worthless sentiment — the only connection I have left to what used to be my home."

"I understand it's made of gold. That hardly seems worthless to me."

"It's just a trinket," he insisted. "I was never told I had to surrender valuables on my capture, so I don't understand why it's of interest to you."

"I've been told that instead of a gem, there is a white-and-blue stone with a family crest carved into it."

"Yes, Your Grace," he replied, trying not to cringe.

"Let me see it."

His hands began to shake, but he quickly steadied them as he reached behind his neck to undo the clasp on the chain as he had when he'd first shown it to Tassia. He felt betrayed by her, knowing that if she hadn't told the queen of his treasure directly, she was responsible for knowledge of it coming to Nalea indirectly. Maybe she had mentioned it to Livia, and Livia had told the queen. He tried not to be angry; he had never even hinted to Tassia the true weight of the trinket and had never asked her to keep it secret. Now he wished he had.

One of the queen's serving girls approached him to collect the ring, still on the chain. She quickly and lightly climbed the stairs and dropped the ring into Nalea's outstretched palm. Sam watched intently as Nalea studied the ring. Her eyebrow twitched upward slightly in both surprise and recognition as she squeezed her fist around the trinket. She looked up at Sam, her gaze intent and grave, before glancing around at her room full of council.

"Leave us," she commanded.

Sam fought to remain composed, but he was trembling and sweating despite the cool air of the keep. Though he had been in her service for two months, he had never met with her alone before. Her council looked startled, but swiftly began shuffling out of the room through its many side doors.

She squared her gaze on him again once the room was empty, her jaw clenched to restrain obvious anger.

"What game are you trying to play?" she snapped.

"It's no game," he whispered, his throat suddenly dry. He did not want to hear what he knew would come next.

"Prince Samleni Teslerin of the Mountain Song dynasty," she said, hurling his true name and heritage at him like a well-laid punch. "Your homeland is just on the other side of these mountains. What are you doing in my court? Has your family run out of proper spies, so they send their kin now instead?"

"I'm not a spy. I'm in exile."

"From what I understand, your exile is self-imposed. What are you doing here?"

"Looking for answers."

"That foolishness might placate Tassia, but it will not work on me!"

"Your Grace, I assure you there is nothing to be suspicious of. I left my family and their titles behind ten years ago and have been travelling, even in the most unsavoury of places, to learn what I can about the world in which I live. I kept that ring, and kept it hidden, only in the case of my death. I know it can trace me back to my family, but I don't want them to know of my whereabouts unless it's to collect my body."

"You kept it hidden, did you? Half my army knows about it. I can only guess you showed it to Tassia. If you had told her it was a secret, I wouldn't know about it. You've either gotten careless, or you're involved in some plot."

"I was careless," he insisted. "I didn't make a big deal of the ring and hoped she would forget about it."

"I don't believe you. You were captured in the compound of one of my enemies, and now I find out you are a prince from a rival kingdom."

"I'm *not* a prince. I abandoned that title when I abandoned my family and homeland. When I entered your lands, I gravitated toward Hetia's compound because it was the worst of them here. The ugliness I see in places like that helps me to better appreciate the beauty to be found in courts like yours."

Nalea shook her head in frustration. "You are every bit as evasive as Tassia has intimated."

"What will you do?"

"What do you think?" Nalea leaned forward, her gaze not wavering for an instant. "You may have abandoned your throne, but it has certainly not abandoned you. Your family is looking for you, and I am obliged to return you to them."

Sam shook his head. "I would prefer death. Please, I have a month left in my service to you. Let me remain in servitude. Forget that stupid ring."

"In a month's time, the snows will have begun in the high mountain passes, and I would not be able to safely return you to Mountain Song until the spring."

"Then turn me out in the spring."

"If you are released from my service in a month, what will you do? Flee back across the plains? All the way to the seas of Glasctinea? I don't believe you will remain in my lands, waiting to be returned to your home in the spring."

"I know what lies behind me, and I don't wish to return." He shook his head emphatically as he spoke.

"Sam, I cannot let a foreign prince remain a slave under my command."

"I'm not a prince! Please, just forget the ring. Forget who I am."

"I cannot."

He nodded, resigned to defeat and sagging under the weight of it. "Very well, these are your lands after all. But, please, don't tell Tassia. At least not until I'm gone."

Nalea arched her eyebrows in surprise again. "Is she why you wish to stay?"

Sam looked away.

"I won't let you harm her," Nalea snapped in a rare show of emotion. "I sent you to her, thinking you were some harmless fool — that you two would be good for each other. This changes everything. I will not let you use her."

"No, because you are a very unorthodox queen," he replied, looking at her squarely. "You make friends of those in your service and refuse to accept any of your suitors. You have no one to answer to — your parents are dead, and you are free to rule as you see fit. To ignore the customs you find foolish. I only wish I had that luxury. You reject the nobility, and yet when it comes time for an heir, I'm sure you'll find one of them to suit that purpose, won't you? You won't mix the bloodlines."

Nalea was smouldering, her jaw clenched, but she remained silent, unable to address the accusations.

"It's a stupid notion — about the bloodlines," he continued, sympathetic now. "We both know it. You would probably marry a farmer if the court wouldn't overthrow you for it. You're a good queen, and they won't question the lineage of your children, should you choose not to marry. But they won't bow to a commoner as a king. It's a small price to pay for the freedom you have, though, isn't it? Exile is the price I pay for my freedom, and I won't have half the choice you do in the matter if I return home."

Still silent, she kept her gaze fixed on him, mulling her options and weighing them against what he had said. Finally, she tossed the ring and its chain back to him.

"You're right, it's a worthless trinket," she finally said in a conspirator's tone. Then she grew serious. "I won't tell her, but you had damn well better. This will not remain secret for long, and speculation about our meeting will grow until someone else hits upon the truth. When that happens, I have to send you home."

Sam was awash with relief. "Thank you, Nalea. My heritage is all I've concealed from you or anyone else. Everything I've said — everything that's happened — has been genuine."

"Sam, this won't end well. Word of your ring came to me via Butch, and I'm sure you understand by now that he's quite possibly the biggest gossip in all my lands."

Sam sighed, squeezing his eyes shut.

"Are many of the people in your kingdom — particularly those inclined to gossip — really that familiar with forgotten old crests of rival monarchies? I'm amazed you knew it, though I guess nothing should surprise me about you anymore."

"I keep close watch on my enemies," she admitted. "Someone will put the truth together eventually. I risk open war with your homeland if I keep this secret after word begins to spread. I understand that you want normalcy and that you're beginning to find it here, but you really can't bet on secrecy now and you must be honest with Tassia."

"She's just my friend. She won't get that upset when she finds out."

"How long do expect mere friendship to hold?"

"I hope not much longer, but she thinks my attentions are rooted in malady. Perhaps I wouldn't have seen her for who and what she is if I had met her under different circumstances, but that doesn't change the fact that she is unique among all the women I've met in my long years of travel. I understand that you cannot risk war on my behalf, but I hope you understand that I would risk death to remain here."

"Sam, you know I sympathize with you. I would let you have Tassia, and I would convince your family of the same if I could, but keep her in mind and don't let her get caught in the middle of this. Tell her who you are and let her know what she really is to you. She'll appreciate the honesty and perhaps even give you some more direction or some notion of how to proceed."

"I'll try," he said with little conviction. "You will let me carry out the remainder of my service to you?"

"Nothing changes unless I'm forced to notify your family," Nalea assured him, though she still seemed reluctant.

"I'm truly sorry that my fabrications weren't the truth and that I'm not a simple commoner because I wish that I could stay here openly as one of your subjects."

"With all the power you have — or could have — do you really wish to be ruled?"

"There's more freedom for me in your service than there is for me on my kingdom's throne."

"If you feel that way, perhaps you should express that to your family. Your parents are still in good health, and I see no reason why they wouldn't be able to continue their rule until your sister can take over in your absence."

"I have a sister?" Sam asked, flabbergasted.

"You really haven't paid any attention to Mountain Song at all? Sam, she's eleven. How did you not know?"

"I've been gone for twelve years. I guess she was conceived around the time I left."

"Intentional or not, she's a replacement, Sam. I think if you go back there now, as a grown man, and remain firm in your convictions — renouncing your claim to the throne and giving your sister your blessing — I think your family will accept that."

"I'm not going back there unless I have to."

"You're going to have to before long. You won't be able to hide here forever. It would be easier for you to go back there now than to be forced back once they discover you're here. If you were hiding among their allies, it would be different, but relations between Wheat Sky and Mountain Song are tense at best."

"I won't leave Tassia," he insisted.

"Then tell her the truth. Maybe you can convince her to go with you somewhere else. Return to your parents from a nation of allies and you will fare better than if you wait for them to find you here."

Sam closed his eyes and tilted his head back, his body sagging. He had begun to hope that he would be able to live out the plans he'd started to make with Tassia, and even now part of him remained in denial. But Nalea was right;

his time was limited now. At most, he could hope for another year or two of secrecy.

"I won't leave her," he said again, looking back toward Nalea. "I'll weigh all that you've said and hope for the courage and opportunity to talk openly with Tassia. But I won't leave her — I can't."

CHAPTER 6

Tassia stood at the southern edge of her barracks and watched the wagons disappear again, this time into battle. Their destination was a colony on the southern border that the queen's advisors believed was plotting an uprising. Sam had joined her just in time to watch the wagons load up, and he stood silently with her as her comrades slowly vanished over the gentle roll of the low prairie hills.

"Is it any easier than last time?" Sam asked.

"This is definitely worse. I thought it would be easier because it would mean this nonsense is almost over, but it's harder to watch them go into battle. Disaster clean-up isn't as dangerous; it's so unlikely that we'd lose any of them on that kind of deployment. This is different. I might not see some of them again."

Sam nodded.

"I knew this battle was coming, but I'd hoped I'd be off my suspension by the time it happened. They're going right past my sisters to get there."

Sam gave Tassia's shoulders a light squeeze. "I think I've found a good place we can go over the winter. It will take us past your sisters, but also provide some much-welcome warmth."

Tassia turned to him, finally smiling.

"There's a wonderful place at the northern tip of the mountains to the south, and I think you'll enjoy it. Have you been to a hot spring before?"

"No, but I've heard of them."

"The one I'm thinking of — the spring comes down the side of a mountain forming a steaming, hot spring waterfall. It's a narrow stream, and the entire cliff face is covered in rich moss year-round because of the heat from the water. At the bottom is a large, fairly isolated hot pool. It's popular, but not so much that it's ever crowded because it's a bit of a climb to get there."

Tassia grinned and squeezed his hand in excitement. "Mountain climbing and an enchanted hot spring? That sounds delightful!"

Her grin was infectious, and Sam was relieved that she liked the idea as much as he had hoped she would. He kept hold of her hand and tugged her back to the road, heading toward her hut.

"There's a nearby city with some stunning architecture, too, and they have a month-long ice festival that starts with the solstice. I've never been there in the winter, but I hear the ice sculptures are unbelievable."

"That would be something! I'm looking forward to it already. Who knows, maybe I'll catch some wanderlust, too. Have you thought of what you'll do once your service is up?"

"I've got a whole week left; I'm sure I'll think of something. I'll need somewhere to live and a way to pay for it. Nalea said I'll be released to a workhouse until I can earn enough to pay rent somewhere, so that gives me a little more time to really think it over. In the past, I've always done farm work or helped at inns when I needed coins, so I'll likely start there."

"The inns here tend to hire children for general chores, so you probably won't have much luck there."

"Well, farm work it is then! There, narrowed it down already."

He was enthusiastic but nonchalant as well, and Tassia wondered how serious he was about it all. She did like the sound of the vacation he was planning, but at the same time, she wasn't getting her heart set on it yet. She still didn't believe he would stay long after Nalea released him.

Tassia had originally planned on going through her drills and then working in the garden, but the day was blazing hot so she changed out of her armour into a blue summer dress, trading her combat boots for sandals, and joined Sam in the park, lounging in the shaded lower branches of a willow that leaned out over the water. Tassia removed her sandals and let her feet dangle into the cool water. Sam was the first to break the companionable silence that had settled over them.

"This is the first time in as long as I can remember when I could just enjoy a place without wondering where I was going next, what I would need and how I was going to get there," Sam said, looking out over the water. "It's refreshing, and it makes me appreciate this place. There's nothing remarkable about this city, but maybe that's what makes it special... it's just a wonderful, normal, safe place."

"I've never thought of normal like that," Tassia said. "It is peaceful. I've never had worries about the future — apart from concerns related to battle."

"I haven't felt this at peace before. I always mistook idleness for boredom, but just sitting at the water's edge on a beautiful summer day and having the opportunity to reflect has calming and healing effects that I didn't realize existed."

She gave him a sidelong glance and was surprised to see he was being serious. "There must be something peaceful about the extraordinary places you've seen. Like that place in the desert that you love."

"Yes, there's a humbling sort of peace to be found in those awe-inspiring places. Where the true power of the world around us — not power exacted by humans, but the power completely independent of us — where that kind of beauty is abundant is soul-soothing, too. But none of those places were places to stay. Before long, I stopped noticing their beauty and wondered about the next journey, where the next dangers might be."

"So staying put is looking more tempting?"

"It is. I just can't imagine doing it forever. I would need to punctuate it with some travel. Even just small trips like the one we'll take in the winter. Staying somewhere forever is so permanent. It will take some getting used to. You need to adjust to some wandering and seeing the world, and I need to adjust to enjoying where I am."

Sam fell silent again. His gaze looked out over the water, but Tassia could tell he was deep in thought. She hoped he meant what he said about the peace he felt in staying. Even if he had never run into trouble in all his years abroad, she still envisioned such constant travel to be chaotic and couldn't imagine being so uprooted. Unlike Sam, she would hate being away from her family. It was hard enough being so far from her sisters.

They remained in the park all afternoon, leaving the willow tree to catch a one-act play at the outdoor theatre. The theatre had been built at the edge of a forested area at the bottom of a hill, and the slope of hill allowed everyone an unhindered view of the stage. Tassia was relieved it was a comedy. She was in no mood for watching something sombre while her comrades were marching into danger.

They had dinner on a patio and wandered the city until well after dark, enjoying the torchlight and the sweet night smells. Sam walked her back to her barracks, more out of a reluctance to head home than any misconception about protecting her. Both of them knew full well he was more likely to need her as an escort than the reverse.

At the barracks, away from the city lights, the landscape was brightened by starlight. Far out on the prairies, they could see pinpricks of light from distant farms and the oily red blossoming of the occasional brush fire. Sam sat with her on the dry grass behind the hut. The garden smelled pungent and sweet in the night air, and the earth, which had baked all day under the unrelenting sun, had now started to cool. Above them, the clear night sky revealed the beginning of a late-summer star shower.

"I forgot about this," Sam said. "It's always so stunning, though some years are more extravagant than others. The prairie skies are the perfect backdrop for this."

"We always try to catch it. It's easier to enjoy than the two over the winter." Tassia leaned back on her elbows, taking in the whole of the heavens. "Have you studied the stars at all? What causes them? And why do the showers happen the same time every year?"

Tassia could make out Sam shrugging in the near-dark. "I'd like to learn more," he said. "There's a university here, isn't there?"

"Yes, and Nalea has been working very hard to establish its reputation. She's been bringing in reputable scholars from all over. I believe there is a small campus out on the prairie just south of here where they solely study the stars."

"That would be something. Do you have any interest in scholarly pursuits?"

"Not right now. But I like books. Livia and I are always sharing the books we find."

"I think I'd like to go to university. Learning from the brightest of minds is something I miss. I had some excellent tutors as a child, and I would like to learn like that again."

"I'm sure you can manage it. I don't think tuition is too extravagant. And you're used to living by narrow means."

"A shack would be the nicest place I've lived in since leaving home," he admitted, sighing at the realization. "I've lived in workhouses, camps, compounds and now the prisoners' quarters. Just having a space that's my own would be a welcome change. Not to have to fall asleep to the grunts and snores of strangers would be a joy."

Tassia smiled. "I'm always relieved that Livia doesn't snore much."

"Well, I should get back soon," he said, suddenly rising. "They will start to think I've managed to run off."

"I'm sure Nalea will know you're here," Tassia commented, but didn't discourage him from leaving.

Tassia had just finished cleaning up her breakfast dishes when she heard the first rumble of thunder. If there had been others before it, they had been carried away by the wind or lost in the din of her morning chores. Now she noticed the sky to the west had darkened as the storm roiled across the prairie from the foothills.

By the time Tassia reached the doorway, she could hear the first drops of rain pattering against the roof and smacking the cobblestone out front. She opened the door and stood in the threshold, watching the rain come down. The drops were fat; it took only one to fill the palm of her outstretched hand.

The day had begun hot, and the morning sun had been busy baking the cobblestones when the storm hit. Now the stones were steaming, and the fresh scent of petrichor, reminiscent of wet dust and green wood, arose. It made her head swim with memories of childhood summers in the garden, dancing in the rain to welcome the end of a dry spell. She closed her eyes to breathe in the sweet aroma of the warm stone and cool rain, her lips relaxing into a smile.

She barely noticed the sound of Sam's boots slapping against the cobblestone, only becoming fully aware of his presence when he skidded on the slick stone and cursed. Tassia opened her eyes to see him bounding toward her doorway, seeking shelter. As he joined her, grumbling about the weather, she noticed his wet hair was plastered to his forehead, the soft fabric of his shirt pressed against his broad shoulders.

"Don't you have a coat?" she asked him.

"Didn't think I'd need it," he said. "The sun was still shining when I left the castle."

"Prairie storms are swift beasts, rolling across the plain with the speed of a dragon," she warned him, grinning.

"Noted." He shook some of the water from his hair and looked out the door at the damp morning. "Are you just watching it?"

"Nothing like a good downpour to nourish the garden. And it will save us more trips to the pumps," she pointed out. "I love the rain — everything about it. Well, except during battle."

Her gaze drifted absently toward the distant, vacant square. She missed battle and was no longer satisfied with drills.

"Now that I'm out of it, I suppose I can see what you mean," Sam conceded, glancing up at the racing clouds just as another peal of thunder rent the air, vibrating the ground beneath them. "The rainfall sounds much like the wind through the trees, and that's something I certainly miss being out here and so far from the forests."

Tassia nodded and ducked back into the hut, just long enough for a quick glance out the window. "It looks to be clearing in the west," she told him.

"Already?"

"Prairie storms are quick," she reminded. "Nalea doesn't have any work for you today?"

"I'm not sure if she will have any more for me. One of her aides just returned from a brief holiday so there's little for me to do. She said I may as well just come join you so you're not alone, especially since I always return from my visits with a better idea of what I'll do with myself."

"Six days left," Tassia said. "Are you nervous?"

"Not really. Going from one dorm to another really doesn't change anything for me. And I almost like this better since part of my work for Nalea seems to involve your garden. I doubt I will get the same treatment in the workhouse."

"I suppose not. Do you know which one she's releasing you to?"

"She said it's on the south side of the city and makes clothing. There's a curfew and the dorms are cramped, but the pay sounds excellent and I will still get a free day every week to give me time to find something new. I think I'll try farms first. Do you know any farmers in the area?"

"Sorry, just the ones in Winterberry. As the harvest nears, I'm sure you'll find some looking for extra help."

"That's good to know." He paused, observing as she strapped on her gear for her morning exercises. "Can I practice with you?" he asked.

She stopped in the middle of strapping on her sword belt and set it aside. She didn't mind the distraction and was glad to see him taking interest in things as the end of his servitude approached. She wasn't sure if he was still serious about becoming a soldier, but anything she could teach him about what she knew would likely benefit him, especially if he still intended to wander.

She took him through each of the stretches, instructing him first and then correcting his form. Even when they weren't training, she and Livia often went through this morning stretching routine in their hut, especially in the winter when the cold stiffened them while they slept. He'd trained with a sword as a child, and she was pleased to see that he still remembered a fair bit of what he'd learned. By the time she had taken him back over the basics of fencing, the sun was out, and they headed out back, each taking up a garden stake to spar.

"I'm not ready for the real sword?" Sam said, laughing.

"Not even close," Tassia countered.

"You don't have to go easy on me," Sam said. "A good whack in the ribs will remind me to keep my arms down, and nearly getting that stake in the eye will remind me not to keep my arms down too far. Knock me over enough, and my feet will eventually remember how to be graceful and keep a proper stance."

"You better start by widening your stance," Tassia instructed, a playful and competitive gleam in her eyes. "And grip the stake better than that. Like this—" she said, standing next to him and holding out her hands so he could copy her grip. "Tight enough you won't drop it or have it knocked away, but not so tight your hands begin to ache — you'll quickly lose strength and that's just as bad as a loose grip."

"Okay, I think I'm ready."

Tassia could see that he wasn't, but only grinned mischievously and lunged forward to attack. He managed to pivot out of her way, but Tassia spun to follow him just as quickly and caught him in the thigh. He was already off balance from turning so awkwardly, and the blow tripped him up. He stumbled as Tassia moved in behind him and swung her mock-sword, catching him in the middle of the back. He ended up face first in the mud, and Tassia couldn't stop laughing.

"Do you know what you just did wrong?" she asked.

"Everything," he replied sheepishly.

"It all fell apart with your pivot. Your feet were too far apart when you landed, making it easier for me to throw you off-balance. You also didn't have your guard held properly. You were too high and off-centre. Your footing was the worst, though."

"Can we just go slowly and concentrate on the footwork?" Sam asked. "I think I will fare much better if I'm not falling down all the time."

"Let's start by making sure you track your feet properly."

"How do you mean?"

"When you take a step back with one foot, the other stays planted, which widens your stance and puts you off-balance. You need to slide your foot to follow the one that moves. Watch," she instructed.

She held her stake out with a firm grip and tilted it slightly forward, adopting her fighting stance. The she took a step forward and pointed to her back foot with her sword so he could see how it slid forward to follow the lead foot. She took a step back again, and this time her front foot slid to follow the lead. She did the same taking steps to the side.

"Do you see now?"

"I think so."

"Don't keep the tracking foot firmly planted, but don't lift it all the way off the ground either. This way you'll be able to stay balanced but move quickly. There's a drill we can do to help. I'll take a step toward you while you take a step away, and then I'll strike so you have to block. When I move back or to the side, you follow me and strike. It's almost like dancing," she said.

It was slow going at first, with Sam frequently stumbling, but he only fell once, and by the time they were ready to break for lunch, Tassia was confident in his ability to keep his stance.

"Now the trick will be for you to keep this up again tomorrow and the next day," she said.

"...and after lunch," he added.

She laughed and shook her head. "You had better be able to do it again after lunch. We can practice in the square if you'd like. The possibility of falling on stone will provide plenty of motivation to keep your footing, but it will also be easier to keep your balance on a smooth, even surface."

They drilled in the square most of the afternoon, and Sam's abilities rapidly improved on the stone surface. The day had grown hot again, and the recent rainfall had made the air humid, so they went back to the hut to wash up when they were done. Tassia brought some supplies out to the square where there was a large fire pit for communal use so she and Sam could make a small stew. The cauldron Tassia had wasn't very big, but was perfect for one meal.

"Where did you get that?" Sam asked. "I've never seen a proper cauldron that small before. I've been burning my stews in a tin pot for a decade."

"They're part of our army gear," Tassia said. "Some of our supplies are sold in the market — not weapons, but gear like bedrolls, canteens, pots and spice boxes."

"That's something else I could use," he replied. "A spice box small enough for just a few meals. I've got a pouch for salt, but it's easy to tire of just salt."

Tassia marvelled at how even the simple life she led seemed decadent compared to his years of travel. She couldn't imagine a stew without some sage, thyme, pepper or basil.

"I imagine the bedrolls you have are lightweight," he said.

"They roll up small, too," she added. "The larger canteens are designed to be strapped across the body. I've even fought wearing one when we were ambushed on a forest path. I didn't even notice I was wearing it until a foe sliced it open. I was so angry! And had to spend the rest of the day in wet boots."

"I can't think of many things more uncomfortable than wet boots," he said. "Maybe a damp bed."

"Yes, that's awful, too."

"So I could easily find some of your gear in the market?"

"Everything but weapons and armour. Well, you can find weapons and armour at the market now and then, but not the same quality as soldiers use. For enough coin, you can commission weapons from a smith."

"Fair enough. Citizens can arm and defend themselves, but the queen's army still has the advantage in case of uprisings."

"That's the intent, yes." She watched him carefully for a moment, and then dipped a spoon in the cauldron and took a sip. "Almost ready... You're awfully interested in the army today. Any reason?"

He shook his head. "Just considering my options. You say the army travels, even if just for battle, and that sort of thing might make it easier for me to stay here. I'm not sure what I want exactly."

"Well, if you still want to travel, farm work is good. You get the entire winter free and clear, unless you work on a ranch — then they might need you to help with the animals."

Sam nodded thoughtfully. "So I'll probably want to stick to working for farmers who focus on crops."

"I think so," Tassia said as she scooped the stew into bowls.

"Excellent! See? Nalea was right; I always find more direction when I come to see you. Oh, and she's invited you to come to her chambers this evening — or any evening this week. She anticipates some free time and thought you might like some extra company."

"Oh good! I'd like that. I haven't had much of a chance to speak to her since — since I told her about Hetia. And that wasn't much of a visit. I'll come back with you when you go tonight."

They grinned at each other as they took their first bites of stew.

Sam was waiting for Tassia outside the queen's chambers the next morning as a line of aides, counsellors and court members began to form in wait of the queen's appearance. Her personal serving girls were in with her, but so far no one had emerged. Sam wondered what was going on, but then Tassia finally appeared, moving slowly and looking ill.

"Everything all right?" Sam asked.

"Nalea had some excellent wine for us," Tassia said, speaking softly. "A little too much wine."

Sam chuckled and guided Tassia quietly back to her hut.

"Will you be all right?" he asked, standing uncertainly on the steps as she went inside.

"I'm going to make myself a good tea and maybe hold my head under some cold water for as long as I can stand. If I feel any better after that, I'll make some porridge. Then I'll be fine. If you want to stick around, I shouldn't be more than an hour. If I'm more than an hour, I'll need the whole day."

"I can muck around in the garden, then. It hasn't been weeded in a while, and I'll bring a basket with me and harvest anything that looks ripe."

"You might need more than one basket," she said with a small smile.

Sam went outside. Eventually Tassia came back out with one of the waterskin canteens strapped across her chest. It was designed to be easy to drink from without removing it, and Tassia drank from it frequently. She also ate almost as much as they harvested from the vines.

"The others need to get back soon so they can help eat all of this," Tassia commented. "Livia is usually out here every day getting her fill of cherry tomatoes and beans. She ate most of my pea crop, too — that fiend!"

"If you're just looking to share some, I wouldn't mind bringing a basket with me back to my quarters tonight. I'm sure it will make me quite popular. We get fed well, but I'm sure the others don't get nearly as many vegetables as they would like."

"Please, take as much as you want. Livia and I can't eat all of this at the best of times, and this year my garden is much larger than normal."

Sam filled the basket and put it on the doorstep to collect when he left, while Tassia remained out in the garden, pulling the odd weed but mostly just enjoying the greenery and the pleasantly pungent smell of the tomato plants. The day was clear and hot, and the soil turned to mud where it mingled with the sweat of her hands and forearms, leaving black streaks when she absently wiped her brow. The sticky air was sweet in the garden, and she seemed content to sit all day in the dirt and watch time go by. She was sitting among the pumpkin vines, retraining them to keep them from growing into the rows of peas, when Sam joined her. He nudged her with his arm, and she grinned up at him for a moment before returning her attention to the garden and what he suspected was a lingering headache.

He was also content to just let the day pass, and his gaze wandered to the mountains on the horizon, hazy blue with distance, and he felt a brief pang of homesickness that he hadn't felt in all his years of travel. He didn't miss his parents, but he longed for the familiarity and stability he'd known under their roof. He knew Tassia was right that he needed a home, and he hoped against all odds that he was sitting in the midst of a new one.

When he looked back, he found her watching him curiously, and she smiled when he met her gaze. He ran his fingers over her midnight tresses that were pulled from her face in a braid, as always. When she reached up to touch his hand but didn't pull it away, he felt a sense of hope rise up and seized it, leaning forward to find her soft lips. Her mouth was small, like the rest of her, but her lips were full and inviting, and he kissed her deeply, gently teasing his tongue along the tip of hers.

She leaned into him, her hand resting on his knee and her breath quickening, and he'd just begun to believe he might finally enjoy her fully when she pulled away, gasping. She let out a little giggle and turned her attention back to her plants. Her mind and heart seemed in conflict, but Sam couldn't understand why.

Tassia got up suddenly, slicing through his thoughts, and he saw her swiftly but carefully picking her way across the pumpkin patch. She stooped down, pushing aside the large fuzzy leaves to uncover a massive patch of dandelions. Their spiky green foliage had blended in with the vines, and their yellow flowers matched the ones growing on the plants. Neither of them had noticed the weeds encroaching.

"It never fails," she said, digging in and thoroughly blackening her fingers. "They always manage to hide under the leaves. There's probably a million of them in the other squash, too."

Tassia had taken over the pumpkins, and Sam moved into the zucchini, carefully pushing aside the broad leaves to see if there was anything growing under them. He found a few stray patches of clover, but nothing like the dandelions Tassia had come across. They were both combing through the vines when the first piercing cries shattered the still summer air.

Tassia swore and stood upright, searching the sky from horizon to horizon. The cries were loud, but clearly still far off.

"Do you see them?" Tassia demanded, her voice beginning to break with panic.

Sam didn't understand and looked around, seeing nothing but cumulus.

"Dragons, Sam."

His eyes grew wide, but he said nothing. The cries came once more, and he could at least identify the direction.

"North."

"Let's go! The city blocks our view of them, so we'll never see them until they're here!"

"Where do we go?"

"Into the city. There are shelters. We'll go to Nalea." She cast a quick, desperate look around at her garden. "Good luck," she whispered to it, and then clutched Sam's hand and began running. She paused at the hut, considering, and took another look around. "We should have a few minutes yet," she said to him and darted inside. She came out a moment later with her soldier's gear and a couple of books. Sam grabbed up the basket of vegetables, and they started running toward the city.

The streets were full of people scrambling for cover. If the dragons were coming in from the north, the brigades along that side would be preparing while the rest took to their shelters. Tassia could have taken them to her brigade's shelter, but she couldn't bear the thought of just two of them in such a large and hollow place with no news of what was going on outside.

They fought against the waves of people who were heading toward the local shelters and away from the castle, and Tassia paused only for a moment to see if she could spot the dragons yet. There were two clans in the nearby mountain range, and they were constantly warring with each other, but only the red clan came after human settlements. All dragons travelled in groups, and it was impossible to tell from their cries if this was a group from the blue clan merely passing over or one from the red clan out marauding. They wouldn't know until they could see them, and by then it would be too late — especially if it was the red clan.

Tassia could see nothing but blue sky and soft clouds, so they kept going, heading for the queen's towers at the heart of the city. Tassia knew they would be safe if they made it to the shelters, which were sturdy and deep underground. The dragons were not out to destroy the city; in fact, there was little damage they could do as most of the city was built of brick and stone. In previous attacks, they had targeted the rulers and left the rest of the population to deal with minor damage. Even so, Tassia knew it was critical to not be caught above ground when they arrived.

She paused to scour the sky once more, but Sam nudged her from behind.

"I'm watching, you lead. They're not here yet."

He was holding on to the strap of the bag she had slung over her shoulder and giving only a fraction of his attention to the path ahead of them as he watched the skies to the north. They could always turn south again and head to the nearest shelter if the dragons appeared before they reached the towers.

A surge of terror rippled through the crowd as people started screaming, "Red!"

"I don't see anything," Sam said to Tassia.

"Scouts to the north probably see them now and have passed the message along. Hurry!"

The crowds were thinning out, and Tassia and Sam were able to go much faster. They reached the castle as the cries became deafening, but there was still no sign of the clan. The guards at the castle recognized Tassia and ushered them in. Nalea was guarded by soldiers and enchanters, but standing in a vast courtyard in case the dragons wanted to negotiate.

"Can I help?" Tassia called.

Nalea spotted her, but waved her off.

"Into the shelter. Gear up, and I'll send for you if we need reinforcements."

Tassia nodded and turned, pulling a confused Sam with her. He paused at the door and turned her around to face him.

"Is it far to the shelter from here?"

"Down the hall, there's an iron door, and then the stairs."

"I just want to see them, just a glimpse. Can we wait here?"

She pursed her lips nervously and glanced to the sky, wincing as another cry came.

"All right," she said. "The instant we see them, we head to the shelter though. It's a long way down the stairs and a long tunnel to the underground compound. It's out under one of the courtyards, not under the actual castle."

"In case they collapse the building." Sam nodded in understanding.

Tassia began gearing up while Sam watched the sky. A few stragglers rushed past them, heading for safety. Sam heard people crying out in renewed terror a moment before he spotted the dragons — far away still, but sleek and glimmering crimson against the blue sky. Sam found them mesmerizing to watch — their movements had a liquid grace that betrayed their size and strength, and their wings seemed to be tinged with silver — but his reverie was shattered by the clang of Tassia's things dropping to the stone as she starting swearing.

He looked in her direction just as she drew her sword and started running back toward Nalea, and he realized she hadn't been looking north at all, but to the southwest. He turned and followed her gaze. A spike of fear and adrenaline tore through his body when he spotted the lone dragon silently sweeping toward the adjacent courtyard where Nalea stood in wait. All eyes were on the northern approach. He dropped his basket beside Tassia's things, but froze, unsure of what to do.

Tassia was already screaming the warning to Nalea and her people, and the enchanters got a shielding ward up against the dragonfire an instant before it exploded off the invisible dome. Cover blown, the beast began screeching. Its cry was enough to bring Sam to his knees; the terrible sound had physical weight at such close range. When he looked up again, he saw the beast streaking across the courtyard, dragging its heavy spiked tail along the ground. It shredded the ward that had been meant only to protect against fire and trained its sights on Nalea. Sam watched one of her guards — quite possibly the largest man he had ever seen — slam a war hammer nearly as large as Tassia into the beast's tail just in time to alter its course around the queen. Her guards swarmed her then, pulling her farther from danger.

Having missed its best chance at eliminating Nalea, the beast spiralled up over the towers to regroup and attack with renewed force. In the aftermath, Sam could see several wounded people and at least one who was certainly dead; they must have been caught outside the ward when the dragonfire hit.

Tassia was still rushing headlong into the courtyard, her shield across her back and her sword held ready, but Sam could see she had only had time to strap on one forearm guard. He looked down to see the rest of her armour beside him on the stones. Nalea, encircled by two enchanters and nearly a dozen guards, was running toward where Sam now stood, heading for the safety of the castle. Sam's feet finally heeded the garbled messages from his brain, and he began to run as well, heading out to Tassia. He fought to keep panic from overtaking him. He reached the edge of the battle zone just as Nalea and her entourage passed him, but none of them took notice.

Sam picked up a lance of one of the fallen guards, and the energy of his fear pushed him forward more quickly than he would have thought possible. He spotted the dragon, crimson death, swooping back toward the courtyard, and it seemed focused on Tassia. She was separated from both groups — the guards remaining to defend and those bringing the queen to safety — and was an easy target.

The dragonfire rippled off the renewed dome of protection the enchanters had erected, but there was simply not enough of them to create a defence that could withstand the physical attack of a dragon. The dragon tore through the shield again, a fiery mountain collapsing on them from the sky, and skimmed the ground with teeth gnashing and claws tearing.

Tassia had her shield out to deflect the claws as she swept her sword at the dragon as it passed, but the rush of air from its wings was enough to knock her to the ground and expose her to the spiked bludgeon of its tail. She rolled backward and came to a crouch, ready to fight. She still had her sword, but her shield had been knocked from her grasp and carried away by the dragon-gale.

Sam wasn't thinking when he swiped the shield up off the ground — he was focused intently on the swiftly approaching tail and trying to calculate its trajectory. He slid to a stop just in front of Tassia, jammed the hilt of the lance into the ground and braced it with his entire body. He got the shield up just in time to receive the strike from the dragon, but the lance had done its job. It wasn't nearly enough to pierce the tough dragon scales, but it caused enough pain for the dragon to swing away from them, dealing only a glancing blow.

The impact was still enough to slam both Sam and Tassia backward a dozen paces, a shot hard enough to cause Sam to black out for a moment. He came to as Tassia was frantically dragging him toward the castle and out of the worst of the danger. The enchanters and castle guards were retreating as well, now that Nalea was safely inside, and the dragon was rocketing skyward again, its battle cries being met by those of the other dragons who were closing in on the castle.

Sam stumbled to his feet, ignoring Tassia as she cursed his foolish bravery, and they retreated into the castle, stopping briefly to collect what they'd dropped when the attack began. The iron door to the shelter still stood open, and Tassia plunged through it, dragging Sam behind her. The stairs were lined with lanterns at regular intervals, and there was another iron door at the entrance to the tunnel. This one was closed tight, but a guard opened it from the inside once Tassia identified herself. The tunnel stretched out into the darkness, and Sam quickly began to feel nervous in the narrow, low passage. It had been designed to be too small for a dragon to follow, no matter how determined, and the door at the end of it was also made of iron, but unlocked.

Tassia and Sam entered a large room, long and arching, with tables and benches running down the centre and bunks along the walls. Like the stairs and tunnel, the shelter was made of grey stone and lined with lanterns. The wall along the back was packed with supplies, and the higher ceiling made Sam breathe a little easier. The shelter was full of people milling around, and Sam recognized quite a few of them as the queen's aides and members of the court.

Nalea spotted Sam and Tassia right away and broke away from her aides to speak with them.

"What the blazes was that?" Nalea demanded, clearly incensed over the attack. "Have you ever heard of anything so brazen?"

"It meant to kill you," Tassia said.

"And it would have if you hadn't seen it." The queen softened a little. "Thank you, Tass. What would I do without you?"

Nalea finally took stock of the pair and laughed a little. "You two look awful! What happened?"

Sam realized that they were still crusted with mud from Tassia's garden, but were also sooty and scraped from battle. He recounted what happened as best he could.

"I panicked, really," he finished. "Not a thought in my head, except getting to Tass because she'd know what to do."

"You saved my life, Sam," she said quietly. "As stupid as it was for you to try. That dragon would have shredded me the way it meant to shred Nalea if you hadn't done something."

The shelter door burst open one last time, and a handful of guards and enchanters tumbled in, a tendril of smoke and fire curling up from the top of the door as it slammed shut behind them. Everyone was startled, and Nalea went to them immediately for an explanation.

Tassia collapsed against the nearest wall and sat on the floor, while Sam sat next to her, silent and anxious.

"That hallway..." he muttered, shaking his head.

"Smothering, I know," Tassia said. "Has to be small though."

"Yes — to keep them out. Still..."

"It's unpleasant," she agreed. "This room is better. We're safe."

Not long after they sat to rest, Nalea stalked past them, looking troubled.

"What happened?" Tassia called.

"One of the smaller dragons chased the last of the guards all the way to the stairs and got partway down them before it got stuck in the corners. A ward held the flame back for a while, but it still reached most of the way to the shelter door once the ward came down. They were quite serious about killing me today. No one seems to know the particular reason why, and I suspect one of my rivals bargained with them."

Nalea moved on, and Sam sat shaking his head in anger and disbelief.

"Only a fool would try to use the dragons as pawns. When this goes badly, they'll just go back to whoever sent them in the first place," he said. "Then there will be two ruined cities, and no one will have come out better for it."

"I can't fathom the kind of bravery or stupidity required to even consider bargaining with the red clan."

"If someone really did send them, we may be stuck here for a while. I've heard of rulers having to send desperate, secret messages to the blue clan for aid. Of course, by then, there's not much left to save."

"At least the shelters will hold that long, and there's still a city full of people left to rebuild."

Sam nodded but remained silent. The last time he'd been in a dragon raid as a child, it had lasted nearly a week, and the smell in the shelter had begun to grow unbearable. The dwindling supplies had tried everyone's patience. Thinking about it made him feel smothered again, like the tunnel had, and he tried to push the thoughts away. Tassia saw his troubled expression and reached out, giving his hand a squeeze. He smiled briefly, a worried half-grin, and squeezed back.

Tassia eventually went to wash up, bringing back a bowl of clean water and a cloth for Sam. Once he'd cleaned the worst of his wounds and wiped off as much mud as he could, they went to sit with Nalea and share the basket of vegetables Sam had managed to salvage. Despite being surrounded by so many members of the court, the queen was friends with very few of them and welcomed Tassia and Sam's company.

"These could be the last things I get out of my garden this year," Tassia said forlornly, popping a cherry tomato into her mouth.

"They came from the north and have no reason to attack the southern part of the city. They may not even notice your garden," Nalea said, trying to reassure her.

"With my brigade gone so much, I'm sure I could get things cleaned up and replanted with my remaining days off."

"They're going to be away another week or so," Nalea said. "The colony wishes to negotiate a truce, and I had just managed to dispatch a convoy before the dragons struck, but your group will have to stay out there until a peace deal has been reached."

Tassia sighed. "I guess I'll just go home for a while again. Maybe I can help Janso in his shop or something." She looked over to Sam. "You'll be free soon; why don't you come with me?"

He looked questioningly at Nalea.

"The workhouse isn't another prison," the queen said to him. "You may miss any days you choose, as long as you understand you only get paid for work you're present for."

Sam nodded. "Maybe I will come. Or if there's enough time, we could meet the others to the south. You can see your sisters, and we'll wait for them there."

"Maybe," Tassia said, but shifted restlessly.

"I wish we had some more of that wine," Nalea commented. "I ought to mandate that the shelters have as much wine as water."

Sam grinned.

"I'm sure we've had enough wine to last us a fortnight," Tassia said, trying to ignore the headache she'd been fending off all day.

The other people in the shelter had settled in at the tables to eat small meals as the day came to an end. Sam and Tassia claimed beds near Nalea and her bodyguards and shared the books Tassia had brought. She was relieved she had been wearing comfortable civilian clothes and not only her gear when the dragons came. She hated trying to sleep in her armour and stashed it under the bed with her boots and the books they weren't reading.

Nalea was much more comfortable — her aides had brought her plenty of extra clothing and some of her more pressing work to pass the time. During the day, she sat at one of the tables poring over correspondence, studying maps and preparing for the carnage they were likely to face once the dragons were gone again.

After two days, Sam and Tassia had each read all of Tassia's books and talked them over at great length. Sam had begun to talk about his travels again and was trying to describe the irrigation systems in the desert to Nalea when the queen's top enchanter burst into the shelter announcing the dragons had finally gone.

"That was too quick," Nalea said, suspiciously. "You're certain it's a full retreat?"

"The scouts have lost sight of them. They left the city late this morning, and we've been tracking them ever since, but we've lost them; they've simply gone too far."

Nalea gathered up the work in front of her and headed for the door, talking with the enchanter as she went. Tassia and Sam gathered up their things and followed out close behind as a crowd formed behind them.

"I want a full report," Nalea demanded. "How many casualties and how bad is the damage?"

"The damage is surprisingly minimal, Your Grace. They focused the attack on the towers which, of course, were designed to withstand it. Our enchantments kept them from ever gaining full access. There's not a spot in your courtyards that hasn't been scorched, but no structural damage was caused."

"No damage to the city?" she asked, stunned.

"Very little. This was certainly an assassination attempt."

"Casualties?"

"Twenty-four dead and fifty-eight wounded, at last count. They appear to have made some random attacks on their way in and out of the city, and we have yet to receive any confirmed reports of damage from the outlying areas."

Nalea was silent for a while, considering the information.

"That's very odd," Sam finally said, breaking the silence. "That's quite possibly the quietest raid they've ever been involved in."

Nalea nodded. They exited the dim tunnel into more darkness. It was night out, and the torches had yet to been lit, leaving the castle in long shadows.

"What time is it?" Nalea finally asked.

"Nearing midnight."

She halted and turned to Tassia. "It's too late for you to head back to your hut, especially since there's a very good chance they will return before dawn." She nodded to one of her aides. "Bring them up to my chambers and see to it they're comfortable. Bring any fresh food you can find and a good flask of wine. Wash water, too, for all three of us."

Tassia and Sam were led away while Nalea stayed with her advisors to gather more information and begin delegating the cleanup. She had to be certain they were prepared for another attack and wanted to know the exact extent of the damage across the city and the outlying areas.

One of Nalea's serving girls brought Tassia and Sam up to Nalea's personal quarters near the top of the tower. They entered into a large antechamber that contained several lounging chairs and an overstuffed but still elegant sofa near a massive mantel. There were two doors across the room, one leading to Nalea's personal library and another to her bedchambers.

Sam was nervous. "I really should just head down to the prisoners' quarters."

"For all you know, there aren't any more prisoners' quarters," Tassia pointed out. "The rest of them might be spending some extra time in the shelter until temporary housing can be built. I doubt you want that."

"No, I suppose not. But still, this is — awkward."

"You'll be fine. Wash up," Tassia said, nodding to the basins and washcloths being set out for them.

While Sam revelled in a bit of cleanliness for the first time in days, washing away dirt still lodged under his nails from the garden, Tassia dropped her gear at the sofa, claiming it, and began gathering up throw blankets from around the room. The serving girl had moved to the hearth and got a fine blaze going before disappearing into Nalea's bedchambers to prepare them for the queen's arrival. There was a wardrobe at the far side of the room, near Nalea's bedchambers, and Tassia searched through it to dig out a few more blankets for Sam.

He was watching her curiously.

"You don't think it's odd that you're so familiar with your queen's personal chambers?"

"She was my friend before she was my queen," Tassia said with a shrug. "You think it's odd?"

"I've never been in the personal quarters of a monarch before. Nalea is certainly rare in the company she keeps. The princess of Elintrin was rumoured to have close friends from lower in the court, and she entertained them frequently, but she also wasn't a queen yet."

"Nalea is different. She's always had some very powerful friends, and she keeps them near, regardless of rank. She keeps in touch with what keeps the lower classes happy while also maintaining a strong authority among the nobles. They have their wealth and their titles, but she does not allow them to abuse that or those in their service. She has done a great deal to pull the lower classes out of misery — and she did it in a short time — so there is general contentment here."

"She's remarkable," Sam said. "Few could manage what she has."

"She's clever," Tassia agreed. "And she has an iron will. She will not be swayed when she knows she is right. But she always seeks a balance."

Tassia handed Sam the blankets she'd found for him and went to wash up. He pulled some cushions off the chairs and set them out on the floor near the hearth, pulling the blankets around himself and settling into a nest of warmth.

"You're not going to wait for wine and something to eat?"

"Depends on how long it takes. My stomach will survive until morning, but my sanity might not without some rest."

Tassia shrugged and got comfortable on the sofa, watching the flames until Nalea was finally escorted up to her chambers. Nalea greeted Tassia briefly and smiled at Sam's sleeping form before vanishing into her bedchambers to change and wash, finally emerging with her fiery locks plaited for the night and wearing a soft, long nightshirt under a silk robe.

One of the aides had left bread, cheese and fruit with a flask of wine and jug of water on one of the tables. Nalea broke off a piece of bread and grabbed a slice of the cheese before collapsing into one of the chairs that hadn't been robbed of its cushions by Sam.

"He couldn't wait?" Nalea asked, nodding to Sam.

"Guess not."

"More for us."

"I think I'll pass on the wine for now," Tassia said. "The rest looks fantastic. I'm famished!"

"I wish there was a way to make shelter rations taste better. Maybe I should get an enchanter or two to work with one of the local bakers."

"You'd be elevated to goddess by the whole of the kingdom," Tassia joked.

"It's probably easier to make the rations taste better than to convince the dragons to stop attacking."

"Did you learn much more?"

"Not yet, but I expect to receive full reports on the damage tomorrow morning. I've instructed everyone from the shelter to remain in the towers for tonight, and we will not update the city shelters that the dragons have left until the sun rises and we can be certain that they aren't lying in wait."

Tassia nodded and reached for some fruit. The two women ate in silence, and then Nalea poured them each a chalice of wine, not letting Tassia protest.

"Just one," the queen insisted. "To help us sleep easy tonight."

When Tassia awoke just after dawn, she saw that Sam was already up, rummaging a poker through the dying coals of the fire, trying to coax a little more warmth out of it. His other hand held a sandwich that he had fashioned himself from last night's leftovers, which he was absently nibbling.

"Did you try the wine?" Tassia commented with a smirk.

"Doesn't seem like the best way to start the morning."

"One cup won't hurt. We might have a very long day ahead of us."

"If the dragons come back, I'm bringing that flask with us," he insisted, giving her a weary look.

"I don't think they will. I really want to get home, though, and see what's left. It's always so hard coming out of the shelter after the dragons have been through."

"Do you want to just go now? Nalea will know where we are."

Tassia glanced over at the sealed chamber doors and shrugged. "We'll give her a few more minutes. Let the sun come up, and if she hasn't risen by then, we'll go."

"How much wine did you two have?"

"I stuck with only one cup, but Nalea had a few. She's had quite a bit on her mind lately, what with some big trials coming up and the difficulty with this colony to the south. Things have been uneasy with the Krunleks for some time, and now there's this mess with the dragons."

"On top of everything else," Sam commented. "I wouldn't want to fill her shoes for all the world."

Tassia agreed. "I'll keep my garden and my sanity."

They packed up and watched as the sun came up over the horizon, brightening the mist-shrouded fields surrounding the city. Usually they would be able to see out almost all the way to the mountains from the height of the towers, but this morning the mist blocked most of the view.

"Let's go," Tassia finally said. "She'll send a messenger if she wants to see us again before you return this evening."

"Two days left," Sam said, "and she won't have to keep tabs on me anymore. That will be one less thing on her mind."

There weren't many people stirring as they made their way out of the castle. All the citizens were safely tucked away in shelters, and most of the castle staff were still asleep. There was some early morning bustle among the guards at the gates, but once they exited the towers into the city, it was eerily silent.

Tassia nervously took Sam's hand as they picked their way over the rubble and some scorched places that were still smoking. Mere blocks from the city centre, everything looked normal again, just utterly empty. There weren't even any birds out.

"Should it be this quiet?" Sam asked.

"Yes. It will take another day for the smaller animals to return to normal activity. Humans aren't the only ones who remain cautious after the dragons have been through."

Despite the eerie silence, Tassia started to feel better as there was no evidence of destruction beyond the towers. She was relieved when they exited the south gate of the city, and she could see all of the barracks there still standing. They turned west and followed the cobblestone avenue to Tassia's corner of the world, and she nearly wept with joy to see her little hut still standing and her garden untouched.

"All right then — to work?" she said.

"Do you need anything from the house? Some fresh clothes or maybe some water?"

"I can't see the point of changing now if we're just going to spend the day in the mud. Are you thirsty?"

"Not right now, we'll stop in later. Shall we find those dandelions?"

"That would be excellent."

They worked their way slowly through the garden, each with a bucket, pulling out weeds and retraining vines as they went. Tassia stopped at midmorning to fetch her water skins. The day was still quiet, but the sounds of the city — the soft thrum of voices and the gentle clatter of wagons — had begun to drift to them as people climbed from the shelters to assess the damage and begin repairs.

They ate lunch directly from the garden since Tassia had little food left in the hut, and spent the rest of the day working quietly. At dusk, they cleaned up and walked into the city to buy some fresh supplies from the market and have a proper dinner. They parted ways near the south gate as Sam headed back to the prisoners' quarters for what would likely be the last time, and Tassia went back to her hut for a proper bath and the first good night's sleep in days.

CHAPTER 7

Sam waded through the vegetation in the late morning sun and peered down every row he passed, searching for Tassia, but there was no sign of her. He finally called out.

"What vegetable are you in?"

There was no reply, and he grew even more confused. He walked the entire perimeter of the garden, grabbing a handful of berries along the way, but found no evidence she had been out that day, so he finally went back to the hut. His knock went unanswered, but he could hear sobbing from within. Gently, he pushed the door open.

Tassia was half dressed for the day, with her long hair still falling in dishevelled knots around her face. She was sitting on the floor against the side of the bunk bed with her knees drawn up to her chest and her head bent, weeping.

"Tassia, what's happened?" he said. "Tass..."

He knelt in front of her, placing one hand carefully on her shoulder, but couldn't elicit a response. He noticed she was clutching a message, and he gently pried the crumpled page from her fingers. It bore the official royal seal of the military council and brought crushing news — he wondered if Nalea even knew, if it had passed her desk before being delivered — Tassia's parents had been killed in the dragon raid.

He let the message fall onto the tabletop and sank to the floor beside Tassia, pressing carefully at her side so she would know he was there. When she leaned against him, he wrapped an arm around her shoulders but remained silent, knowing there was nothing he could possibly say to console her.

He didn't know when the message had been delivered, but since Tassia was only half dressed — in her trousers and boots, but still wearing her nightshirt — he suspected she'd known since early that morning. It was nearly lunch now, and he needed to get her moving before she sank into herself for good. He stood and took her by the arms, lifting her despite her resistance, and helped her sit on the edge of her bed. He pushed her matted hair from her face and tilted her chin to catch her eye.

"You need to get moving," he said softly.

Sam went into the latrine and retrieved a washcloth and the basin of fresh water. He washed her puffy, tear-stained face. He hastily pulled her hair back into a clumsy ponytail and then handed her a clean shirt.

"Fresh air will do you some good," he said. "Get dressed and join me outside."

She was nibbling on a slice of plain bread when she joined him on the front steps, squinting against the sunlight, but she was dressed and had properly plaited her hair. Otherwise, she still looked terrible.

"Are you there now?" he asked her, searching her expression for signs of lucidity.

Tears began brimming up in her eyes again, but she nodded and refused to let them spill.

Sam gestured for her to sit on the steps beside him, and he patted her knee but kept silent. She finished her bread and sat staring forward but not seeing.

"Can I get you anything?" he asked finally.

She shook her head.

"You should have some water," he commented, going back in to retrieve a canteen. "We should work in the garden," he said as he came back out. "We didn't get all the weeds yesterday, and last night's rain was sure to make everything grow again. Or would you like me to take you to Nalea?"

"Garden," she whispered, sucking back a sob.

"Don't think. Let's go get our hands dirty."

She reached out and took his hand, much as she had as they'd walked through the empty city the day before. He led her into the pumpkin patch and left her with the weed bucket beside a persistent patch of dandelions, while he sat to train the pumpkin vines that were still trying to encroach on the rest of the garden.

"Tass, it's midday; you should have something to eat. I'll go get some sandwiches."

She reached out, lightning quick, and caught his hand. "Please stay."

"I'm afraid you haven't taught any of your plants to grow us a proper lunch, so why don't you come with me?"

She nodded wearily and got up to follow him. She sat on the steps while he rummaged through the pantry. He took stock of what she had in her cupboards and decided they would need to stop at the market for some fresh meat and a few supplies so he could make them a stew for dinner.

He returned with some sandwiches and fruit, and they sat on the steps to eat.

"What am I going to do?" Tassia finally said. "I don't know if Janso is okay. And what if no one has alerted Mernia and Varia?"

"I think if your brother had been hurt, word of that would have come with the message about your parents."

"But he lives right next door."

"Tassia, we have no idea what happened. Maybe he wasn't home when the attack came... Your brother could have very well been the one to get the message to you. How else would it have arrived so quickly? You can't worry yourself with these what-ifs. We'll get a messenger to send word to your sisters, but for now you need to get yourself together. I'm free starting tomorrow, and I'll come with you to find your brother as soon as you're ready for the trip."

He saw the first attempt at a smile — just a brief upturn of the corners of her lips — since he'd arrived there that morning, and she clutched his hand and leaned into him, her lips briefly brushing his.

"Thank you, Sam. Tomorrow is probably no good, but perhaps the next day."

"It's up to you. Given the circumstances, I think Nalea will let me go a day early if you want to go home now."

She shook her head. "I have no idea what I'm returning to. If the house was destroyed, I couldn't bear to face that yet."

"When you're ready, then," he assured her. She leaned against him and slid her arms around him, burying her face against his chest. He rested his chin on the top of her head and stroked her braid as he waited for her to compose herself. When she'd finally calmed herself, he kissed the top of her head and began to stand, intending to head back into the garden.

Before he could climb to his feet, Tassia grabbed the front of his shirt and yanked him toward her with surprising strength and ferocity for someone her size. She'd pulled him off-balance, and he had to brace his hands on either side of her to keep from falling. She held fast to his shirt and pulled his face to hers, her lips hot and urgent against his. She leaned back and brought him with her so that he lay across her.

He lost himself to her, unaware of the passing of time, but just managed to maintain control. One arm was pinned behind her shoulders, but the other rested on her waist, and he used every ounce of will left available to him to keep that hand from sliding any lower. But Tassia was insistent and gripped his belt, tugging his hips firmly against hers. Gasping, he pulled his lips from hers and caught her eye, trying to determine her intent. He could see that she longed to be with him, but it was a desperate longing. The desperation was enough to fully restore his senses and cool his desire.

"The garden is waiting for you," he said, taking her hand and bringing her with him as he rose.

Sam wasn't sure if there was a full afternoon's worth of work in the garden, but Tassia needed to be there, in the only healing place she had. Sam did little work, mostly keeping an eye on her and telling her stories from his travels now and then to keep her mind occupied. She worked slowly and stopped frequently to hug him or just sit in the dirt beside him. She wept a few times as random things triggered memories of home, and Sam let her sob, holding her silently.

As the sun began to sink toward the horizon, they were both covered in dirt and exhausted, although they had accomplished very little actual work. Tassia had only filled her weed bucket once, and Sam had concentrated on the vines. With sunset approaching, he encouraged her to wash up and then brought her with him to the market to buy some supplies.

"Will you come with me to the towers tonight?" he asked her.

"I want to stay at home."

"I should get back there and collect my things. I don't have much, but I don't want to lose what I've managed to accumulate and I don't know if they'll hold it for me once I'm not officially a prisoner."

"Nalea will hold it for you. Please, stay with me," she pleaded, catching him by the shoulders and holding him until he promised.

"All right, I'll come back with you and stay. I'll have to send a messenger in the morning though."

"I'm sure Nalea will know where you are."

"Yes. But I want to make sure she knows what happened. She's been busy and may not have seen the message before it reached you."

Tassia nodded, sinking into her thoughts again now that she was assured he wouldn't leave her. He wanted to get her to

Nalea before long because even with his presence, he didn't think the isolated hut was a good place for her to be. Her garden was a healing place, but also reminded her too much of her time gardening with her mother, and before long it was apt to only make her feel worse.

The best thing would be for her to go home where her brother would be able to help her, and she would have the comfort of family. Sam hoped to convince her to leave before too long.

He insisted on making dinner and instructed her to pick a book to read while he cooked. Tassia sat on the edge of her bed and stared at the pages for only a moment before giving up and sitting at the table to help Sam cut vegetables.

Every time she tried to speak, the conversation always led back to her parents, which only brought fresh tears. Finally, she gave up talking, and they sat on the front steps, watching the deepening eventide, and ate in silence.

"I think I need to sleep now," she said, finally speaking.

"It's been a long day. I'm getting tired too."

He helped her up and they retreated inside. Sam had expected her to go into the latrine to change, but instead she merely stood with her back to him as she pulled off her clothes, stripping down to her britches and pulling her nightshirt over her head. He tried to look away, but was entranced by the colour of her skin and her alluring shape, rippling gently with muscle from a lifetime of strenuous work. He finally looked down at his feet before she could turn around to see him watching, but Tassia had felt his eyes on her anyway and hadn't minded. She slowly unravelled her braid as she sat on the edge of the bed, watching him closely. Sam's focus was on her fingers as they deftly worked through her tresses and dropped her locks down her back to her waist.

She turned the lantern down low, but just sat staring at the bed under her as if trying to divine its purpose. Sam sat next to her and took her hand, giving it a squeeze.

"Sleep will do you good," he insisted.

"It's like a tomb in here," she said, her eyes darting around the close, dark quarters. They'd had the door open all evening to let in the air, but now only the one window stood open and the hut felt stifling. Sam had been there when it was hotter and knew Tassia could manage, but tonight was different. Sam stood and opened the door, knowing there would be little in the way of intruders with everyone gone, but the air outside had grown still.

He looked out into the clear, humid night, wondering how he'd get Tassia through it when a bright starburst trailed overhead. He realized it was the peak of the summer's star shower, and it gave him an idea. There was a soft, thick quilt folded at the end of Tassia's bed, used in cooler weather and all but forgotten in the height of summer, and he draped it over his arm and pulled some of the linens off the bed.

"Come on," he said, taking her hand and guiding her back outside. He'd discarded his boots earlier in the evening, and they were both barefoot in the cool grass. She sighed in relief and took a deep breath of the fragrant night air, rich with damp summer smells and fresh sweet grass.

He led her around the side of the hut and out to the garden where rising mist clung to the exposed earth and the season's last firefly drifted through the corn rows, mistaking the starburst for kin. Tassia stood watching the star shower while Sam spread the thick quilt over the grass and the linens on top. He sat at the edge of the blanket and lifted the linens to cover her when she crawled across the blanket to join him. Sam draped the linen over them both before lying beside Tassia and gathering her in his arms. She brushed his hair from his forehead and stroked his cheek for a moment before kissing him soft and deep — a long, slow kiss.

"Thank you," she whispered, curling against him with her head at his chest and her hand resting at his waist.

His heart began to beat so fast and hard that he thought it might break through his chest, but Tassia didn't seem to notice, stealing glances at the stars now and then. Sam watched her for a while, enjoying the damp earthy smell of the garden lingering in her hair, before he turned his attention to the star shower.

Sam wasn't sure when he'd fallen asleep, but he felt as though he had barely slept at all when Tassia stirred at his side and woke him. It was nearing dawn, with the faintest traces of grey light to the east, but the stars were also still clearly visible and the last starbursts raced overhead. Tassia looked calmer now, and Sam was relieved, hoping a solid night's sleep had helped improve her spirits. She smiled up at him and drew his face to hers, kissing him deeply and intensely, pushing her body tight against him. The warm swell of her breasts threatened to weaken his resolve. He extracted himself from her embrace and moved away from her, sitting near the edge of the blanket next to the garden. She was insistent though and crawled toward him. He didn't resist any further.

She straddled his hips and leaned tight against him again, pressing her lips fiercely to his and knotting her fingers in his short, dark hair. He slid his hands up her sides and under her shirt, riding it up past her waist while he stroked the soft, firm skin of her back. When he felt her pull away from him, he eased his embrace, expecting her to back away completely, but she only wanted room to pull her nightshirt over her head, tossing it aside to expose the porcelain teacups of her breasts. Sam was amazed by the stark contrast between the paleness of her chest and the tan of her arms and shoulders.

She rocked back, bracing her arms against his legs and arching her back, pushing her breasts out further, and Sam sat straighter, burying his face between them, kissing her there. He slid one hand around her back and kneaded her breast with the other when she leaned down to kiss him again — hungry and intense.

She leaned over him, pushing him back to brace one hand against the ground, but was barely touching him, only one hand on his shoulder while she continued to kiss him. He realized after a moment that she had distracted him as she discarded her undergarments. She pushed his shirt off over his head and lightly ran her nails down his chest and over his abdomen. He lost any caution he may have had left and quickly slid out of his trousers, as she nibbled at his neck.

Tassia slid her arms around the back of him and pressed hard against him, squeezing her thighs around him so he could feel the damp heat of her loins. Her breathing quickened as she trailed kisses down his neck and shoulder and slid down his body, raking her nails down his torso as she went. Bracing one hand at the base of his shaft, she pushed her hair out of her face with the other in order to nibble at him playfully before taking his full length into her mouth.

Sam groaned softly, and the heat of her lips and tongue melted through him and spread across his whole body. She worked him until he was right at the edge and then nipped at his abdomen as she climbed back up his body, straddling his hips. She arched her hips away from him, but only to find him and properly guide him into her. She gasped initially, but began to breathe deep, hard and quickly again as she eased back down with her hips tight against his so that he was fully inside her. He grunted a moment, startled by the sensation, but sighed as he relaxed into her heat.

He thrust clumsily for a moment, lost to the warmth of her and the salt of her lips, but he arched his back with both arms braced behind him, allowing him to push deep and find a rhythm with her. Once comfortable, he brought a hand forward so he could clench her long black tresses, his fist between her shoulder blades holding her tight to him, never wanting to let go, yearning to feel her skin and her heat, her lips and her breath for the rest of his life.

He'd had his eyes squeezed shut to focus on every pinprick of bliss tingling through him. When he opened them again, he could see nothing but the vast expanse of the heavens above them, dark and moonless with bursts of light from the racing stars. Tassia saw him watching the skies and tilted her head so that they both looked starward during the frenzied final moments of their act.

Her breathing became shallow and quickened, and she pressed her face to the side of his head so each gasp was delivered directly into his ear, causing hot shivers to dance across his skin. Then her body tensed and she arched backward, her head snapping back to expose her neck to him as she cried out. He kept his arms hooked around her, watching her now and thrusting quickly. She arched forward, her dark eyes focused intently on his, and she cried out again and again until he finally joined her in climax. She fell against him as he slid back against the grass. They were both slick with sweat, and he kissed her slowly, running his hands across her back, up her sides and over her breasts.

Still gasping and not saying a word, she rolled onto the blankets. He stretched out beside her, still stroking her abdomen and squeezing her breasts, until his heart finally settled and his skin began to cool in the damp night air. He pulled the blankets around them again, and they both drifted off to sleep.

It was full morning when Sam awoke again, the sun shining brightly, though they were shaded by the hut, and he and Tassia were still lying intertwined. He disentangled himself from her limbs and propped himself up on his elbow, leaning over her as she smiled up at him. She brushed her fingers over his cheek, and he stroked her long hair fanned out across the blanket. He leaned in and kissed her, slow and soft, but still hungry, and she hooked her arms around him, holding him close.

He cupped her breasts, squeezing and massaging them, then kissed her mouth, her cheek, her neck, and nibbled her ear. Her breathing had begun to deepen, and Sam ran his hand down her stomach and abdomen, surprised to find that she was ready for him. Still kissing her deeply, he slid two fingers into her and pressed the heel of his hand down, working her inside and out until her thrusting was in time with her breathing, which came in short gasps. He removed his fingers and rolled onto her, carefully parting her legs and pressing himself between them, entering her easily.

She wrapped her legs around him, locking them at the small of his back and using them and her arms to pull him closer. It seemed like every part of him was tight against her or deep inside her, and they both lost themselves to the heat and rhythm. Sam climaxed first and then Tassia cried out, but neither of them slowed and she held him tightly, still rocking with him, until they climaxed together.

Sam collapsed against her, spent, but she held him there, still inside her, though he was withering now. Their heat and sweat mingled as they gasped for breath and tried to regain control. Sam finally removed himself from her, but slid to her side, still in her arms, and held her. They were covered in a sheen of sweat, their hair damp and matted.

They dozed, but reality quickly began to set in for Sam as the sun crept over the hut. He finally disentangled himself from her still-sleeping form, gathering her up among her blankets and bringing her back to her bed. Then he retrieved all their clothing and went to wash and dress. When he had freshened up, Tassia was still asleep, so he took the opportunity to venture to the market and find a messenger. He wouldn't leave Tassia long enough to bring a message to the queen himself, but he had to be certain that Nalea knew what had happened to Tassia's family and that Sam would remain with her until Livia returned. In a brief message, he told Nalea he would begin his work only once he knew Tassia had someone else to help her face her grief.

When he returned, Tassia wasn't in bed anymore, but he could hear her crying from the latrine. He tapped softly on the door.

"Tass?"

At the sound of his voice, she began to wail, and Sam became alarmed.

"Tassia, what's going on?"

When he tried to push the door open, she slammed it from the other side.

"Stay out!" she cried.

"What's going on? Are you hurt?"

"Don't come in here. Please, just leave."

"You need someone here with you," he said, staring at the door in confusion. "You shouldn't face this so alone."

"I don't want to see you. Just go."

Sam winced, realizing what she meant, and he sat on the floor and leaned his head against the wall, closing his eyes for a moment. When he opened them, he could see her nightshirt and clothing still piled on the floor.

"Tassia, I'm sorry. I thought you wanted—"

"I did! That doesn't make it right."

"I don't understand. You were there for me when I needed it most, and you've allowed me the opportunity to put my life back together. For the first time ever, I have a prospect of a life. I know you see how much you mean to me. Do you really insist on just friendship after all this?"

"I'm sorry," she said quietly, and he could hear her soft voice break with tears. "I know what you want, and I took advantage of that to alleviate my loneliness. It's not easy to be a woman in the army; it gets lonely in so many ways. With Livia drifting away and now my parents gone—" A sob escaped her, and she fell silent for a moment. "When I've gone so long without the attention of men, it's hard to resist one as persistent as you. I let my grief cloud my judgment. Sam, I'm sorry. This is all a mistake."

"Tassia, we're friends," he insisted. "Don't tell me you don't care about me at all."

"Friends don't do this sort of thing!"

"Butch and Livia do."

"Just stop!"

He sighed and got up, saying nothing, but he refused to leave her now that she'd made herself even more vulnerable to misery. Hope melted away from him, and he wanted nothing more than for her to come out, kiss him softly and tell him that it had been real. It had felt right to him and still did, but she guarded her emotions so closely that he was left with only her words.

Sam put a kettle of water on the stovetop and dug through the wardrobe to find some clean clothes for her. He folded them and left them neatly piled just outside the door.

"Please, just leave," she insisted from behind the firmly closed door.

"Not until I know you're going to be all right."

"This changes everything."

"Why?"

She didn't respond.

"We're friends, aren't we?"

Still silence.

"It was a mistake, fine. Forget it ever happened."

"You're not going to forget."

"Maybe not, but that doesn't matter right now. Your pain is bigger than what I might feel. We can return to this once the wound of losing your family has had time to heal. If you need to forget, then forget. Get washed up, and let's finish in the garden and pack your things so we can go find your brother."

"I don't want you to come with me."

He sagged under the weight of her words, relieved the door between them kept her from seeing how badly they stung.

"All right," he said. "I should start work anyway. You still need to get on with your life." He paused to set the hot kettle down outside the door. "There's warm water and fresh clothing out here," he said. "So get cleaned up and come out of there. Lying naked in your latrine isn't going to solve anything."

While digging through her things, he'd come across soap and a washboard, and he said nothing else to her, but he gathered the soiled blankets off her bed and went out.

Tassia peeked out the latrine door in time to see him disappear toward the central court, where there was a large washbasin near the main pump. She felt even worse that he had taken it upon himself to wash away the evidence, despite how much it must have hurt him to be rejected so forcefully. He'd resisted her all the day before and had tried again that morning, but she had been persistent. She had wanted him, and it had felt so right as it happened, but it was a terrible abuse of his friendship, and now she felt as low as she had when she read the message about her parents.

She was cold and numb from the hard wooden slats of the floor. Slowly, she picked herself up and grabbed the kettle. She crouched in the large tin basin and scrubbed away all evidence of him on her body, feeling relieved but also like she was betraying them both. Once she was washed and dressed, she combed out her hair and plaited it, and then she had a slice of bread and went out to find him. He was already back, hanging the clean, wet linens over the line between her hut and the next.

"Please, just go. This doesn't help."

"Why not?"

"I — we can't pretend that nothing happened."

"What do you want then?" He stopped with the quilt hanging awkwardly on the line and turned to face her. "What do you need? You said it was a mistake, so you need to move on. You're in emotional agony, and I'm just trying to make things go easily for you. Chores are the last thing you need to worry about, and I doubt you wanted Livia to discover these." He gestured towards the sheets on the line.

Tassia's jaw dropped, and she turned away from him quickly. She could feel his hurt, but he was right. She hadn't even thought of Livia finding out. Livia would have taken one look at her bedsheets and known the truth. And, if Tassia was still away, there was no guarantee Livia wouldn't share her suspicions with the others. But the fact that Sam was right didn't make it any easier.

"I don't want to see you. Please, just leave!"

"I'm not leaving you like this," he calmly replied. "Pack your things while I finish this up, and I'll take you to Nalea. Otherwise, I'm going to stay right here." He turned from her then and continued spreading the damp quilt over the line.

Tassia stormed back into her hut. She grabbed her sword, ready to make him leave whether he wanted to or not, but stopped just at the doorway, sense suddenly returning. She couldn't do anything to hurt him more than she already had. He had done nothing wrong but to care about her — to be there for her when she needed someone — and that was all he was continuing to do. It wasn't his fault that simple gestures of kindness made her feel guilty.

She put her sword away and began to pack up her things, preparing for the journey home. If Nalea was still busy dealing with the fallout of the dragon raid, then Tassia wouldn't linger in the city. It was almost midday now, and she could be in her village before dark if she left soon.

She was almost finished packing when Sam came back in.

"Would it be too much to ask of you to put the blankets back later this afternoon, once they've had time to dry?" she said.

"This is my free day — I can do that."

"Thank you," she said, struggling to keep her tone even. The knowledge that he was going to spend his free day showing her more kindness made her feel small and petty. "I think I'm ready to go."

Nalea was seated behind a table that had been dragged before her throne, poring over maps and half listening to reports of the dragons' damage while she made notations. Her hair had been hastily clipped from her face with bone pins, and she wore a simple brocade corset and skirt over cool linens. She hadn't seen Tassia be escorted in, but raised a hand to halt her advisors' reports the moment she spotted her friend. Tassia was pale with swollen red eyes, shifting restlessly amidst the queen's audience. Nalea sent her advisors to wait in the crowd and signalled Tassia to come forward.

"Tass, I'm so sorry," Nalea said, moving around the table and embracing her. "I got Sam's note this morning. I didn't know. I'm so sorry."

"Thank you," Tassia said simply. "You're still quite busy then?"

"They marauded heavily across the entire north of the kingdom — all the way to the mountains. I'm still receiving reports of the damage. I can't understand why they inflicted so much damage so far from me and the city, but they seem to have done most of it on their way in, as our scouts were watching them closely as they retreated."

"I'd like to go home now," Tassia said. "If you're busy, I'll let you do your work. Is there an escort for me?"

"Sam isn't going with you?"

"He needs to start work," Tassia said flatly, but Nalea could see the twitch of her bottom lip as she fought to keep her emotions straight.

"I see," Nalea said, confused but not pressing the matter. "There are messengers going back and forth frequently, and I can make arrangements for you if you'd like, but you can ask around at the northern gate and you'll find someone going this afternoon. If you're quick, you'll catch the eastern brigade on their way out there to help with cleanup."

"I'll do that then. You've got enough to worry about. I just want to get home and see if I can find out anything about Janso."

"If it's any consolation, I searched all the registers this morning when I found out about your parents, and his name didn't come up. He's quite likely safe."

Tassia exhaled in relief, but only nodded and left. Once she was gone, Nalea turned to one of her aides.

"Go to the prisoners' quarters and bring Sam Ta Nalertan to me," she instructed and turned back to the business of dragon cleanup. When she left the meeting an hour later, heading for the war room for a further round of consultations, Sam was among those waiting to speak with her.

"Sam, go in and wait for me. I need a moment's rest," she said. She retreated through a side parlour to a balcony for a breath of air and to gather her thoughts before confronting Sam.

When Nalea entered the war room, Sam was standing near the empty hearth, staring at the cold ashes with sagging shoulders and his hands clasped tightly in front of him. He tensed and stood erect when she dismissed her aides, leaving them alone.

"Did you finally tell her?" Nalea demanded, not wasting time with pleasantries.

Sam shook his head.

"Tassia is not herself, even for someone who's lost her parents. She's specifically angry at you."

"She's not angry with me," he insisted, refusing to clarify.

"She's angry. It's buried under her grief, but it's there. And she doesn't want to see you. So what's—" Nalea halted abruptly, her eyes widening with shock and understanding. "You fool!"

Sam opened his mouth, some witty defence trying to bully its way past his brain, but he wisely pursed his lips and stood silently for a moment. Nalea waited, watching him intently, as he carefully ordered his thoughts to address not just one of Tassia's closest friends, but the kingdom's ruler as well.

"I appear to have been in the wrong place at the wrong time. Or maybe the right place at the wrong time. I don't know," he finally said.

"She'll tear you apart if you tell her the truth now. What were you thinking?"

"When was the last time one of your lovers resisted you?" he shot back. "I thought she was muddling the lines of friendship on purpose, not out of grief. We've been subtly muddling those lines for weeks. How could I have known?"

Nalea leaned against the table and looked across the room, thinking and refusing to meet his gaze. She turned to him finally and did nothing to conceal her anger, speaking concisely in a slow and threatening tone.

"You need to leave."

"I don't want to hear those words anymore today," Sam protested.

"Before she gets back from her village, you need to go. If you're quick and the weather holds, you can be home before the snows bar the higher passes."

"I'd never make it, even if I was willing to leave."

"I'll drive you out if I have to," she swore hotly, standing erect. "Go south then. It's time for you to leave my lands."

"You think my abandonment would help anything?" Sam argued, taking a dangerous step toward her before checking his emotions. "She's going through a deep loss right now, and I admit she's not likely thinking clearly, but she might be lying to herself. I won't know until I hear from her when her judgment is sound again. Until then, I won't leave."

Nalea paused, considering his words. Tassia was a stubborn, blind fool when it came to men, and she knew Sam's love was sincere. She didn't want to drive Sam away before Tassia had the chance to realize the full truth, even if Nalea couldn't see how the situation could possibly end well. Sam would have to leave Wheat Sky soon or be forced back to Mountain Song, where he would have absolutely no chance of being with Tassia. She finally decided that she had interfered enough, part of her wishing now that she hadn't at all, and she decided to just let the situation play itself out. She would get involved only when it was time to send Sam home for political reasons, just as she had promised him.

"When you have that conversation with her, I expect you to be honest about who you are. You can't ask her to commit to you when you can't commit to the truth."

Sam nodded, and she gestured his dismissal.

Tassia was beyond relieved to walk through the southern gates and see the barracks brimming with life. She still wasn't prepared to see Sam, but was even less prepared to return to a barren home. If Livia wasn't in their hut — and she suspected she wouldn't be — she could mingle in the centre courtyard with the others and find out how battle had gone.

She adjusted the bag slung over her shoulder and marched along the avenues, waving to her comrades when they called out to her. She wondered if many of them even knew about the dragon raid, since there was little evidence of it in the southern lands or in the city. It had been over a week since she'd left, and much of the damage to the towers had been cleaned up. There were still scorch marks, but they'd been scrubbed down, and some of the sections affected had already been repainted. All the vegetation that had burned had been replaced, so only structural damage remained to be repaired, but even that was minimal.

She pushed open the door to their hut and was relieved to see that Sam had made good on his word and remade her bed — the hut was spotless — but she was even more surprised and relieved to see Livia sprawled across her bunk, reading.

"Tass!" she called, excited and concerned at once. "It's so good to see you! I'm so sorry! How are you doing?"

Livia jumped down from her bunk and crossed the room in two quick strides to embrace Tassia. Tassia suspected her friend didn't mean to hug her quite so fiercely as her face was buried in Livia's generous bust, but by the time she was released, she was grinning for the first time in days.

"It's so good to see you again!" Livia said. "I just can't get used to battle without you. I wish Nalea would end this foolishness!"

"One more battle left," Tassia pointed out.

"It won't be over soon enough! How are you holding up?"

"I'm all right. It's easier now that I've been home, but it's hard to deal with. The house is gone completely."

Livia sat at the table, looking pained.

"Mamma's garden is still there, but there's no one to care for it," Tassia said, sitting on the other side of the table. "Janso is so busy with arrangements and his own land — there are so many families that need help right now, and it's going to keep everyone in the village busy. He says if it does well on its own, he'll get some locals to help harvest it. There are families that lost everything — crops and home — and he thinks once their homes have been rebuilt, they'll welcome the chance at some crops, too."

"At least it won't go to waste. I know you wouldn't tolerate that."

"No, but I don't think I can go back there — especially not with the garden standing there like nothing's happened. Waiting for Mamma to come out and care for it." Tassia's voice caught, and she paused to compose herself again. "Maybe next year once the land has been completely cleared — but then there will just be so much emptiness where my whole life used to be."

"How are the others doing?"

"Janso got word to the girls, and Mernia is going to make arrangements to go home for a week or so. Varia is still too frail to travel."

"Were the girls upset about missing the funeral?"

"There wasn't one," Tassia said, looking away. "The house was their pyre."

"What! Why weren't they in the shelter?"

"I didn't realize, but Pa had been injured in a riding accident and was bedridden. Mamma refused to leave him." Tassia paused for air and forged ahead. "Janso is pretty sure she was trying to carry him out to the shelter on her own because their remains weren't far from the door, but the house still came down around them."

Livia closed her eyes and held her hand over her mouth. She finally looked up at Tassia again and merely reached out and squeezed her hand.

"Janso was in the village buying supplies when the attack struck. He tried to get home, but the dragons got there first and he ended up in a neighbour's shelter to avoid death."

Livia gave her hand a final pat, and they sat silently until she sensed Tassia's emotions had levelled off again.

"Where's Sam?" Livia asked.

"I'm not sure, probably at the workhouse," Tassia replied.

"He didn't go with you?"

"I left before he had all of his arrangements made," she lied. "I wanted to make sure he got settled in and adjusted to his freedom. It was hard, but he's been so excited about starting something new — something permanent — that I didn't want to pull him away for something so sombre when he was right in the middle of his transition."

Tassia had managed to keep calm, and Livia didn't detect the lie.

"He'll be back before long, I'm sure," Livia said. "We just got back yesterday, and someone has sure been keeping your garden in top shape!"

"He mentioned he'd keep an eye on things while I was gone."

"That was nice of him. He must be busy with the workhouse."

"I don't really know. He hadn't started yet when I left, so I don't know his schedule. He mentioned he was in one nearby, though, so he may have been stopping in at the end of the day to check on things. We might see him tonight."

They didn't see Sam for weeks, though, and Tassia was relieved, both that he didn't show and that if Livia noticed, she made no comment.

CHAPTER 8

Sam stood at the end of the lane and knew he was in the right place when he spotted the scorched patch of land surrounding what had likely been the house foundation. The garden had been more difficult to find, completely overgrown and almost smothered by the surrounding grasslands. Then he heard a man shouting.

"I won't have any more looters!"

Sam turned to see a short, dark-haired man rushing across the field toward him, brandishing a pitchfork.

"Janso! It's all right, I'm not a looter."

Despite his confusion as to how a stranger knew his name, he slowed his pace.

"I don't know you," Janso called warily, still gripping the pitchfork.

"No, we've never met. I'm a friend of Tassia's."

"Sam?"

It was Sam's turn to be confused.

"She spoke of you when she was here. It's too bad you weren't able to come with her."

"It was a family time," Sam said. "And I had plenty to keep me in the city."

"What brings you here now? And without Tass?"

"She's angry with me and still upset about this," he explained, nodding to the ashes that had once been her home. "I wanted to bring something to cheer her up, and I know how much she loved her mother's garden."

"Tassia and Ma were out here for hours," Janso said. "I

wish I had been able to keep it up, but underneath all that wilderness, there are still plenty of vegetables. I've had some, and in a week's time, one of the harder-hit families from town is going to come take the rest."

"I just want a pumpkin," Sam said. "She loves the seeds, and I promised her a stew."

Janso nodded, giving Sam a bemused look. "She's got plenty of her own pumpkins, doesn't she?"

"A whole patch," Sam agreed. "But your mother didn't grow any of those."

Janso nodded again, understanding now. "How long have you fancied her?"

Sam flushed, but chose honesty. "Since the moment I met her."

"Give her time; she'll come around. My sister is nothing if not stubborn and blind. Take any of the pumpkins you want. Anything else you can carry if you think it will help her."

"Just the pumpkin will do," Sam said. "I've got a long journey back to the city today, and my pack will only hold so much."

"You came all the way out here just for a pumpkin? I don't know what you did, but if that doesn't buy you her forgiveness I don't know what will." Janso clapped him on the back and smiled. "Good luck, my friend. I hope to see you around here again."

"I was beginning to think we'd seen the last of you!" Livia cried out when she saw Sam standing at their door.

"Things have been busy, and I know Tassia needed some time to get over all that happened. I found a place of my own. It's farther away than the workhouse was, but it will be a little more flexible, too."

"That's excellent! Come in," Livia said, opening the door wider.

Tassia was sitting at the table, finishing her lunch, and she looked nervous to see Sam again, but composed herself before Livia could notice.

"What's the pumpkin for? Did you snag it out of our garden?" Livia asked.

"No, it's from your mother's garden," Sam said to Tassia. "Your brother said a family from the village is coming next week for what hasn't been driven out by weeds, so I got there just in time. I promised you stew."

Tassia looked away and drew a breath to steady herself.

"Pumpkin stew?" Livia asked, giving Tassia the moment she needed. "I've never tried that before. Never would have thought they were good for anything but sweets."

"Cooked with the right ingredients, they make a very rich stew. I brought mushrooms too," he said, holding out a small sack. "Pumpkin mushroom stew. It's very rich and earthy. It's my favourite thing this time of year, when you can start to sense the frost in the air. The stew just *tastes* warm."

"Did you bring everything you need?" Tassia asked him, noticing that the sack was far too big for just mushrooms.

"Some spices and a larger pot than you have. I have to cook the pumpkin first."

He set everything down on the table and opened the pumpkin to collect the seeds. Tassia put them into a shallow pan, drizzled them with oil and spices and put them into the oven to roast. Livia tended to the fire while the other two made preparations. Sam dug out the stringy bits and then peeled away the hard outer shell of the pumpkin, leaving the firm inner shell, which he boiled. Tassia had forgotten how much she loved the smell of cooking pumpkin. She helped Sam drain the pot and mash what was inside it.

"Have you had it mashed like this with just cream and some cinnamon?" she asked.

"Oh, that was my favourite as a child!" Livia said.

"I haven't tried that," Sam replied.

"Do we have cream?" Tassia asked.

"I brought some with me," he said. "For the stew."

"Try just a bit with the cream then. We've got cinnamon."

Sam was surprised that it tasted almost like the filling of a pie and was relieved that Tassia was sharing and acting naturally again. He set the pumpkin and some cream and spices on the stove to simmer and began chopping up mushrooms. He sent the women out to get onions, carrots, beans and any of their favourite vegetables to chop into the stew as well. It would be two more weeks until they had the time off to harvest their garden fully.

"Do you think you'll be able to help us?" Tassia asked.

"I'm not sure. I'm working on a farm south of here, and they'll expect me in their fields from sunrise to sunset."

"Is it far? Where are you living?"

"It's nearly a league away, but I'm living on the farm in a shack near their barn. It's not much, but it's big enough for a small stove, a cupboard and a cot. That's all I need right now," he said, shrugging.

"You sleeping better now?" Tassia asked.

"Away from the snoring of strangers? Of course! It's cozy and comfortable and so far away from the city it's amazingly quiet. I didn't realize how poorly I was sleeping in the dorms until my first night out there."

"I'm glad to hear you're faring well."

"It's an interesting change, that's for certain."

Tassia and Livia had to return to the courtyard for an afternoon drill, so Sam stayed behind to tend to the stew. Both women could smell its rich aroma from three huts down as they returned near dusk.

"You two got yourself a chef?" Butch teased.

"You just wish you had one," Livia replied, giving his arm a playful squeeze.

They found Sam had everything set out on the table, which he had moved so that they could sit on the bed to eat, since there were only two chairs. He'd put the roasted seeds into a bowl near the centre with another bowl of mixed greens from the garden. Wine and bread rounded out the feast. The loaf had been sliced and toasted, and he'd spread some of their spiced butter on it. He was just working on melting a layer of sharp cheese over the stew when they arrived.

"Can Butch join us for dinner?" Livia asked.

"I insist!" Sam replied. "This is a large pot, and I think we'll need some help with it. We may end up needing more wine though."

"Oh, we've got plenty of that," Livia promised with a wink.

They sat for dinner — Livia and Butch sitting together at the edge of Tassia's bunk, and Tassia and Sam in the chairs — and Sam told them a little bit about where he was living now. Livia and Butch talked about what they anticipated their next deployment would be — heading north again to help build more shelters for those still homeless after the floods of the spring — and about their trip to the southern colony which had thankfully ended with little loss and a successfully negotiated treaty.

"What were the particulars of the treaty?" Sam asked.

"We never heard much. Nalea is keeping most of it to herself," Livia replied. "She's promised them protection in the event of an outside attack, and in return, they must continue to pay taxes, but I think she's going to otherwise treat them as an independent nation. She's monitoring them, of course, and they realize that. They refused to disarm themselves but have signed a treaty swearing allegiance to Nalea. As long as they maintain peace, Nalea is going to leave them alone."

"We were only sent out there because rumours of an uprising were reported," Butch added. "We still haven't figured out why, after all she's done for them, they wanted to overthrow her in the first place, but we've put an end to that foolishness so she's going to continue to let them be."

"Did the trip south reduce your desire to come south again in the winter?" Sam asked.

"Not at all! I still think it would be fun," Livia said, shovelling in some stew.

"Butch's family is to the southeast, and Livia's is in the east along the forest boundary, so they'll take a longer route to come home so they can visit," Tassia explained.

"Everyone's making a family trip out of it then. Well, that's good."

"Do you think you'll head for Sletrini any time soon?" Livia asked him.

"I have absolutely no desire."

"You don't want to see your family at all?"

"I was never close with them, and it's been so long since I've had any contact that they hardly matter to me anymore. It would be strange to go back after all this time and try to make up for it, to fill in the blanks. I'm much happier here, building a new kind of family."

"You going to be a farmhand your whole life?" Butch asked.

"I doubt it. I'm not sure what I'll do later, but for now I just want to build a base for myself and see where that leads. I need to get used to permanence and remember what it's like to actually make plans."

"Are you still thinking of the university?" Tassia asked.

"Definitely," Sam said, brightening at the thought. "Right now I'm more concerned about buying some quality pots and accumulating quilts for the winter. It's a good shack, but it's still a shack and I need something to keep me warm. I guess I'll need winter clothing. That's about as far as my planning goes. Whatever I manage to earn before the snows come will be spent on essentials, so I will have to wait until spring to try to figure out how I could pay for an education."

"So you've got a plan then?"

"Yes, at least until spring. Then I'll make a new one. I'll still be needed a little bit around the farm over the winter months, but once the harvest is complete, they don't mind if I take a lot of time away — like to head south for a spell."

"Why don't you talk to Nalea about any positions in the court?" Tassia suggested. "You were in the court for so long, even if just as an aide, that I'm sure you could make something more permanent out of it."

"I'm not friends with her — I haven't known her for years the way you three have, and it's difficult for me to approach her like that. To me, she's the queen."

"She's spoken with you in private before," Butch pointed out. "Twice, as I can recall."

"Yes, and both times were terribly uncomfortable for me. Staying in her chambers after the dragon raid was nearly unbearable."

"You've met with her in private twice?" Tassia questioned, surprised.

"The first time she was inquiring about my ring. She was concerned it was something it wasn't — a ring of power — and wanted to question me in private in case the situation became delicate. It's just a trinket, as I finally convinced her."

"Can we see it?" Livia asked.

"Now that I've got somewhere safe, I don't really keep it with me very often," Sam admitted with a shrug. For not the first time, he wished he'd never kept it at all. "I'll try to remember it next time I come around."

"Why else did you meet her in private?" Butch asked.

"It was right after the dragon raid. She was concerned about Tass and didn't think it was anyone else's business how

Tassia was doing. I can appreciate that you have known her possibly all your lives, but I'm not used to being on casual terms with heads of state — or members of the court at all."

"I'm sure you'll get used to it before long. Between the three of us, Nalea is hard to avoid."

Sam nodded. "I've noticed."

They finished their meal and broke out a second and third bottle of wine. Both moons were edging their way down from their peak when they pushed the table back where it belonged and Sam gathered his things for the long walk back to his new home.

Tassia was glad to have Sam with her as she watched the others depart again. He'd found out the deployment date and had made sure to get at least part of the day off. She was thoroughly relieved that there would be no danger involved on this trip, as the soldiers of her brigade were going to be rebuilding and nothing more. Her main concern was staving off boredom in their absence.

"You're awfully pleased about this," Sam commented as they headed south again.

"No more being left behind now! When they get back, it's done with, and at least this time I can rest assured they're all coming back. I love these rebuilding missions — they have all the sense of purpose to them that a battle has but without any of the negative aspects. It's almost like being in the garden."

"What are you going to do without that?" he asked her.

"Go crazy!" she laughed. "There are still a few things left to harvest, and I can probably do a little more canning. We've got some space left under the bunk for storage, so we might as well use it. And then I can spend a day or two in the market selling off what's left. I will need at least another day to pull down the plants so they can compost over the winter."

"I wish I could stay to help," he said. "But they expect me back some time before the sun goes down. There's a lot of work left in the fields."

"Why don't I come with you? An extra set of hands this afternoon will make up for your absence this morning. And then I can finally see where you live."

"I'd like that."

They stopped at Tassia's hut for soup and bread, and then she picked up some of her gardening tools and they headed out of the city, going south on the main road. They finally turned east after a half-league and continued down a narrower, rutted road that was barely more than a path, which was lined with farms.

"Will your garden and the market keep you busy through the entire deployment?"

"Probably not. I've cleared it with Nalea to head south to see my sisters; so if I'm still gone when the others get back, it won't be a problem. I'm sure my absence will please Livia and Butch for a little while."

Sam smiled. He turned down another lane, and she could see a farmhouse up ahead and that the fields around it were full.

"Do they have many workers?"

"Mostly children and some extended family that live in another house at the other side of the property. There are only two other workers here who are not part of the family. They live in smaller outbuildings, too. It's not bad, really, and everyone is friendly. Obviously, I haven't told them much about where I came from — I prefer to not talk about Hetia's anymore. Just that I was at the workhouse for a time."

Tassia nodded.

"Come meet the heads of the house," Sam said, leading her over to the barn where a man and woman just a little older than Tassia's parents had been were loading bales of hay into the loft.

"Trom, Nisa," Sam called. "Since I missed the morning, I've brought a friend to help for the afternoon."

"Your soldier friend?" the man, Trom, asked.

"She was raised on a farm," Sam explained. "She can harvest and defend all at once. You should see her with a garden stake," he joked, giving her a conspirator's wink.

Nisa smiled. "Certainly, Sam. You know we never mind the extra help. Show her around some, and then you can grab a barrel and head into the orchard."

Tassia waved to them as Sam brought her around the side of the barn to a little shack with a door and one sad, little window.

"This is it," Sam said. "Home sweet home."

He pushed the door open and ushered her in. The small window was on her left and to her immediate right was a cot that took up the entire length of that wall and almost jutted in front of the door. There was a small wood stove in the far left-hand corner and a small cupboard over the window. There were shelves above the cot and beside the stove, but these contained only some food supplies and the three books he'd accumulated while in Nalea's service. The cupboard contained only clothing.

"You've been collecting quilts, I see," Tassia commented, not sure what to think of the cramped space and not wanting to discourage Sam since he seemed so pleased with his first real home since his youth.

"I'll need a few more, and some furs, to get me through the winter, I think. My little shack isn't nearly so well-built as your hut."

"The queen wouldn't let her defenders freeze," Tassia admitted.

"Well, it's a small space at least, and the stove will warm it enough. I'd like to get some more books, and perhaps find some art. Or a nice vase so I can keep some wildflowers in the summer."

"That would certainly add to the cozy feel."

Sam laughed. "You mean it would make it actually seem cozy? Rather than like I'm living in a closet?"

"If you insist," she said with a grin.

"Really, I have just as much space as you do."

"How do you get that?"

"You have to share your space with Livia. Your hut is twice as big as my shack, but only half of it is really yours."

"I suppose, but the bunk helps. And we have a latrine."

"Well, so do I! I just have to walk a little farther to get to mine."

"All right then. You want to show me the rest of the place?"

Sam stepped back out into the cool, sunny day. "Well, there's not a whole lot to see. You've been introduced to the barn, and there are some storage sheds over by the main house. And the house, of course. It has two latrines, but that's for the family. The shared one is over there, by the brush."

Tassia followed where he was pointing, sort of behind his shack, and saw a dilapidated structure some distance away near some sad, scrubby trees. She said nothing, knowing the conditions were below anything she'd want to live in, but then again, she hadn't been living from a bag for a decade. She figured Sam must be more enamoured with the permanence and sense of ownership than the actual rustic nature of his surroundings.

"I know, it's not much," he said, reading her expression. "It's a wonderful start though."

"Beats sharing your space or sleeping under the stars, I suppose."

"Sleeping under the stars isn't all bad," Sam countered.

"It is in the winter," Tassia said, trying to keep her thoughts from straying to the night they'd shared.

He shrugged and conceded.

"I'll find something better before too long, but this will be excellent while I start at the university. I asked around about tuition, and it will take me until next autumn to save up for it, but a year or two will be plenty to get me an apprenticeship. Even just two years will get me into Nalea's court again, and then maybe I'll get a proper house of my own."

"Is that what you've decided on then?"

"I think so. I had everything given to me as a child because my parents were well off. I miss those comforts, but like the idea of earning them for myself. And I think I see how I can do that."

"I'm glad you're settling down so much. But aren't you going to miss the travelling?"

"There's always the breaks between the winter and summer semesters. The winter break is an especially excellent time to travel. And I know how to travel quite cheaply, so I don't see that getting in the way."

"All this time out in the silence has given you time to think, hasn't it?"

"It's really helped me put things into perspective. I certainly don't want to live like this for very long, but it's easy to do when it helps me work toward something better. I wouldn't mind living in the homestead and being an actual farmer, instead of just a farmhand, but I don't think I'd make a very good farmer. I haven't had enough practice at it in my youth, and it doesn't seem like the sort of thing someone my age can just pick up."

"You might be surprised," she said. "But you've always seemed more academically inclined anyway. Your face positively lit up when I told you about the university."

"You're right. I think I could be content doing just about anything, really, but I would be happiest if I could learn a bit more and do something in the court. I think I could make a good ambassador or foreign advisor, given that I've travelled so far."

"You're right! I hadn't thought of that."

"I'd love to help Nalea expand her network of allies. And that sort of work would probably allow plenty of opportunity to travel."

"Undoubtedly! You could travel comfortably, too, and likely be paid for it."

"Now you're talking!" he said, grinning. "I've got to actually go into the university and see what their training is like. I'll have to take some entrance exams as well, and I'd like to get an idea of what those are like, too, so that I can prepare. I have plenty of time in the evenings to sit and read, so I can study and be ready for the autumn enrolment."

Sam was beaming now as he further considered his plans, and Tassia was happy just to see him so enthusiastic. She followed him to one of the storage sheds where he grabbed two barrels — one for each of them — and continued across the vast yard of the farmhouse and through one of the fields that had already been harvested.

"Corn?" Tassia asked him, bending to inspect the remainder of one of the stalks.

"I think so. I wasn't working this field when they cleared it. I was in the wheat."

He walked on, and she eventually spotted the orchard, which had only one other person working in it — a horse and cart of apples patiently waited nearby. She could only see apple trees from where they stood, but the trees farther back looked different.

"What are they growing out here?"

"There were pears and some fuzzy orange fruit, like a peach, that I'm unfamiliar with. There are only apples left now, though."

They approached the other worker, the owners' oldest son, Luuko, who was at the top of the ladder, intending to work his way down the tree, slowly filling the cart full of empty baskets beneath him. There was another ladder nearby, and Sam propped it against the trunk so Tassia could work the other side of the tree while Sam picked everything he could reach from the ground. She and Luuko passed their full baskets down to Sam who would pass empty ones back up to them. With a system in place, Tassia was surprised by how quickly they were able to get through the tree.

When they ran out of baskets, Luuko set out to empty the cart and fetch them some more, leaving Sam and Tassia with one basket between them to share until he returned. They had worked out a system quickly and picked until evening when Luuko suggested they head in before they lost all light.

"My parents didn't have an orchard," Tassia said. "That was wonderful! I imagine I'd have spent whole summers among the branches of the trees if they'd had any."

"I know we certainly did," Luuko commented. "Until we were old enough for the more strenuous chores, we passed our summers in these orchards, climbing the trees and eating what ripe fruit we could reach. My oldest sister would always make herself sick from eating too many apples."

Tassia helped unload the apples from the cart and then followed Sam into the farmhouse for dinner.

"I should probably go home," she said. "I've got plenty to eat there."

"Nonsense," Nisa said, appearing in the doorway. "You were such a help today, and we would be honoured to have one of the queen's elite dine with us tonight."

Tassia blushed. "I'm hardly elite! I'm only mucking about with Sam today because I'm on suspension."

"Sam says you're among the queen's high command."

"Well, I suppose. I'm second rank in my battalion, in the top ten for my brigade."

"He also said you're on suspension because your commander is unfair. He said you disobeyed orders in order to stop one of the queen's enemies."

"Yes, but it was also incredibly stupid. I almost got killed."

"You're a soldier," Nisa said. "Come, join us for dinner. We can talk about working the land if you prefer to stay away from military conversations."

Tassia was still reluctant, but quickly grew relieved that she'd stayed, as it reminded her so much of home, with the warm scent of home-cooked meals and the room full of light and welcoming chatter. It was an atmosphere she would never see again, with her parents gone and her remaining siblings scattered, but rather than lamenting that fact, she found herself laughing and enjoying her evening.

Tassia could see the bustle of her brigade as she approached home, and she was glad they had returned. She had been gone a full week, and Nalea hadn't been certain how long they would be when Tassia had finally left to visit her sisters. She had been worried about them, particularly Varia, and the journey to visit them had put her at ease. Varia was much stronger than the last time Tassia had seen her, and had been in the dooryard chopping wood when Tassia had arrived. The last time Tassia had seen her, she could scarcely walk across a room.

Tassia had also been able to meet her new niece — Mara. Varia and her husband had recently brought home the child from an orphanage, and hadn't even had time to send Tassia the news before her arrival. The little girl, a six-year-old with blonde ringlets and a heartbreakingly sad gaze, had done much to bolster Varia's spirits, even in the aftermath of the loss of their parents. Varia was doing everything she could to make the little girl happy and get her adjusted to life outside the orphanage. Toward the end of her visit, Tassia had seen Mara come out of her shell and shout and giggle like a small child should.

"You're going to do wonders for each other," Tassia had assured Varia on parting.

Mernia had been so happy to see the effect Mara and Varia had on each other that she was talking about motherhood for the first time in her life. It was almost enough for Tassia to start considering the same, though she doubted she would tire enough of military life any time soon. Even so, she was starting to think that maybe it was time to take the strategist's training so that she would be ready to enter the queen's court when the time came for her to leave behind her role in combat.

"Tass! Welcome back!" Livia called from the front steps of her hut. She was sitting with Butch, but he gave a little wave and walked off.

"Everything going all right?" Tassia asked, surprised Butch hadn't stuck around to get caught up on any gossip Tassia might have.

"He thought we could use some time together since it's been over a fortnight."

"That was kind of him. Odd, but kind."

Livia laughed. "He's getting used to my needs, I think. He knows he'll hear all the gossip before long anyway. So? How was it?"

"It was fantastic! Primarily because this marks the end of my suspension. No more staying behind, and that couldn't make me any happier!"

"How are the ladies?"

"Wonderful! Oh, Livia, Varia has a daughter now!"

Livia gasped. "Tell me everything!"

Tassia did, including her belief that it was just about time to start the strategist training.

"I'll do it with you," Livia said. "This thing with Butch is it. Without a doubt. I've got to think about the time when we make it proper, and I'll have to leave battle to mother."

"It would be good to have someone help me with the studying," Tassia admitted. "You know I've never been good at it."

"It will be more difficult this time. There's more book knowledge and less physical work for the strategist's training. But we'll still get instruction from Nalea's top general."

"I'll find out from Nalea what we should study, and we can prepare over the winter and see about taking the entrance exams in the spring."

"You want to do it so soon?"

"I'm sure by spring you'll want to as well. How much longer do you think it will be before you move to Butch's?"

Livia was quiet for a moment. "We're certainly not getting any younger."

"You're about ready to see the end of battle," Tassia pointed out. "You're probably ready to see the end of the military entirely."

"Aye." She sighed. "I suppose I am. What else would I do?"

Tassia shrugged sympathetically. She couldn't imagine leaving the military entirely. It would be nice to be in the court and working with Nalea directly, but she also thought she might enjoy being a military instructor and training new recruits. Showing Sam some basics over the summer had renewed her desire to teach. She would have to pass the strategist's training either way.

She stayed with Livia, unpacking and listening to how the rebuilding had gone until after lunch. It was good to have her back, but it was also Sam's day off, so Tassia decided to go visit him for the rest of the afternoon while Livia got Butch caught up on any gossip he'd missed.

"You sure? Butch can wait," Livia said.

"I haven't seen Sam in over a week, and I found something for him in the market. His place is so small and pathetic and empty, and I saw a canvas at the market when I was selling off the last of our vegetables."

"Oh, can I see it?"

"Of course," Tassia said, pulling out a tin storage tube. She'd stored it in the wardrobe while she'd been at her sister's and was surprised that Livia hadn't already found it and snooped.

It was a small canvas with a painting of a red arch of rock in a desert, set against the most brilliant blue Tassia had ever seen.

"What is it?" Livia asked, tilting her head sideways trying to make better sense of it.

"I think it's of this place in the desert Sam has been to. I told you about it, I think. Cathedrals of stone was how he put it. From what he described, I think this is it."

"That's a real place? A real thing?"

"I think so. The vendor said she picked it up from an artist to the south who claimed to be from near the eastern sea. Sam said the place was southeast, so if the tale the vendor told me is true..."

"He's going to love that! You sure you want to risk igniting his wanderlust again? It sounds like you just convinced him to stay put for once."

"Might make him less likely to wander off if he's got a small reminder with him. I wish I'd had time to get it framed for him, but I guess that can be his solstice gift," she said, smiling.

"You going to be long?"

"Not sure. It's such a beautiful day — likely the last we'll see this mild until spring — and the family he's working for took a shine to me. They might invite me to stay for dinner, so don't wait around for me."

"All right. Definitely a good day for a country walk. I'll have to come out there with you before the snows begin. Today, I think I will enjoy the last taste of summer in the company of my man."

"Have fun," Tassia said with a wink.

Tassia set out southward again, enjoying the grass against her sandalled feet and the feel of the unusually warm breeze. This last taste of summer was always particularly sweet. She was wearing a simple, faded blouse and a long brown skirt that flowed lightly around her legs. She easily found the place again by memory and was surprised by how quiet it seemed this time. There was no activity at all in the yard. She had expected to see at least a couple of the family members out doing chores, but they all seemed to be taking the day off, or at least working somewhere out of sight. She spotted Sam sitting in the grass in front of his shack, leaning against the wall with a book in hand.

"Tass! How good to see you! What brings you here?"

"Brought you a housewarming gift," she said, waving the tin at him. "Where is everyone?"

"I'm not sure. I think mostly in the house, taking some rest. Some of the others are in the city — probably at the park enjoying the weather."

"Everyone gets the same day off?"

"Yes, and they take it off completely. The only chores involve making and cleaning up meals. It's quite wonderful."

"I'm sure it is! What are you reading?"

"Astronomy. I picked it up in the market just after you were here. I thought it would be nice to start some hobbies again, and reading seemed like a good place to begin. The clear winter skies will enable me to put this into practice once I'm through the book."

He ushered her into his shack and set the book on one of the mostly bare shelves, closing the door behind them. There was a new addition to his home at least, a chair stood just in front of the wood stove, and she saw he also had a new quilt folded at the foot of his bed.

"Looks like you had a successful trip to the market," she commented.

"They feed me well enough that I don't see much need to spend any of my earnings on food just yet, especially when I've still got all the preserves you gave me."

"Where do you keep them all in this little space?"

"Took some of your advice and put them under the bed," he said with a grin.

Tassia crouched and saw that he had lined the floor under his cot with jars of canned goods from her garden.

"Well, I'm glad to help out! You may as well enjoy it. I had some success in the market, too. When I was selling off what I had left, I came across a vendor with a piece of art that I thought would interest you and make this place a little more homey."

Sam was grinning anxiously at the mere gesture, and she was a little nervous handing the tube over to him, not sure how he would react.

"I hope you like it," she said, passing it to him. "It looks right based on your description, though."

He gave her a puzzled look for a moment and popped the lid off, pulling out the canvas and carefully unrolling it. His expression was unreadable for a moment, and she was concerned she had found something entirely wrong.

"It's your desert, isn't it?" she asked uncertainly.

She noticed his eyes had begun to well up with tears and became even more concerned.

"Sam?"

"Tass, where in the name of the moons did you find this?"

"Just at the market," she said, with a confused shake of her head.

"This is it! I've seen this very arch! It was a mammoth of rock, Tass. I just — I can't believe you found it — that you thought of me—"

"It's all right then?"

"This is my first proper gift in over a decade, Tassia. It's perfect," he said, his voice growing quiet with sentiment.

He set it down on his chair cautiously, revered, and turned to her suddenly.

"You continue to amaze me," he said, still quietly, cupping her face in his hands. He leaned down to her, pressing his lips fiercely to hers, completely overcome with emotion. She realized his cheeks were damp with uncontained tears.

He'd completely caught her off guard, and his unrestrained elation swept her away as well. When his hands slid from her face and wrapped around her, holding her tightly, she wrapped her hands around the back of his neck, keeping his lips on hers. He lifted her, pulling her legs up around his hips and her skirt up around her waist, pressing her back against the wall. Bracing her there, he unbuttoned her blouse and cupped her exposed breasts, while she clamped her thighs around him, locking her legs together behind him. She pulled his shirt over his head while he nipped at her breasts and ran his hands through her long tresses.

She wrapped her arms around his shoulders, pressing tight against him, breathing deep and hard against his skin and locking her mouth at the side of his neck. He nibbled her shoulder and began to slide her britches down while she continued to hold herself up with her arms around his back.

They both worked at his belt, and he slid his trousers down, still deftly balancing her between his body and the wall. She felt the heat of him against her thigh and moaned softly in his ear before pulling his mouth to hers, kissing him greedily. He'd slid his arms around her inside the blouse that still hung from her shoulders and pulled his fingers down the skin of her back, where sweat was gathering between her shoulder blades.

"Tassia," he gasped against her lips. "I—"

She wasn't interested in words and silenced him with her tongue, drawing him even closer to her, pressing her skin fiercely against his. With one hand still firmly around her back, he slid the other down her stomach and over her thigh, sliding two fingers into her and working until she was slick and thrusting her hips against him. He readjusted her position against him and then carefully slid into her. She felt the bliss of his warmth filling her again and never wanted to be away from him. A satisfied moan slipped from her lips as he entered her, and she began to gasp in quick, shallow breaths. Sam was unable to find his rhythm though and carried her to his bed, lying her across the cot and following her down quickly, pushing back into her before either of them could lose any of their heat.

Still thrusting, but harder and steadily now, he pushed her blouse away completely and stroked her shoulders, finally running his fingers down her chest to her breasts. She had her fingers laced behind his neck and her head thrown back, arching feverishly against him, wishing she could fit his entire being inside of her.

Tassia could feel him watching her, and she turned her head to face him, not flinching from the intense expression he wore. Her mouth curled up in ecstasy, but her strong gaze never left his, even once they both began to climax. She looked away only as she began to cry out, jolting against him in orgasm and squeezing her eyes shut involuntarily. When he tried to pull back from her, she held him steady, not wanting the moment of bliss to be broken, wanting to stay in its enveloping warmth — a shield against the reality beyond their act.

He still held her, but finally pulled out of her and rolled beside her, still lying in her arms, with one of her strong legs draped over his hip.

"Tassia."

She silenced him again with a kiss, not wanting to let words break their spell, not yet. She didn't know what to call what kept happening; she just wanted to feel his skin and hear his breath. She slid out of the skirt that had bunched around her waist and pressed herself at his side, continuing to kiss him and stroke his chest.

He kissed her lips and then pressed them against her ear, nibbling, finally finding the opportunity to speak.

"You have to face this," he whispered, running his hand down her neck and over her firm breasts.

"Not now."

"Then when?"

"When all heat is gone," she whispered lustily, stroking her hand down his abdomen, cupping him and massaging him. His body responded, but she could still feel the heat slipping out of him. She doubled her efforts, pressing her breasts and groin firmly against him, and drawing his lips to hers, kissing him hungrily. But his passion had faded, and she couldn't bring herself to coax more out of him, like some desperate enchantress.

"You're going to say it's a mistake again, aren't you," he said sullenly, looking deeply hurt.

"It can't be. It feels so right." She couldn't maintain his gaze and looked down, staring at his chest but not really seeing.

"You've felt that before," he pointed out.

"Then it must be right."

"Tass, I never know what to believe out of you anymore. One minute you hold me at bay as a friend and the next you're pulling me into you as a lover, all the while insisting it's right and then wrong."

"But it is. When I'm with you like this, when I feel you inside me and we're together like this, it feels right. But when I think about it, when I examine this, it seems that it must be a mistake, that I'm just some foolish, lonely girl desperate for the attention of men. And here you are, paying attention to me."

"You said last time that you were just using me. Taking advantage of my attentions to satisfy your loneliness. But what about your spirit? We're friends, aren't we? So don't I satisfy you fully?"

"I don't know," she said quietly.

"You have to name it eventually, Tassia. You can't just keep letting this happen and then denying me and pushing me away again. Make it real or push me for good because I can't bear to keep being pulled in only to be cast aside." He tilted her chin up, forcing her to look at him. "Tassia, I want you to be with me wholly until the end of your days."

"Something like that requires certainty of intent from both of us."

"I'm certain," he insisted.

"But are you? When my body is entwined with yours, I'm certain, too. And yet later, there are strong doubts. You can honestly tell me you never have doubts? Sam, how long has it been since you had a lover — Hetia obviously doesn't count — how long since you had even just an innkeeper's daughter for one night?"

She saw doubt creep into his expression, and he sighed and looked away from her. "Elintrin. Four years ago, maybe five," he admitted.

"But you don't believe you want me out of a need to fill years of loneliness? Not to mention the harm Hetia did?"

"I'd never considered it."

"But now?"

"I don't know," he conceded miserably.

"We've always been friends," she said, wrestling with her thoughts, but unable to concentrate on them, only noticing his flesh and yearning for it.

"This is more than a friendship."

"Right now. Can we keep with 'right now'? Can we let 'later' worry about itself? I just want to stay in this little house with you, in this bed, and feel your heat."

"For how long?"

"I don't know. For today. Can we just start with today?"

"I've lived day to day for too long to let it extend into my romantic life, too. It exhausts me too much. Please just name this."

"I can't, and right now neither can you. Let's be temporary lovers until we can give this a real name. Let me feel you one more time and take that home to think on."

She could see that Sam wanted an answer more than anything, but wanted her too badly to press the matter any further. When she pressed against him again and continued to knead him, he responded and didn't back down. His passion returned, but the intensity of earlier had gone out of both of them. She kissed him slow and deep, letting her hands explore his body while he let his lips explore hers. He nipped at her abdomen and thigh, tickling her and making her gasp. He pressed his face between her legs and his tongue deep into her, and she was startled at first by the new sensation, but quickly eased into it and relaxed.

She took his shoulders and pulled him up, wanting to feel his skin on hers. She guided him back into her, and they moved slowly, drawing out each kiss, each tingle and each spike of pleasure — neither of them wanting to let the moment end nor let reality back in. They climaxed again before they began to hear the voices of the others returning and he slipped out of her for good.

Neither of them spoke for a long time, and Tassia held him and stroked his hair while he kissed her gently. She wouldn't let any thought in at all and concentrated on the murmured voices from the family as they returned and to the sound of Sam's soft breathing. He continued to let his hands explore her body and finally sat up, tracing every line of her with his eyes.

"You know what I want," he said. "What I *think* I want," he amended. "I want you to decide what you want — what you want independent of me. I've always been a wanderer, Tassia, and I will wander to new places and look for new companionship if your heart truly decides that this is wrong. But I'm here now, and if you want me to remain, I'm fully prepared to do so. I want you to know that this is real. That I've travelled far and never before have I cared for someone the way I care for you. I will meditate on my intentions, to be sure my desires aren't borne of loneliness. All I ask is that you do the same."

"I need more time," she said, beginning to pull her blouse back on, slowly buttoning it over the swell of her breasts. "I will give it proper thought now. My head is clear of grief, and after this, my heart can't plead loneliness. I have so much to think about. My sisters left me with a lot to consider, and I need to give my entire future more thought because I never have. I know what you want, but I have little notion of what I want — especially in the long term. Does it help to know that I certainly want this — want you — for the short term?"

His lips smiled, but his eyes were still touched with sadness and longing. He leaned into her again, kissing her deeply but briefly. She wished she could give him more of an answer, pained by his obvious disappointment, but they would both continue to get hurt if they didn't properly sort out their needs before things went any further.

"I'm sorry that I don't have any water for you to wash up with," he said, looking around sheepishly.

"I can wash up when I get home. I've got plenty of road dirt to wash anyway."

"Livia will notice," he cautioned.

"Only if she's not out with Butch when I return," she sighed thoughtfully. "If she's there when I return, I will just take it as a sign it's time to tell her what's happened anyway. It keeps happening, and I think it's going to keep happening, though I'm not sure why. Maybe she'll have some insight."

Sam nodded. He was surprised when Tassia, now fully dressed, kneeled on the edge of the bed and leaned in to kiss him again.

"If you don't want to explain this to your hosts, you may want to wash up yourself," she said with a wink.

"Right," he said, shaking his head like a man waking from a dream. "And Tassia, thank you so much for the painting. I just—"

"I'm glad you like it even more than I hoped you would. Make this a home independent of me, all right?"

He nodded and she slipped out the door, making it back to the road without being seen by the others.

"Tassia!" Livia cried out from her seat at the table on seeing her walk through the door.

Tassia was relieved to see that Livia was alone and immediately collapsed onto her bunk, gasping and nearly sobbing — trying not to weep.

"What in the name of the moons is going on? Didn't he like it?"

"A little too much," she said, bewildered. "I should have expected he would. I just—"

"What did he do to you?" Livia demanded, growing concerned and angry. She moved from her chair to kneel in front of Tassia.

"Nothing I didn't want him to. Nothing he hasn't before."

"You must be joking."

"When you were away before — in the south. It was just after the dragon raid and I was such a wreck and he's always been there..."

"You saying you let him have you because you were a lonely, emotional wreck?"

"Not at first, but then in the morning, once he went out to send a message to Nalea to make sure she knew about my parents, I was alone with my thoughts — away from him, I couldn't keep reality out anymore. I had doubts. I thought then that it was just a mistake borne of my grief and profound loneliness. But what excuse do I have this time? I've just been to see my sisters, just seen you and Butch. I haven't been lonely in ages! I don't know what to think, but I've just got to get washed up."

She disappeared into the latrine, shutting Livia out behind her and relieved that the weather was warm enough she could just bathe in the cool water sitting in the basin. She didn't want to sit feeling the remains of him on her while she waited for the water to warm. She changed and tossed her soiled clothing in with the rest of the laundry from her journey south.

"You're just leading him on," Livia said, getting angry. "You can't just let him latch onto you like he has so he can scratch your itches."

"I know that! I'm just not so sure if that's what I've been doing all this time. When I'm with him — his skin on mine — my heart says it's right and there can be no other way, and my mind is silent. But as soon as I'm away from him again and that heat is gone, my mind won't be quiet, but it won't talk any kind of sense either."

"You love him then."

"I don't know. Is that what you feel? With Butch?"

"It was at first," Livia said. "Now I'm more certain of how I feel. All of my future plans involve him now, and I couldn't imagine planning my future without him in it. I guess that's how I know for sure that I'll marry him when he asks me to."

Tassia nodded.

"That doesn't help?"

"I can see him in my future, yes, but I can see so much else still, too. I have no problem making plans that don't involve

Sam, or anyone really. Right now I just see me working toward becoming a strategist — maybe to work with Nalea and maybe to train new recruits. Sometimes I see myself with just some idea of a companion — a phantom lover — and sometimes I see myself alone."

"Have you tried before now to place him in your future?"

"Not as anything more than a friend. I see him in my future the same way I see you or Nalea."

"Then you need to try to put him in your future. If you can't comfortably place him there, then he doesn't belong there. And, Tass, you should probably stay away from him until you decide."

CHAPTER 9

Livia was startled when the man who caught her shoulder in the market wasn't Butch but Sam.

"Sorry, I thought you heard me call to you," he said.

"I'm just not really paying attention, sorry. How have you been?"

"I imagine you must have an idea." He looked at her squarely and pulled his cloak tighter around him to ward off the biting prairie cold.

"Aye, Tassia told me. I gave her some advice that you may not appreciate."

"You told her to stay away from me until she gets her head and heart sorted out?"

Livia looked away.

"Good," Sam said and smiled at her startled expression. "It's what she should do. I hinted that she should do the same. It's hard on us both with this back and forth, and I just want to know where her heart is before this goes any further."

"Well, she's been giving it some thought, but she hasn't said a thing to me since she first spoke of it the last time she saw you."

"She hasn't given any hints? As her best friend, you haven't had any intuitions?"

"No, I haven't. She can be hard to read and she's closed this part off. She's dealing with it silently, and we've been so busy. I moved out, you see. I live with Butch now and see less of her. She doesn't talk to her new bunkmate very much, and the girl has no idea. Tass is under stress, but we both are, what with the strategist exams coming up."

Sam tilted his head curiously.

"She didn't mention it? We're taking the strategist training entrance exams in the spring. If we pass, we start new training in the autumn. She just can't make up her mind exactly what she wants, and I think that partly includes what she wants with you, but she's got her mind set on the strategist training now. She either wants to work in Nalea's council or train new recruits."

"She'd excel at either, I'm sure, but something tells me she would probably enjoy the training more."

"She did mention she showed you some things," Livia said with a grin. "I'm trying to talk her into just doing the recruitment first and entering Nalea's council later, once her body begins to protest the strain of constant training."

"If you think it will help her in her decision, tell her I agree with you."

Livia nodded. "Look, Sam, I hope she gets this all sorted out soon, and I wouldn't mind it one bit if she decides to keep you as a lover. You're a worthy man. But I can't say what lies in her heart, not even after all these years. She still comes up with things that surprise me, so I can't give you any indication of what to expect. I have none."

Sam spotted Butch approaching. Butch wore a serious expression — with no evidence of his usual good cheer. Sam turned back to Livia.

"Is everything all right?"

"Haven't you heard about the war with the Krunleks? It's been going on since late autumn."

"I'd heard there were problems." His face sagged with understanding. "You're being deployed."

"Nalea rotates a new brigade in every two weeks, and we leave tomorrow. It will be eight weeks or more before we're back again. Maybe you should break my rule this one time and come with us back to the barracks to see her before she goes. Give her a reminder of what she's got to think about if she comes back alive."

Sam nodded solemnly. He followed awkwardly as Butch and Livia finished making their purchases and went back to their hut. Livia stopped only long enough to drop some things off and then continued with Sam to find Tassia. Luckily, she was outside doing some stretches, and alone.

"Good luck," Livia whispered to him and left him to approach Tassia alone.

"Sam!" Tassia said, shocked. She looked a little scared to see him.

"I ran into Livia and Butch by chance in the market, and she told me you're being deployed to war," he said, letting his fear through even though he hadn't meant to.

"You've seen me in battle," Tassia said. "I'll be all right."

"You can never promise such a thing in a war. I've heard of the Krunleks' viciousness. I fear for you, Tass. I can't help it."

"I never worry too much. Not for myself, but I appreciate your concern."

"I spoke with Livia briefly, and I'm sorry if my sudden appearance has thrown you off, but I didn't want you to go to war — not with the chance that you might not return — and not come to see you before you leave."

Tassia nodded. "I had hoped to have answers for you by now, but I've been too consumed with the strategist training."

"That's good," he said. "As long as you're not idle. Make your plans and let them include me only if you feel they must."

Tassia took his hand and drew him around the back of her hut where no one would be able to see them. She kept her grip but stared down at his hand for a moment before speaking.

"Thank you for coming to see me," she said softly. She was shifting her weight from one foot to the other. He wasn't sure it was a gesture of nervousness as much as an attempt to fight the cold as the snow rose up over her ankles. "I've missed your company and I do value your friendship. You want me to give you a final decision, but I'm not ready. I don't see my path in life clearly enough yet to see if you belong on it or not."

She touched his cheek and drew him down so she could kiss him. Fearing it was the last time he'd hold her, he pulled her tight against him, feeling the gentle warmth of her body against his. The sharp wind was at his back, tugging his cloak around them both. She lingered in the warmth of his embrace and pulled his lips to hers again before parting.

She sighed heavily, still holding his hands between the two of them.

"It's hard not to invite you in," she admitted. "But my new bunkmate, Grea, will be back from the market soon. Besides, I don't think that would be fair or help the situation at all."

"Probably not," he agreed, knowing he would not be able to resist the invitation against his better judgment. "Perhaps that's a sign?"

She smiled at him, and his fears vanished for a moment.

"I'd like it to be. I want this to be right, Sam. I do. But I have to be certain."

He understood. He'd known from the outset that it wasn't going to be easy — not after it had taken over a decade to find her. He knew her well enough to know that she had to be completely certain of how she felt, but that once she sorted it out, she would throw herself in headlong. But now she was off to war, and he was afraid of losing her.

"I'll do my best to return — I always do," she said, seeming to read his thoughts. "I'll try to give you an answer when I get back. War has a way of setting the world into perspective. On one hand, you are uncomfortable and get little rest, but on the other, the moments that you get to yourself are strangely clear and powerful. That's always the way it seems to happen. The danger and adrenaline wear thin, and I start to look for the meaning underneath it all."

He kissed the back of her hand and nodded.

"I am sorry that we'll be gone all winter. I had really wanted to travel south with you. Will you still go?"

"I think I might, especially when I know for certain I won't hear from you for so long. Take care and come home safely."

She answered him with a final kiss — warm, desperate and hungry — then she let him get back to his errands.

Tassia dropped sideways under the attack, feeling her right knee squelch into the bloody muck, and swung her blade up with all the strength and momentum she could muster, catching her foe in the thigh and nearly taking his leg off. He collapsed toward her, and she rolled left, trying not to think of the reason the ground was so soft when it should have been frozen; the metallic stench was enough to remind her. She rolled to her feet, plunging her sword into the man's chest.

She had no time to think about the filth she was covered in, though, as she spun to address the brute she could hear clomping up behind her. When would they learn not to run? No one ever snuck up on an enemy while sploshing heavy boots across a blood-soaked battlefield. She swung her blade into the spin and caught him in the ribs. He was one of the few wearing armour, so it did little damage, but he was caught off guard by her attack, truly expecting that he was about to take her by surprise, and her blow knocked him off-balance. She put a boot into his stomach and pushed him to the ground before he could regain his footing, bringing her sword down under his chin and taking his head off.

She was trying desperately to retreat and find the others, unsure of how she had ended up so thoroughly exposed to her enemies and so isolated from her comrades. She had been careful to strike a balance, following her instincts as much as possible while obeying the commander's every word. She'd had an uneasy feeling when he'd sent them down into this valley and instructed her to the front. Now she could see no one but her enemies, and was concerned she would end up breaking her promise to Sam.

It wasn't as upsetting a thought as she had expected it to be, though, and she quickly pushed it from her mind. Now was not the time to panic. She wasn't too heavily outnumbered — some of the Krunleks appeared to be charging to a battle she couldn't see and the others were launching a scattered attack on her. As long as they didn't organize themselves and attack all at once, she could keep fending them off until she found her platoon or retreated successfully.

She heard a twig snap behind her and spun again, plunging blade-first into a woman with an axe who had managed to get a little too close for comfort. It was a good reminder that at least some of her enemies had the sense to creep up and she had to keep moving.

She slashed at the ankle of one of them as she charged by, pushing her way between the falling man and his comrade, and made a run deeper into the forest. It was a rocky, treed area — not quite mountainous, but getting steep and craggy. The snow had been packed down everywhere so it would be difficult for her enemies to track her. She kept her eye on the hills for enemy archers, but she saw no one and hadn't seen any arrows on the ground in quite some time. She kept casting her glance back over her shoulder, but there didn't appear to be anyone giving chase. That concerned her, too.

She finally stopped moving up the hillside and dipped in between two large pines, letting their dense, drooping branches offer her some camouflage while she tried to assess the situation and get her bearings. She couldn't understand how she had managed to get so lost. The commander was going to tear a strip off her.

She could see the valley below was red with blood, but she was too far away to identify any of the bodies as those of friend or foe. She scanned the surrounding hilltops, looking for any sign of her comrades or landmarks that might help her regain her bearings. She would need to figure out where she was if she was going to try to sneak around the many battles and get back to camp for new orders. She wanted to use that retreat as a final option, though. Her first priority was finding her line. She hoped they hadn't all been killed or taken prisoner. She couldn't remember if the Krunleks still took prisoners. She sighed wearily and looked back to make sure there were no more clever women sneaking up on her with axes, but saw that she was quite alone.

She had hoped her private perch would give her a better idea of the lay of the land, but she wasn't familiar with the area and the overcast sky made it difficult for her to judge direction. She knew she could use the trees to gauge north, and she knew her camp was east of the main battle, so she shifted her attention from the hills and the sky to study the bark of the trees she crouched beside. She found a mossy patch running up one side of the tree to her left. She was certain that moss pointed north and couldn't waste any more time second-guessing herself. She had to keep moving before someone found her. She pushed herself back to her feet, and spent a quick moment wishing someone would blow a battle horn so she would know for certain which way to go. She decided to trust the trees and head along the rim of the valley, in the direction she believed and hoped was east.

She crested the hill, being cautious not to expose herself to whatever might lie beneath, and was devastated by the carnage below her. These bodies she recognized as belonging to her comrades, but not many appeared to be from her line. There were at least no living Krunleks visible, and she darted down the hill and continued to charge in the direction she hoped was east, trying not to look at the bodies. For now, she had to think of them as only obstacles not to be tripped over, not as people she had known and cared for.

At the edge of the next valley, she found a stream, red with blood, and she ran along its bank, darting between looming evergreens, still seeing very little signs of life. She at least remembered the stream and knew if she followed it, she would reach her camp. However, she had no way of knowing what waited for her on the way there. She forged ahead and kept her sword at the ready, fearing an ambush at any time.

Finally, as the snow became white again and the frozen ground more solid, she slowed and took a look around. There was no underbrush to mar her view, though the trees grew close together. The forest was still, not a whisper of breeze drifting past, and she could hear nothing but her pounding heart. It was eerie, and under the circumstances, she'd have been terrified if she had been the type swayed by superstition. Still, she felt confident in taking a moment to catch her breath. She had left the reek of battle behind her and now breathed in the sharp scent of new snow and the pungent, heady scent of pine. It cleared her head and calmed her emotions. She could see no one at all now, only the trail they had made through the snow as they marched into battle. The Krunleks lived in these hills, and she had thought it foolish to charge into an environment so foreign to the entire brigade. She had tried to voice her concerns, but to no avail; now she was certain that if she saw the commander, she was going to cut him apart. All of the footprints in the snow seemed to be running into battle; there were no signs of retreat.

She spotted a scout half hidden by pine boughs and called out in joy and relief.

"Comrade! Any news?"

"News?"

"From the others? Surely there must have been others retreating."

"Not this way. Why would we retreat?"

"We didn't have the upper hand at all. I don't understand how I'm the only one to have come back this way. You're certain no one has past you?"

"Not a soul. There's the southern flank though — maybe others came that way instead."

"I pray to every spirit that ever existed that you're right. Otherwise I'm all that's left of my battalion."

His jaw dropped. "Comrade, are you certain?"

"The only thing alive that I could see in those hills were Krunleks. I got separated from my line, though whether by death or some act of the terrain I don't know. How much farther to the camp?"

"A league."

She nodded and ran on, still alert. She couldn't let her thoughts linger too long on what the scout had said. She reached the camp, a huddle of tents in the forest that now stood nearly empty with only a few dozen soldiers visible, and burst into tears when she saw Livia.

"Tassia! By the moons, where have you been?"

"I could ask you the same thing!"

"That blood—"

"If it's mine, I don't feel the injury," Tassia said. "What in the name of the hills happened back there?"

"I don't know. The formation was deeply infiltrated and broke apart into chaos. I didn't need the call of retreat to tell me that battle was done for. The commander should have heeded your advice — not to mention that of dozens of others. We should have drawn them out of the hills or made the advance more slowly."

"If I see him, I'm going to cut him apart and to hell with the consequences."

"When he gets back, I'm sure no one will stop you."

"He's not here?"

"He was with your line. I'm sure he'll be here with the others before long."

Tassia bit her lip and shook her head. "There was no one left alive when I came out of those hills. It's only by the grace of the spirits and pure fortune that I made it out."

Livia looked around at the near-empty camp; her eyes grew wide with terror.

"Livia, is this it? Was there really no one else on the southern flank?"

"I came back from the south, and Butch was one of the last ones out of there. He said there were maybe two dozen left behind him still fighting for a retreat, and he expected most of them would make it. I haven't paid attention to the numbers coming in. Once he got here, I just started searching for you. I think this is it. This is all of us."

"We need reinforcements. Now. Who's left in charge?"

Livia went blank.

"I don't even know... We've lost so many, I just... My stars!"

"Let's go to the command tent and see who's there."

They pushed through the camp to the tent at the centre, stunned by how few people remained. The only consolation was that those who had managed to escape had done so with little to no injuries. Livia pushed back the tent flap and paused again. There were four men in there, one of them was Butch, and they all looked equally confused.

"What news do we have?" Butch asked.

"We're blind," Tassia said. "There was no one left alive when I left the field, and I was the last one to come down the eastern flank. I didn't even hear a call for retreat."

"This makes you in charge," one of the other men said to Butch. "Until we find the commander. *If* we do."

"We'll likely find him in a pool of blood, along with everyone else who hasn't made it back," Tassia said grimly. "I saw no one left alive and far too many dead. I don't believe the Krunleks are taking prisoners this time."

Butch turned to the man beside him.

"Get the first scout you find to take the quickest steed we've got and have him ride to the western brigade. They're the closest reinforcements we've got. We hold this camp until we get some better idea of our resources, but we will certainly need help if we hope to hold even this bit of ground for long."

Tassia and Livia exchanged frightened glances.

"Shouldn't we retreat?" Livia ventured.

"Not yet," Butch said. "It's grim, but we need more information before we decide to give up this much land. You know that."

"This is unbelievable. How did this even happen?" Livia quivered.

"Commander went soft on us," Butch growled. "We've seen it coming for so long, not least of all with that business he pulled on Tassia after Hetia's. If he's still alive — if they've taken him prisoner — I say let them keep the stupid lout!"

"We'll get everyone else together around the central fire pit," Tassia offered. "We should see who's left and if anyone saw what happened — especially to the commander."

Tassia and Livia walked out into the cold evening and were just in time to see the scout depart for the west.

"How long do you think it will take him to get to the next brigade?" Tassia asked.

"We won't hear anything before dawn."

"I hope the spirits are still on our side then. We'll be lucky to survive until nightfall if the Krunleks know of our decimated numbers."

"Let's hope we've got a good number of enchanters left to at least give us a ward to hold them back from this camp."

"Is that the best we'll get?"

"It might be."

Tassia sighed wearily.

"You about as tired of battle as I am now?" Livia asked.

"Just for the moment. If we live, I think I'm just that much closer to needing to be a strategist. If Nalea had replaced the commander when the rest of us began questioning him, then maybe—"

"A lot of people would still be alive," Livia agreed.

They searched the camp, finding only two hundred of their comrades; three thousand had come into camp with them. Tassia's new bunkmate was among the missing, and Tassia's heart grew heavy with doubt and worry.

"Did you see three thousand dead?" Livia asked Tassia. "You were the last one out there by all accounts."

"No, definitely not three thousand. Maybe close to it, but they certainly weren't all ours. I know I saw a few hundred Krunleks bleeding into the snow as well. I wish we had more numbers to go back out into that wretched valley and see who out there is bleeding because they're still alive. No one was moving, but that doesn't mean they were dead. And yet we have to leave them to die or risk the last of us being slaughtered or captured."

"Let us hope the Krunleks choose to take ours off the field on stretchers along with theirs."

"They have to have taken a few prisoners. We can only hope they will take some of the injured as well."

"Do we have enough enchanters left, do you think?" Livia asked.

"Twenty-nine will do us for a while. But it will depend on how many enchanters the Krunleks send when they attack."

"How long do you think we have?"

"I hope they choose not to attack until dawn. If we had better numbers, we'd have the advantage in this terrain. If they don't know what kind of numbers we have, they might hold back until daylight," Tassia reasoned. "Fighting us in the dark would be foolish regardless of our numbers because it will needlessly cost them extra lives to drive us back or finish us off."

"What do you think they'll do?"

"I don't know enough about their kind to make a guess. Butch looks concerned though, and he knows better."

Livia nodded wearily. "Yes, he's worried. I'm worried, too."

"We should rest then. We only have a couple of hours until nightfall."

Livia stopped to see Butch, and he echoed Tassia's sentiments. They should rest now; there weren't enough of them left to afford the luxury of sleeping once the darkness had swallowed them. Every last soldier left had to remain on alert.

"He thinks that if all of us are out patrolling tonight, it will make it seem like normal guard duty and like we've still got a fair number of soldiers in the tents sleeping," Livia explained. "It's the best shot we have of keeping them at bay until dawn."

"He's probably right."

"I just want to go home. I don't remember it ever being this bad before — being this close to the losing side. To death."

Tassia nodded.

"Tassia, do you ever remember it being like this? Ever?"

"I've never been in this kind of mess before. But I've heard of it. Other brigades have survived with such decimated numbers. It takes good leadership, and Butch will certainly keep everyone together better than the commander ever did. Everyone respects him already, and I think this might improve the spirits of some people here, even if the situation is grim."

"I just can't help but think that all the others must be dead," Livia lamented.

"Not taking prisoners is just foolish. They need something to bargain with if the war goes badly for them, and the commander will make an excellent bargaining chip. Or so they'll think. If I have a thing or two to say about it, Nalea will let them draw and quarter that man!"

"She'll likely bargain for everyone else before him after this mess," Livia said fretfully. "I just can't fathom that they're all gone."

Tassia held little hope of finding many of the others alive, but she wouldn't upset her friend by saying as much. Those left in camp would be lucky to escape with their own lives, especially if the Krunleks chose to attack before dawn. Retreating through the dark would be difficult, and they would be unlikely to be able to bring many supplies with them.

Tassia and Livia only spent a few minutes trying to rest on their bedrolls, and then they began wordlessly packing up their things, ready to flee at a moment's notice. Tassia left the water skins, knowing they wouldn't need them with such deep snow around to melt. She packed only a few dried food items, tea and the lightweight cauldron Sam had been so impressed with. If they were to retreat, they would join up with the western brigade first before gathering some more supplies to either settle in with that brigade or start for home.

"They'll send us home if we ask, won't they?" Livia asked.

"I'm sure of it. If you're shaken badly enough to ask it, then they won't put you into battle — especially under an unfamiliar commander — and risk losing you needlessly."

Livia nodded, looking relieved.

"We just have to make it through the night and get to the western camp," Tassia said. "Or hope they send enough reinforcements to hold this camp until Nalea can send relief."

"You're hoping for the latter, aren't you?" Livia said, shaking her head in bewilderment.

"I don't have the same prospects to live for as you do. Do you think Butch will leave with you?"

"Tassia, be serious. Most of the others are going to want to leave as soon as possible after this."

"I suppose."

"You really wish to stay and fight?"

"It's not out of me yet. I haven't got any idea of what my future will be or who I will share it with, so it's hard for me to forsake this — the only thing I've known and something dear to me — when I have nothing to replace it with."

"Think of your sisters! And what about your garden? Or Sam?"

"My sisters are building their own lives and will move on without me, the same as they're moving on without our parents. It will be hard on them, but they would overcome losing me. I do miss my garden, but I'm not prepared to make a life as a farmer. As for Sam — I just don't know. I thought of him when I thought I would die out there. I guess I felt disappointed that I would break my promise to him — to return safely. But that was it, just disappointment. I was more concerned about your safety than in ever seeing him again."

Livia nodded. "I hope you find a place for him in the centre of your life," she said.

"Why?"

"You work well together. He's willing to stay put for you, and he's not intimidated by your sword. Do you think you'll find anything better?"

"Do I need to find anything at all?"

"I guess that's the real question, then. You've got to square that away first, and if you decide that you really do want someone, it ought to be him. You two wouldn't be that much different together than me and Butch."

"Yes, you're right. I just need to decide what I want."

"Right now, I just want those of us left to make it out alive."

"I'd drink to that."

"Too bad we don't have any wine."

Tassia set her bag aside and stretched out on her bedroll again.

"That's all you're going to pack?"

"It will get me to the next camp," Tassia replied. "I don't want to take too much and risk it slowing me down. They may just chase us all the way to the western front, and I, for one, am not going to die over a few unnecessary comforts."

"You really think they'll chase us the whole way?"

Tassia looked over at her grimly. "You didn't see what was left in that valley. I will not underestimate their brutality."

Livia hesitated uncertainly and then dumped out her bag and began repacking, lightening her load and following Tassia's lead, leaving the water skins behind.

"I wish we'd been able to go south with him," Tassia lamented. "If this war had waited even a month, we would have been gone and likely not returned in time for deployment."

"Nalea wouldn't have sent messengers to find us?"

"Oh, she would have, but we still would have missed deploying with the others. I imagine she would have sent us with the western brigade when they came."

"I did want to see that hot spring. And I was so looking forward to the return journey and getting to meet Butch's family and introducing him to mine."

"I wanted to see something new," Tassia said. "Something new and not covered in blood. Just once. And I wouldn't have minded so much if I had gone with him alone, even if things had gotten — interesting again. I guess you're right. I need to sort my life and see where he fits."

Tassia lay back and closed her eyes, trying not to think about anything but surviving the night.

Tassia glanced back, but could see very little through the snow. She wondered now if they were even going the right direction anymore. She thought about calling ahead to their leaders to suggest they try to assess their surroundings and make sure they were at least still trekking westward. She didn't want to think about what would happen if they had circled back toward their enemies.

She spotted Livia looking at her and beginning to slow down; Tassia drove the heel of her hand into her friend's shoulder, driving her forward.

"Don't stop."

"Are they still back there?"

"I can't see a thing, but it's not worth the risk."

They both stole a glance anyway. A line of their comrades stretched out behind them, disappearing into the thick snow, and Tassia was relieved that they at least didn't appear to have lost anyone yet. She hoped Butch at least had his bearings.

Finally, he blew a horn, signalling them to stop. They quickly assumed their formation, forming a tight circle around the three men left in command, facing out with weapons drawn. Tassia scanned the snowy forest but saw no signs of movement; she wasn't sure if she should be relieved or concerned. The enchanters were placed at the innermost part of the circle, waiting for sign of danger to throw a ward around them. Tassia glanced between the others and could see Butch consulting a map, and she was relieved that, at the very least, if they weren't on the proper trail now, they would be very soon.

She heard him curse and gave Livia a brief look of concern, but Livia didn't react, as if she did not want to think about what could make Butch so upset that he would risk causing the others to falter.

"We're off course," he called. "We will have to ford the river ahead of us or risk drifting further from our route to find safe passage. We are too far from the bridge to get back to it if we hope to reach the western camp before sundown."

Livia finally returned Tassia's concerned look, but Tassia only shrugged.

"We'll be cold and wet, yes, but if we keep moving, we'll be able to dry off and warm up at the next camp. I'd rather face the river than certain death."

"What if the Krunleks stopped chasing us?" Livia said to Tassia. "What if they realized we were veering off course and have gone on the proper trail? They could be waiting for us on the other side of the river!"

"My love, I've thought of that," Butch said from behind them. "If we hurry and are able to ford quickly, we should be able to beat them back into the forest. Now that we're off our desired trail, it will be difficult for them to track where we will regain our course again. We will be on the lookout, but the closer we get to the western camp, the more likely reinforcements will be waiting to aid our retreat. Now everyone move out. Make haste if you wish to see the sun rise tomorrow!"

Both women held their ground as the rest broke formation and finally followed behind. Tassia was relieved to be bringing up the rear now that she had less reason to be concerned about an ambush from behind. The Krunleks had likely given up following them directly. She hoped the storm had caused them to give up entirely, but wasn't counting on that. At the very least, they had a hope of still getting past them.

"If they have any sense, they'll leave us to this storm," Livia said.

"That's our best hope right now," Tassia agreed. "They have more supplies and are more familiar with the terrain than we are, but it's really not worth it for them to chase us when there are barely two hundred of us left."

"We haven't seen them since the snows began, so hopefully they came to their senses and turned back."

They reached the river where it passed through a ravine, rushing too quick and deep to cross. They were forced to hike along a ridge, descending to a field where the river slowed and spread out. They scanned the far shore and saw nothing alarming, so Butch remained with a small, highly skilled group to guard the rear while the rest plunged into the icy, fast-moving water, holding their packs above their heads. Tassia followed them in, gritting her teeth against a rising scream. She concentrated on keeping her footing and making her legs move while she fought the current. The water never got higher than her thighs, but she couldn't feel her legs in the slightest by the time they reached the shore.

"How much farther?" she asked Butch when he joined them.

He shook his head, uncertain, and consulted his map again. He finally concluded that the trip downriver had taken them closer to the right path, and they had roughly three leagues left to go before they would begin to see signs of their comrades. Now that they had forded the river, Butch sent scouts ahead to alert the camp of their position and to see if any enemies waited along the way. They lit a fire and made some tea, pacing to bring warmth back to their frozen legs and taking turns standing around the small fires to dry out their clothing. Finally Butch decided they could wait no longer, shovelling snow into the fires and instructing them onward.

They had gone another two leagues when one of the scouts returned with the first piece of promising news they had received in days. A large party of soldiers from the western camp was heading out to meet them, and there was no sign of the Krunleks. They reached safety before nightfall.

CHAPTER 10

Tassia returned home to an empty hut and didn't even bother unpacking. She dropped her gear onto the floor just inside the doorway, opened the window to let the stale air out and immediately went to find Livia and Butch. They had left once Nalea had sent the word that the remaining soldiers from the southwest brigade could come home. The northern brigade had been sent in ahead of schedule, and Tassia had volunteered to go with them to reclaim the land she and her brigade had been forced to forfeit. Only a dozen others had also elected to remain.

Despite the initial crushing defeat on the southern front, Nalea's army had regrouped to ultimately overwhelm the Krunleks. Tassia had been pleased when the northern brigade's commander actually sought her input on the terrain and what she thought had gone so terribly wrong in their first offensive. She hadn't held back, and with a renewed effort, they had pushed the Krunleks past the ravine which had turned into such a massacre and had driven them back into the mountains.

The failed southern attack had set the victory back by over a month, and it was early spring by the time they were able to return home. The commander and several others from Tassia's brigade hadn't been killed after all, and they were returned to Nalea after she claimed victory. Although many people pushed her to try the commander, possibly for treason, she had instead stripped him of all his titles and levied him with a hefty fine, keeping Butch in command of what was left of the southwest brigade.

Tassia hadn't heard much news regarding who had survived. She knew some bodies had been recovered, but she hadn't heard whose they were. She had hoped to come home and find her bunkmate, but there was still no sign of Grea.

It was a quiet walk across the barracks to Livia and Butch's hut. She did her best to ignore how empty the square was and hoped they would get enough recruits before long to make up for the losses they had suffered.

She found Butch and Livia on their front steps, enjoying the early spring warmth.

"Tass! I was beginning to think we'd seen the last of you!" Livia called, standing excitedly to greet her.

"It never got so bad as those last two days before you left," Tassia replied, giving Livia a long, fierce hug before finding a seat on the stones in front of her friends. "It was better for me to stay. I don't think I could have dealt with coming straight back to these empty barracks knowing others were still in the foothills fighting and dying."

"Livia and I fell ill on the way back," Butch said, shaking his head, "so we really wouldn't have been any use had we stayed."

"Has it been good to be back?"

"At first, it was, but we quickly started to feel isolated with so few of us here," Livia replied. "We ended up taking the tail end of that trip we'd originally intended for the winter."

"You went to visit your family then?" Tassia leaned forward, curious.

"Yes, we didn't make it all the way to that city Sam mentioned, but we did get far enough south to enjoy some midwinter warmth before heading to visit our families."

"It was healing for you then."

Livia nodded slowly and cast a glance to Butch. "It certainly helped."

"What has Nalea decided for us? Have you heard any news on who we lost and who was taken prisoner?"

Livia was silent for a moment and continued slowly, choosing her words carefully.

"Everyone who was captured has been released and returned now."

Tassia nodded and took a deep breath, looking down the row of huts.

"Nalea is going to wave our entrance exams to the strategist training and expects us to help Butch with the recruits coming in."

"Good." Tassia nodded. "That will keep us busy. I expect we'll still study?"

"Of course. We're getting a free pass into the training but not a free pass through it."

"Are there a lot of recruits to train? Will they fill the barracks?"

"Nalea doesn't expect to replace the losses until autumn," Butch explained. "She's sending everyone to our brigade first, so we should be replenished by midsummer, but it will take quite some time to replace all those we lost in other brigades."

Tassia sighed and stared at her hands. "So I'll likely have an empty bunk for company for some time yet."

"It looks that way," Butch said. "Sorry, Tass."

"Have you been to see Sam?" Livia asked.

Tassia looked up. "No, have either of you seen him at all over the winter?"

"He's remained pretty scarce, but I'm sure he'll be glad to know you're back."

"Well, I'm in no mood for any more travelling today, except maybe to the market for some good wine."

"No need to head to the market for that," Livia said with a chuckle. "We haven't been training since everyone has been gone, visiting family and just taking a leave. So we've had no shortage of wine."

Livia disappeared into the hut and emerged almost immediately with three cups and a flask of wine.

"Have you had the chance to do much thinking?" Livia asked.

"Not really. It was intense and all I could think about was what happened to the others," she said, tipping back her cup and nearly draining it at once. "When does Nalea want us to start the strategist training?"

"The classes don't start until the autumn. We'll be learning informally from Butch until then."

"Neither of you will be commanding any time soon," he said, "but Nalea has a lot of top positions to fill after this, and I think you'll both move up. Tass, I'll have you in the front line where you belong."

She nodded and half smiled, but wasn't in a frame of mind to celebrate that small victory when it came at such a high price.

Tassia was playing cards with Livia and Butch at the table in their hut when the knock came at their door. They were all surprised to see it was Sam.

"You're back!" he said, giving Tassia and Livia a hug and Butch a bow of greeting.

"These two have been back for quite some time," Tassia explained, nodding to Livia and Butch.

"Every time I came by here to come into the city, it always seemed empty." Sam glanced out the door to the quiet barracks.

"Really, it still is empty," Livia said.

"I've noticed, but I ran into one of the soldiers as I passed through this time and I asked about you. I hadn't heard any news about Tassia's return, but they said you guys were back. I thought I'd come for some answers, and here she is." He gestured to Tassia and smiled. "What happened out there? I heard it didn't go well."

"That's quite the understatement," Livia said sourly. "We lost almost our entire brigade. Only two hundred of us walked away from the battle. Thankfully, over eight hundred were taken prisoner and have since been returned. Still, nearly two thousand soldiers died."

"My stars," Sam gasped.

"It didn't go so badly for everyone else," Tassia said bitterly. "There was no reason for us to lose nearly as many as we did."

"The commander went soft on us and led us into a slaughter," Butch growled.

"He's our new commander now," Livia said, nodding at Butch. "The old one has been sacked."

"He deserves worse after nearly costing us the war and wasting two thousand lives," Tassia said. She looked at Sam. "Grea didn't make it."

"Tass, I'm sorry. You're alone then?"

"I've only been back for three days and spent most of my time here."

Sam's brow furrowed, confused. "Why were you away so long?"

"I joined another brigade and helped reclaim the land we initially lost. It made it easier for me to return and carry on as a soldier."

"Still, it can't be easy."

Tassia sighed wearily. "I was just getting used to Grea. It will take some time to build up this brigade, and I expect it will be near the end of that before I get a bunkmate again."

"It's too early for spring planting, so I've been doing very little work. I could stay with you," Sam offered.

"That's kind of you. I'll see how it goes in the coming weeks. I'm still adjusting to just being out of the wilderness and back in the city."

Sam nodded. "Well, now that you're back, and I know that you are, I hope you don't at least mind my company. It's been a long winter, and I haven't been very good at making new friends."

"Well, you're welcome to join us if you'd like," Butch offered.

"Yes, that would be wonderful. I was on my way to the market and would like to go pick up some supplies now before it gets too late, but I'll be back in about an hour's time. Do you need anything?"

"Why don't I come with you?" Tassia said, setting down her cards and getting up to follow.

"I'm glad to see you," Sam said once they were outside.

Tassia grinned, genuinely happy to be with him again. She took his hand, and they walked in comfortable silence. Once they were beyond the barracks, she stopped him again and leaned against a low wall. Though he was tentative, he bent down to steal a quick kiss, and she was relieved for it. It was only a peck on the lips, but it was enough to ignite long-cooled passions, and she didn't let him move away from her. She pulled him close, kissing him more deeply, and then just remained in his arms for a moment until she felt steadier.

"How was your winter?" she asked.

"Likely, it was infinitely better than yours."

That earned him a grin.

"Did you make it south?" she asked.

"I did."

"That's it?" She tilted her head in confusion, watching him closely, but not seeing anything amiss. "You're usually so full of tales from the places you've been to, and this one is fresh!"

"It was nice to be somewhere a little warmer. It will certainly take me some time to adjust to these bitter winters. But the travel wasn't the same — I just felt alone the whole time. I think I spent more time trying to remember the parts of the trip to tell you than actually enjoying what I saw."

"You've lost your ability to enjoy travel then?"

"Seems I now require companionship." He squeezed her hand and watched her solemnly.

"Well, believe me, I certainly would have preferred to go south with you." Her heart danced along, and she secretly fought to keep herself composed, knowing exactly what Sam meant.

"If you're not going to be officially deployed or even training for a while, then why don't we take the trip soon? We can probably get there and back before spring planting begins," Sam said.

"I think I might like that," she said, surprised that she meant it. "It might give me the opportunity to finally think on everything like I was supposed to over the winter."

She could see the disappointment in his face and wished again that she had the answers he wanted.

"I know it's not what you want to hear," she said, squeezing his hand, incapable of letting it go. "But I still want to be with you."

"You just don't know for how long."

"As far into the future as I have solid plans," she said. "That only takes me to completing the strategist training, but it's something." She paused, hitting on a realization. "Sam, I think it's hard because both of our futures are in flux. We're both trying to decide what we want our lives to look like. Maybe I can't place you in my future because you're still trying to place yourself in yours."

He looked startled by the thought, but he was still smiling. She could see him gathering himself to say something, and fear touched his expression for a moment before he finally spoke.

"Maybe we should collaborate then." He paused. "I'm sorry, Tass. I shouldn't have put this all on you — if we're to be together, you're absolutely right that we should both have a say in what that looks like. I can do anything and go anywhere, as long as it includes being with you."

She frowned. "So really, you're waiting for me to decide what I want, and then you'll just follow along? Sam, that's hardly fair!"

"You're right," he conceded, sighing. "Shall we make a deal? When the spring planting starts, I'll be sure to be free from farm work when you have time away from soldiering. We've done some excellent scheming in your garden, so let's put our futures together there."

"One condition," Tassia insisted. She kept her tone serious but couldn't stop herself from smiling. "Can we live in the moment until then? Will you come back to my place after the market? Stay awhile."

A relieved grin broke over Sam's face. To see him smile made Tassia hope with an urgency she'd never felt before that they would be able to forge a future together.

Sam was nervous as the guard ushered him into the rookery at the pinnacle of the tower and closed the door, sealing him in with Nalea. He had been awkwardly pulled away from Tassia's bed after spending the night — thankfully, the guards hadn't walked in any earlier. Nalea had instructed her messengers to go to Tassia's if they didn't find him on the farm he worked. There had been no explanation, and Tassia had been as alarmed as Sam was as he was escorted out. He was worried that he would be forced to tell the truth, and he had no idea how to explain it to Tassia after so much time had passed and so many better opportunities to do so had come and gone.

Nalea was standing near one of the many open windows, stroking one of the messenger birds tethered to a perch. She didn't turn toward him as he approached the centre of the room.

"I have to tell them," she said, her voice touched with regret.

"No!" he cried, startling them both with his ferocity and his desperation. "No, please, it's just finally started to go right. She's finally started to take all this seriously, and we're set to plan our future together come spring. I was going to use it to tell her the truth — I can finally envision how. Just a few weeks, Nalea. Please!"

"I'm sorry, Sam. You're out of time." She half turned so that he could see her in profile, still stroking the bird and watching him askance. "Your identity is widely known now. You'll have to give up the shack on the farm — I can't allow you to remain in such conditions, whether you enjoy them or not. Guest chambers have already been prepared, and I've ordered some fine cloth for you in the fashion of your homeland."

"There must be something else you can do," he pleaded. "I don't want to stay in these towers."

"I gave you your options long ago," she said, turning now to fix him with a fierce gaze. "You had the opportunity to be honest with Tassia and to take her with you to your kingdom's allies before going home. You have had opportunity to leave here altogether, but you have refused to. You have had plenty of options since the summer, and you've refused them. Now, you have no choice. I have to tell your family that you are here, and I have to treat you as a visiting monarch because that is what you are."

"I'll leave now then." He spoke in a desperate rush. "I'll go south, where the passage isn't still barred by snow."

"It's too late." She shook her head and gestured to the bird. "This is my largest, fastest rook, and I will be lucky if it beats out other messages to your family. I must dispatch her immediately because I am certain others already have sent messages of your whereabouts to Mountain Song."

Sam took a half-step away from her, slouching sideways as he tried to think of other options, of a way out.

"I have no choice but to reveal that you are here," she said, her tone softening. "But there might be a way to keep you here publicly. I have two messages, and I will let you choose which one I send."

He saw there were two tiny scrolls set beside the patiently waiting rook, and Sam gave Nalea a curious glance. She approached him with quick, efficient strides and, still intimidated by her, Sam retreated, backing into a support column. She stood before him, so close her body nearly touched his, and she let her thick fur cloak fall from her shoulders, revealing a red silk gown she wore underneath. It clung to her every curve with a deep, plunging neckline that barely covered her breasts and high slits on both sides, all the way up to her hips.

"You have no doubt realized by now that I prefer the company of women," Nalea said carefully. "But you were right so long ago when you said I wouldn't mix the bloodlines and that I would find someone to provide me with an heir."

"This hardly seems wise," Sam stammered with a sudden flash of insight.

"We both get what we want." She ran her slender hand over his chest. "You can remain here, and I will have a suitable mate to give me an heir."

"My parents wouldn't allow it," he insisted, forcing himself to meet her gaze and not notice the rest of her.

"They would not risk war, Sam. You've been away for so long, you don't realize that they have softened a little in your absence. They would prefer a reason to make an ally of me.

We can build allies and a future for this kingdom, and after I've caught with child, you can have Tassia."

"She'd never have me," he insisted. "She wouldn't share me and I'd never ask her to. I would have to wed you to guarantee avoiding my father's wrath, and I will not make Tassia my mistress."

She leaned into him, pressing her body against his, and whispered into his ear, "We have a few moments before I send word, so think this over carefully."

Her lips brushed his cheek, and he could smell her sweet breath as she pulled back only slightly, taking his hand and pressing it to the ample swell of her bosom. Sam's heartbeat quickened, but more with panic than desire. Nalea was hot-tempered and unwavering, and she seemed to have her sights set on him now. Despite his revulsion at the offer, his resolve was melting under her heat. He couldn't help but notice her now, just as she had planned. She was warm, soft and strong-willed — so many things that Tassia was. It was a reasonable offer and probably a smart one — but it was also the kind of arrangement he'd forsaken his throne for in the first place.

Nalea twined her fingers in his hair and pulled his face to hers. He lost himself for a moment when their lips met. And then he pulled back.

"I can't," he said, more firmly now. "Please, Nalea, understand."

"You're the noblest of fools," Nalea said, but without malice — there was an undertone of admiration in her voice. "I understand perfectly. This is why you left Mountain Song in the first place. It's not as bad as what your parents would offer you — I don't want you, just a child, an heir — and then I would release you to the woman you love. I would let you have her, Sam. They won't."

He shook his head.

"I had to try — for both of us." She sighed.

"There really aren't any nobles in your kingdom you find suitable?"

"You've seen them," Nalea replied with a throaty laugh. "So hung up on their titles and their privilege, their stupid customs and their own arrogance. I placate them at every turn, but none of them is worthy of providing me with an heir. You are a true noble, Sam."

"Have you looked beyond your borders?" he asked gently. "There must be a noble somewhere who lives up to the title."

"I'm uncertain. My travels aren't nearly as extensive as yours. I've spent all of my reign and most of my life before it here, building myself into this position."

"There's a prince in Sletrini — I chose that country as my false home because of him. We were friends, not just because our kingdoms were allies but also because we were always very alike."

"Which prince?" she asked, tilting her head curiously. "The queen of Sletrini has four sons."

"Four now? There were three when I last spoke with anyone in that court. He would have been the youngest at the time, so second youngest now. He's a little, uh, *timid* of women, and I think your arrangement might benefit him as well."

Nalea smirked. "I suppose I should work on strengthening my bonds with Sletrini then. Thank you, Sam. More than anything, I needed a little hope. Are you sure, though?"

She shrugged herself back into her cloak and retrieved the scrolls, holding out both messages to him. He glanced at them briefly. The shorter of the two simply stated that he was in her court, and she awaited instruction from the monarchy of Mountain Song. The other informed of his whereabouts, but also announced their plans to wed and asked for a blessing and a new alliance. Sam sighed wearily and held the second over the fire of a nearby torch.

"They'll want you back, without a doubt," Nalea said, feeding the first scroll into the little tube on the rook's ankle. "They are also likely to welcome you as a traitor for being in my service."

"This is the only option left."

"Very well." She freed the rook and cast it out into the cold air. "I'll summon someone to take you back to the farm for your things. Now is the time for you to be honest with Tassia."

"I'm not sure that I'm ready."

"You have to be. Butch has been holding his tongue for days out of respect for the both of you. Others around Tassia will not be so tactful. Not after this. Tell her on your way to collect your things or you leave me no choice."

Sam hung his head in defeat. He knew Tassia well enough to anticipate the fury the truth would elicit now. He went out into the hall and waited while Nalea summoned her aides. One of them came out quickly again and led Sam away, finding him an escort back to the farm. He paused briefly as they passed the southern barracks, considering stopping to see Tassia, but decided he would need a little more time to order his thoughts.

He stopped at the farm, gathering his quilts, books and the painting from Tassia that he'd had framed in her absence. He still hadn't accumulated much of any value, and now that he was expected to act according to his title, he imagined he would need very little of the things he had collected in the last year. He stopped at the farmhouse.

"I'm sorry, I've been called into Nalea's court, and I won't be able to help you any further. You can have everything left in my home, and I thank you for the opportunity you've provided me with," Sam said.

Trom and Nisa were bewildered, but said little in the intimidating presence of the queen's guards.

Sam paused again on his way through the southern barracks, but this time resolved it was time for the truth. He went first to Tassia's hut, hoping to find her alone, but it was empty. He headed to Livia and Butch's next.

Sam knocked on the door of the hut and was shocked to see Nalea answer it, wearing the same fur cloak but now robed in an emerald brocade gown. Livia and Butch were nowhere to be seen, and Tassia was sitting on the edge of their bed, her face teary and red.

"You couldn't wait?" he snapped at Nalea. "You couldn't give me an hour to collect my thoughts and tell her myself?"

"You've had a year!" Nalea hissed, taking a threatening step toward him. "You've had a year and what would seem like endless opportunity to tell her the truth. I warned you before you left the tower. She had to hear it from one of us, and I didn't think that was ever going to be you. Someone was going to say something, and soon. Especially after I met with you privately — yet again. I came here intending to console her, only to find out you'd neglected the truth again. What choice did I have?"

Sam looked past her to Tassia.

"I'm so sorry. Can I have a moment?"

"Just leave," she snapped. "After all this time — I have nothing to say to you. Just leave me alone."

"The only thing I've been dishonest about is my origins," Sam said. "I've gone this long without anyone knowing who I was, and I thought that even despite the rumours that have started here, that I would be able to remain undetected — that I could have a normal life."

"You've said you care about me, and yet all this time you've been toying with me!" Tassia snapped.

Nalea ushered Sam in the door and left, waiting outside and beyond earshot with the envoy. Sam stood helplessly in the centre of the hut, trying not to wither under Tassia's furious glare. He finally approached her carefully and knelt before her, speaking softly.

"I haven't toyed with you, Tassia. I wanted you to make a decision based on your feelings."

"How could I possibly make a decision regarding you and my future when you left out a very vital piece of information?"

"It wasn't vital. It has no influence on me and who I am."

"Are you blind!" She sprang to her feet, seething, and he stood and took two quick steps away from her. "It has everything to do with who you are! You have been wandering for a decade, for your entire adult life, because you didn't want your parents to force you into a marriage. You've spent your life as a nomad because of who you are. You've been *running* from who you are, and it has *everything* to do with who and what you've become!" She jabbed her finger at him, emphasizing her words.

Sam was silent, not sure how to meet her argument head-on, to make her see that the life he had built was his own and always would be.

"That was the life I didn't want." He shook his head emphatically. "I want the life I've had — the one here with you."

"It's too late for that. Nalea has explained the situation to me. Beyond all of that, I just don't know how I can forgive you for keeping this from me. Have I been nothing but a plaything to you?"

"No!" He looked to her desperately, grasping to keep it all from unravelling. "Tassia, I've stayed here because of you. If it hadn't been for you, I would have almost certainly moved on the instant my service to Nalea was complete. I've done everything I can to stay here, and I see now that I should have told you this so much sooner, but it always seemed like you were keeping me at bay. I wasn't sure if I was ever going to mean enough to you for it to matter if you heard the truth. I've wanted to tell you, but you've never expressed with certainty that I was something that would be a permanent part of your life, and I couldn't risk exposing my past needlessly. We had a deal for the spring, and I meant to tell you the truth then."

She shook her head and stood with her arms crossed, staring at the door. When she finally looked at him again, her eyes gleamed with fury and anguish. "You should have told me the truth long ago. It's too late now, and I won't even entertain this as a possibility. There's no place for you in my future because you will be returned to a hostile kingdom and it's unlikely I will ever see you again. You'll be lucky if your parents don't have you executed."

"You don't know them. It won't be that bad." He took her shoulders and tried to get her to meet his eyes, but she pushed his hands away.

"You don't know them anymore either. Nalea is much more in tune with your family than you — they are her enemies and she has to be. Have all these years of nomadism really made you so blind?"

Sam sighed.

"Just leave." She shook her head and gestured to the door. "This is over. I was prepared to consider you as a part of my future, but I won't have a liar and your family won't have me. Just go back to the towers and bide your time. Leave me alone!"

Sam slouched out the door, defeated. He spotted Nalea standing next to her palanquin with her envoy, and he scowled, still furious that she hadn't given him the final chance he needed to be honest.

"It was too late even if you told her now," Nalea said. "Butch and Livia both knew the truth already, and she would have still become this angry when she found out they knew before she did. Your last chance was probably a week ago, right after she got back from war. All I did by telling her myself was spare her the grief of hearing it from someone less tactful."

Sam shook his head, heading back for the towers while Nalea remained behind to try to console Tassia.

Sam cautiously entered the rookery and found Nalea by the window, looking out over the spring landscape but not sending any messages.

"I was told I would find you here," Sam said.

"I took your advice and just sent a message to the court of Sletrini to invite the queen and her sons here on business," she said with a smile. "What do you think the odds are of it doing any good?"

Sam shrugged. "I'm not aware of the intricacies of your relationship with their court, and it has been a very long time since I've been there."

"Of course, I didn't tell my council my true motives, but they seem to think the visit is good politics, at the very least."

He nodded and then sighed. "Tassia absolutely will not have me now, so if relations with Sletrini don't pan out — and my parents haven't executed me — maybe I'll come back. If your offer still stands."

"If this plot with Sletrini doesn't work, then I'm sure my offer will still stand. Are you really going to abandon your principles so readily?"

"I left my parents' world to avoid deals like yours, and I went in search of a reason to reject a privileged life." He paused and looked past her out the window to the mountains that lay beyond. "I was beginning to think I'd never find it until I met Tassia, and this year in your kingdom has certainly been the happiest of my life. I don't believe I need to live as a nomad any longer. I've found the answers I was looking for. But I can't have what I wanted, so I may as well find something better than what my parents will."

Nalea gave him a curious glance. "She's still furious, is she?"

He nodded. "She refuses to speak to me."

"Perhaps she just needs more than a week to calm down."

"You've known her most of your life; do you believe that's true?" he asked hopefully.

"Sam, she certainly cares about you. She's going through a lot — it's been a difficult year for her. But a delightful one, too. Your presence has forced her to give her future more consideration. I think she might be so angry because she was trying to fit you into things and now you're being taken from her."

"I'm not convinced," he replied solemnly. "We were friends — and lovers, too — but anything beyond friendship was likely just her being lonely and responding to my attentions. She may not want to admit that's the truth."

"The best lovers begin as friends, Sam. That is what the happiest unions are built upon."

"And sometimes people aren't meant to be more than friends, and crossing that line only dissolves the friendship."

Nalea nodded but looked saddened, her brows furrowed in concern. "You're giving up then?"

"What choice do I have?" he asked with a frustrated shrug and turned away. "She won't speak to me, and we both know what the response from Mountain Song is going to be. That's why I came to see you. I'd like you to send them another message. Let them know I will return voluntarily as soon as the mountain passes are clear."

Nalea watched him closely for a moment, but he couldn't meet her eye. He wondered if she would try to talk him out of it, but there was no way around the fact that his parents would want him back. If he volunteered to return, that might work in his favour when it came time for him to account for his absence and being discovered in a hostile kingdom.

"I'll send it now," she promised, and he saw her pull out another of the tiny parchment pieces.

"Actually, let me write it," he offered.

She passed over the quill and scroll and let him compose the brief message to his parents:

> *I have found the answers I sought when I left so many years ago, though they aren't necessarily to my liking. I return to you now, as soon as the mountain passes will allow.*
>
> Samleni

Nalea had summoned a rook while he wrote, and she took the note from him and paused to give him one final chance to change his mind.

"I'm sure," he said.

She slipped the note into the tube and sent the rook off. Both of them stood at the window and watched it disappear toward the mountains. Sam sighed wearily, but it wasn't as upsetting as he had expected. He had already made up his mind when he decided to come to the rookery and any pain he had felt at the decision had already passed.

"We should hear their response to the first message in two or three days. Assuming they reply right away."

"I hope they think on it for a little while," he admitted. "They're not the sort of people who make good decisions in haste."

"Believe me, I know." She smirked.

"Has there been much communication between you and them?"

"I did my best to establish dialogue with your parents after I gained the throne. It has been strained at best. I hope for your sake these messages are received better than the ones before them. Before sending them news of you, my last message was one of defiance in response to what I hope was a hollow threat."

He winced. "It's been bad, has it?"

"Not entirely. That they're keeping communication open is encouraging, even if that entails a lot of sniping and positioning."

"You've done what you can for me." He turned to face her and bowed deeply. "Thank you, Nalea. For everything. If my parents see fit not to execute me on my return, I will do what I can to ease tensions between Wheat Sky and Mountain Song."

"I would certainly not be averse to having your kingdom as an ally, Sam. Are you certain you're prepared to go back?"

"I'm idle here, and it's not something I'm used to. I want to work the fields or help Tassia prepare her garden — or begin a journey to some new and wondrous place. I can't sit here and wait with this hanging over my head."

"If this mild weather holds, the passes will be clear in a week. A fortnight at the most."

"I would prefer to leave as soon as possible."

"I will begin preparations, then," Nalea said. "I will see to it that you have a proper escort and scout any dangers that may lie in the mountains so that we can send you back by the safest route."

"You could just let me hide my identity again and travel as a nomadic pauper."

She shook her head. "You know I can't do that. You are my guest, and I have to be certain that you are treated accordingly. I don't believe it would ease tensions with Mountain Song if I just let you wander back with no guard to ensure your safety."

"I suppose you're right."

"You will be well-guarded, but it will not be an extravagant convoy. I'll be certain that you're more than comfortable on the trip and send plenty of skilled blades to keep you safe, but it will still be a simple voyage."

Sam bowed out of her presence and returned to the library where he spent most of his days now. Unless he could convince Tassia to speak to him before he left, he would pass the rest of his days in the kingdom among its books.

CHAPTER 11

Tassia was washing up after a long day turning the dirt in the garden and preparing the soil for planting when there was a knock at the door. She paused, her arms still dripping water into the basin, and wondered if she should just pretend to not be at home. It was her first day out in the garden that spring, and Sam's absence had been heartbreaking. She was in no mood to entertain. Of course, she'd lit the fire already, so it was obvious she was there. She grabbed a towel and dried off as she paced across the hut to the door. She threw open the door and was surprised to find Nalea standing there.

"Nalea — Your Grace — what brings you to the barracks at this hour?" Tassia asked, still wringing her hands dry. Nalea was wearing a military riding cloak with the hood pulled up over her head, concealing most of her features, and she wore plain riding leathers and a military sword at her hip, with throwing daggers strapped at each ankle. Looking past her, Tassia saw that the queen was alone, disguised as a simple soldier to slip through the city undetected. This was a private visit.

"You know that Sam is leaving in three days' time," Nalea said.

"Yes, I've heard he's finally returning home," she replied, trying to keep her tone neutral.

"Do you know that he doesn't want to leave?"

"I'm not sure that man knows what he wants," Tassia said sharply, ushering Nalea into the hut.

"He wants to stay here. Can you really not see why?" Nalea stood calmly in the middle of the room; she pulled back her hood and focused on Tassia. Tassia stood across from her, arms folded at her chest, leaned forward in stubborn defiance.

"He fixated on me because I was the first proper woman he'd seen in these lands. I showed him some kindness after such a long spell of ugliness. Who can blame him? I'm glad he's moving on and going home."

"Tassia, don't be a fool! He's travelled to places that would dazzle even the traders — to every shore of these great lands except for the frigid North. He has seen much worse things than Hetia's dungeons — you've said so yourself. He's remained in exile for vindication, looking for proof that he was right to abandon his titles and privileges for his beliefs. He's fixated on you because *you* are the answer he has been looking for all these years."

Tassia sat down hard on the edge of a chair, burying her face in her hands.

"You never fully considered it, did you?" Nalea said gently.

"I asked him once — addressed it head-on — but only once. I asked him to consider if his interest in me was borne out of loneliness. He never did answer."

"I suspect he was waiting for more indication of your true feelings," Nalea said. "After all he's said about staying here — after the effort he put in to be near you — you just didn't see why he was doing it?"

"Why would I?" she answered, her voice wavering. "I never would have imagined — after all he's seen — that I had anything beyond friendship to offer him. And when I found out he was a foreign prince, I became certain it was just foolish infatuation — that I was merely another in a long line of trifles to meet his needs before he moved on. I just can't believe this. Are you certain?" She'd been speaking down to her feet, but looked up at Nalea now, searchingly.

Nalea nodded and sat next to Tassia, gathering her thoughts. She was staring out the window as she finally began to speak.

"When I first found out who he was — when I met with him in private that first time last summer — he begged me to keep his secret as long as possible in the hopes he could stay here undetected. Here with *you*." She gave Tassia a significant glance before continuing. "When I had no choice but to alert his family, I offered him a way to stay — to be my suitor and give me an heir — but he won't be shared. Tassia, it's you or nothing. He is fully sincere."

"And after all that, he's running again," Tassia said, shaking her head, confused and frustrated.

Nalea patted her knee and watched her closely. "He thinks that you don't care about him. But I see now that you thought he was just a fool and purposely maintained your distance — as best you could. You kept him at a friend's distance and, until recently, wouldn't even consider anything more. Even now, now that you have the truth, do you know what you feel?"

Tassia shook her head again and stared at the warm glow from the wood stove.

"I haven't completed choosing his escort yet. I want you to go with him."

"What? No!" Tassia stood and paced the room, finally stopping to lean against the table.

"This is not a negotiation. He trusts you and enjoys your company, and I think you need more time with him now that you know the truth."

"But my garden — I can't just—"

"If Livia and Butch don't want to keep it up in your absence, I'll send servants. I've got a few who are skilled with plants, and I will have them here daily."

"I can't just leave like that!"

"You would if it was any proper deployment."

"But you can send anyone on this. It doesn't have to be me." She shook her head emphatically, wrapping her arms around her middle.

Nalea leaned forward, her gaze steady on Tassia. "I think it does."

"What about my strategist training? I need to study!"

"Take books with you and read in the evenings. It will take you a month to reach the heart of the Mountain Song dynasty, so I expect that if it all goes well, you should be back by midsummer with plenty of time for your plants and to enjoy the harvest. I will provide you with a tutor when you return, if it's needed."

"What if it doesn't go well?"

Nalea sighed. "Either Sam will take leave of his family again or he won't. Either way, his parents won't risk open war with me over one small convoy. I don't expect they'll hold you up. So start making your preparations for the journey."

Tassia shook her head. "Nalea, please—"

Nalea gave her a stern glance that silenced her. "Tassia, if you can look at me and truthfully tell me you have no interest in seeing him ever again, then I will remove you from this mission."

"I can't have him, and you know that. Why are you doing this?"

"You can have him for a month, Tassia. That's more than some of us ever get. If his parents don't outright execute him on his return, then there may be room to negotiate. I don't believe that he is doomed. There isn't much hope, but there's enough for me to find reason to send you."

"I don't want just a month."

Nalea let out a frustrated growl. "If only you could hear just how much you sound like him now. This may be your only chance at happiness, Tass, and I think you should take it, even if it ends in sorrow. You are working your way up the ranks in my court, not only because we are friends, but because you are remarkable. So go with him; show your integrity to his family and hope he can persuade them to change their minds. He has a sister, Tass, and there's no reason not to let him continue to denounce his titles. Well, there's no valid reason, and I hope that King Dantrin and Queen Kelteni are getting more reasonable as they get on in years."

Tassia didn't respond, and Nalea got up to leave.

"You're sure?" she asked before the queen left.

"I wouldn't send you if I wasn't. So set your affairs in order."

Sam carried only a small bag with him as he left Nalea's castle. He kept his favourite of the quilts he'd collected, along with all of the books and the picture from Tassia, which he had removed from its frame and rolled back into the tin. He left behind his ratty old clothing and the remainder of his bedding, since finer cloth and travelling supplies were being provided for the return trip. Nalea had insisted on returning him looking like the prince he was.

He left the state room he had been occupying for nearly a fortnight and was escorted out to the courtyard where the rest of his convoy was waiting with mules to carry them over the mountains. The courtyard was full of tents and supplies, along with servants, who would set everything up, act as guides, and prepare meals as they travelled. There was also a respectable contingent of soldiers, and he was pleasantly surprised to see Tassia astride the lead mule. Most of the soldiers accompanying him on his journey were from Tassia's decimated brigade.

"Tass!" he called out, jogging to where she waited. "I didn't think you'd come."

Her expression was impenetrable.

"Are you ready?" she asked him. "We've got a long journey today."

He nodded and found his mule, securing his pack to it before wishing Nalea a final farewell. She waved as they left the courtyard, but had disappeared back into the castle before the convoy had turned onto the wide northern avenue leading out of the city.

Sam guided his mule to the front of the line, hoping to speak with Tassia.

"May I join you?" he asked.

"Your Grace is free to do as he pleases," she replied tonelessly.

"Tass, you didn't sign on for this to make the trip a living nightmare, did you?"

"I didn't volunteer."

Sam sagged under the weight of her words.

"Are you really only here because of more of Nalea's meddling?"

She sighed wearily and finally looked to him. "Not only because of her."

Sam looked around and could see that they were well ahead of the rest of their group. No one was listening.

"Tassia, do you know what you want? Or are you here still looking for answers?"

"I want you," she admitted. She looked around shyly before continuing, "I do love you, Sam. I still don't know what my future will look like, but that hardly seems to matter. A month is all we've got left, and I want to spend it with you."

Sam reached across and took her hand for a moment, smiling.

"We might get more than a month yet."

Her smile faltered and she shook her head. "I don't think so. While we're still beyond your homeland, I can pretend you're my Sam — the same one I've always known. But once you return to Mountain Song, you become Sam the prince again, whether you like it or not. Even if your parents don't execute you on your return, they won't let you have me. We both know that. And even if, by some miracle, they do let us stay together, you won't be the Sam I've always known. Here in the wilderness, I can pretend nothing has changed. But there, I won't be able to deny it any longer. I don't want Sam the prince."

"I'm not a prince!" he insisted.

"You will be again. Or they'll execute you. Don't you see that?"

Sam fell silent, though he remained at her side. Neither of them spoke again until they stopped to rest at midday. Sam could see Tassia was struggling with the situation, still unable to let go. He stayed with her, but little conversation passed between them before they started moving again. When they stopped at the end of the day, he was prevented from helping to build the camp, gather firewood or even light the fire. He sat by idly, hating it and wishing he'd never kept the cursed ring that had given him away.

He had been wearing the ring on his index finger since Nalea had sent the rook with news to his parents, but now he took it off, tempted to heave it into the forest. He was surprised when Tassia knelt beside him and closed his hands around the ring again before he could get rid of it.

"Losing it now won't change anything," she said.

"Do you forgive me for not telling you sooner?"

"No," she said crisply. "But I think I understand why you didn't. You believed you would never be found — that after a dozen years, the world had forgotten about you. And if you had told me when you first showed that to me, I don't think I ever would have become involved with you. I have a hard time getting past your heritage as it is."

"Maybe it would be easier if you guys would let me help with dinner."

She smiled. "We have our orders, direct from Nalea. You're to be treated as any other dignitary under our protection. I know you hate it, but she doesn't want to give your parents any excuse at all to be hostile."

He sighed. "Is that why you're being so formal with me?"

"To an extent. While in uniform and in command, I feel honour bound to act according to my station. I need some more time to process everything. Now, shall I fetch you one of your books to help pass the time until dinner?"

Sam shrugged, so Tassia went and got him a book. She smiled to herself when she saw the tin with the painting inside poking out one of the pockets of his bag. She left him to his thoughts while she helped set up camp and went over plans with Traxin, the commander of the night watch. Though Tassia was in charge of the mission, she wasn't expected to lead all hours of the day, and Traxin, another strategist, was on hand to spell her off and to offer support.

Once Tassia had relinquished command to Traxin until dawn, she left her weapons in her tent and went to seek dinner and Sam. Some of the others were gathered around the camp's central fire to eat and hear Sam's stories. He had a dozen years' worth of tales to entertain them, and there were many yet that Tassia hadn't heard. He was talking about Elintrin when she joined them, and she sat to listen with the rest.

Night finally came, and the others slowly made their way to their tents, one by one at first, but then in groups. As the last of the serving staff left, they put out the fire, leaving only Sam and Tassia sitting across the ashes from each other in silence. Tassia didn't mind the lack of fire; it wasn't too cold and the darkness revealed the stars. Sam sat with her by the cold remains and watched the others make their way to their tents.

He didn't say anything and she was glad for it; she wasn't sure she could handle natural conversations with him anymore. It had been so much easier before Nalea had revealed why he had stuck around.

She finally heard the rustling of Sam heading into his tent, and felt strangely at ease with the solitude until he softly called to her.

"Come on, Tass. You're not fooling anyone."

Surprised and bothered by the comment, she got up and followed him to his tent, where he'd lit a lantern.

"What's that supposed to mean?" she asked, sitting across from him on the pile of furs that lined the tent floor.

"Everyone knows why Nalea picked you to lead my military escort."

Tassia blushed and hoped he couldn't see in the dim light.

"We don't have to talk about it if you don't want to. You don't have to say anything. Just please, let me in," he pleaded, reaching out to touch her face.

She didn't flinch away this time, letting her heart make the call. Sam was relieved and slid his hand to the back of her head, pulling her toward him as he leaned into her. His lips barely brushed against hers at first, as he tested her response, but she slid her hands up his chest and laced her fingers around the back of his neck, holding his face to hers. He ran his hand over her dark braid and started nibbling at the side of her neck, his hot breath on her skin making her tremble with desire.

He eased her onto her back, his lips still at her neck, while he stripped off her armour and began peeling back her clothes. Her breathing grew deep and quick with anticipation as his warm, rough hands roamed over her skin, caressing her breasts and sliding up and down her sides. She entwined her fingers in his dark hair, and pulled his lips against hers again, kissing him deeply.

But when his hands began fumbling at her belt, she couldn't ignore the doubts that kept creeping into her head. She pushed his hands from her body, sinking against the blankets and turning away from him.

"Tass, what is it?"

"This just can't happen. Not now and maybe not ever." She turned to face him again, and he backed away, sitting up.

"Why? What's wrong? You wanted this."

"It's not right," she said simply, propping herself up on her elbows. "We're surrounded by far too much uncertainty. You don't know what's going to happen when we reach Mountain Song. I don't want you for the next month, only to have you torn away from me. It's all or nothing. You can't have me until I know I can have you. To keep you."

"It will be all right. This is just a formality."

"You keep telling yourself that because you want it to be true, but you don't know what will happen," she said, and sat up, brushing him aside. "I have to know that you'll leave there with me or this can't happen. You can't assure me until we get there," she explained, hastily buttoning her shirt and gathering up her armour.

He caught her arm to keep her from rushing out.

"Please, just stay. We can still talk, can't we?"

She faced him cautiously. "What's there to say?"

"You understand now that I stayed because of you? You know why I left my family, and I wanted to return to them with proof that I was right. I was looking for a reason to justify what I did, and I'd begun to doubt myself until I met you. You are the answer I was looking for, and you give me justification for abandoning my throne. I was looking for love — for someone who would mean more than all the riches being a king can provide."

"I understand," she said softly.

"This is not about loneliness, and it means nothing if it's not reciprocated. I need to know what you feel."

"I feel that what happened after my parents died wasn't a mistake," she said, her voice still hushed. "I let my grief cloud my judgment about how I responded, but after the way everything turned out, I don't regret pushing you away again. To have let our love flourish for nearly a year, only to be faced with this now, would have been unbearable. It's so difficult as it is."

Sam held her hand firmly.

"You say that you love me and yet you continue to deny me — to deny us both."

"I feel like you're getting too caught up in your emotions and in this relationship and its possibilities to really consider the danger you face. Your denial isn't going to save you if your parents are as unreasonable as you remember."

"I fear that they are every bit as unreasonable as I remember, and that's why I want to make the most of the time we have left."

"I won't be just another notch in your bedpost," she snapped, and she hit him, open-handed, on the side of the head. It hurt enough that he was forced to let go of her, and she once again collected her things and fled to the safety of her tent.

CHAPTER 12

Sam lay curled wretchedly among the soft furs Nalea had provided, trying to resist the urge to walk out into the night and let the elements take him. Tassia had refused to speak to him for two days now, and he was losing the courage to face his parents. His options seemed terribly bleak.

He looked up, startled, when he heard the tent flap open, and was surprised to see Tassia's tiny frame silhouetted in the faint moons' light.

"Tass! Is everything all right?"

"Of course it isn't," she whispered, approaching him cautiously. He couldn't read her expression in the darkness, but her voice sounded pained and raw, yet there was no sign of her previous anger.

Sam pulled back the furs, and she slipped in beside him, her mouth finding his immediately. It was Sam who halted things this time.

"Tassia, what's going on? One minute you're colder than the mountains, and the next you must be pried off of me."

"It's always been like this for us," she admitted. "I keep finding reasons not to give myself wholly to you, but I love you too much to stay away. Nalea sent me here not just to keep you safe and try to convince your parents to be lenient, but to let us have time together. It's likely to be the last opportunity we have. I keep getting so angry at you because you seem almost naive in your insistence that your parents can be convinced to just keep letting you do as you please. I don't believe that for a moment. I think that the best you can hope for is that they allow you to live — not anywhere near me ever again, but alive."

"Yes," he said, softly. "I fear that you're right."

"Do you really?"

"It's not something that's easy to admit." He paused, hanging his head before meeting her gaze again. "I don't want to think that I'm heading to my doom — either death or misery. I begin to fall to pieces if I think on it too long. So I scheme and I deny and I hope. It's all I've got left."

"It's not quite all," she replied. "You've got me, and we've got nearly a month. If these are our last days together, then let us make them worthwhile. I don't want to leave you in Mountain Song regretting that I didn't let myself be properly loved or love properly in return."

She found his lips in the dark once again, and all resistance washed away as he kissed her. She gasped away from him only long enough to struggle from her riding cloak. Then she pulled his face to hers again, their kisses intense, hungry and desperate. When she felt the hot bulk of him against her hip, the longing became more than she could bear, and she pulled away from him again, gasping for air against the need, but only long enough to expose enough of herself and enough of him to pull him onto her and then into her.

She moaned softly in his ear as his heat began to fill her, but his lips sealed over hers again and he thrust into her softly and irregularly, more interested in being near her than in the act itself. He felt overwhelmed by the need to touch her, and he pulled off their undergarments, using his feet to carefully push them away without pulling out of her again. His lips left hers only long enough for him to lift his shirt, and then slide hers up over her head, though it still remained pinned under her. He was unconcerned, needing only to expose her flesh and press his against hers.

Skin on skin again, she could feel his heat filling her, and the feeling was more intense than she had ever felt before. Her legs entwined his, and her arms pulled him tightly, pressing him so hard against her and into her that he felt as though she were trying to physically join them as one flesh. They moved as one and climaxed as one, she burying her face in his shoulder and he pressing his face to her neck to muffle their cries. But still they pushed on, one climax rolling into another and another, until they lay spent, barely able to move.

As morning began to light the interior of the tent, she got up and left, embarrassed and not wanting the rest of the camp to know what had happened. She was cleaned up and dressed again, secure in her own tent, when the dawn fully broke and she took formal command of the convoy again.

Through the day, she remained friendly but still in command, speaking with him about light matters. She listened to his tales of travel in the evening with everyone else and went to her tent alone afterward. But she came to him again, once the camp was settled in to sleep, and this time the travelling cloak was all she wore.

Eventually most of the camp became wise to what was happening, and Tassia gradually felt more at ease being open about her intentions. She stopped setting up a tent of her own and shared his. She still remained more distant during the day, while in uniform and in command. But once evening came, she relaxed, setting aside her sword and removing her armour, releasing her strong will to her stronger emotions.

"We need to talk," Tassia insisted, and laughed when Sam's expression fell. "I'm fully committed to the weeks we have left," she reassured him. "But I want to explore the possibility of extending our time further. We had a deal, remember? We've established that this isn't the product of loneliness, so it's time to deal with the rest. We don't have my garden to plan in, but we've got an expanse of mountains instead. What are your options? Let's consider them and see if we can still put our futures together."

Sam, who was riding beside her again, grinned. It had been a week since they'd left the city — and a day since they had made it out of Nalea's borders — and Sam hadn't felt freer in his life. The river valley stretched out before them, and in the distance, he could just make out the snow-covered pass they would take.

"My options are not good," he finally replied. "Most likely, as you know, I will be executed as a traitor. I've learned that I have a sister, which should make me quite expendable in my parents' eyes. There is Nalea's offer, if you think you could stomach it. I'm not sure that I could."

"It might be worth exploring," she admitted. "But is there anything else? Anything better we can hope for?"

"Oh yes! There's always the possibility of my delusions becoming a reality," he said with a little laugh.

"All right, then, let's talk on that. What would it take for your parents to let us be together?"

"Well, if they both die before we get there…" He sighed. "You are low-born, Tass. That will not go over well with them."

"Yes, I can see that being a problem. But I will enter my queen's court before long. By the autumn, I could be a strategist, and within a year, I'm sure I could earn another promotion. To hear Nalea talk, I've earned it already, and she just wants to let time pass so that her rivals don't think she's merely favouring me."

"What kind of promotion are you talking about?"

"A full commander. That would grant me a minor ladyship."

Sam nodded, eyes fixed on the horizon. "That might be enough."

"But it might not?"

"You would still be a soldier. My family holds soldiers in esteem, but does not believe that a woman should be in such a position on the battlefield. Strategizing from a war room is the limit of what they deem acceptable. And a minor ladyship might still not be a high enough title considering your origins."

"But could we try that as a bargaining chip?"

He looked at her and grinned. "Oh, yes. I insist."

She smiled. "These are just words right now, and I want to assume that we can make it happen — but what in the name of the moons would that look like for us? What would your family expect of me? Where would we live?"

"I will continue to renounce my claim to the throne — letting my sister have it all. I will press to be an advisor, to build peace with other nations, and I will press to begin a truce with Nalea. That would mean we can return to her court for at least a while. My family would expect us to wed immediately, especially after all the…" He rolled his hand in an awkward gesture. "You could be with child and that would not do at all if we are not wed."

He was surprised when she nodded solemnly.

"You would really be my wife?"

She was the one startled now. "I couldn't possibly see myself as the wife of anyone else. If I'm to marry anyone, it would be you."

He immediately reined in his mule, and she stopped hers suddenly beside him. The entire convoy halted behind them, watching curiously.

"You mean it? Promise me."

"Yes, I promise," she said, bemused.

Sam turned then, raising his voice and addressing the convoy.

"I, Samleni Teslerin, crown prince — at least for now — of the Mountain Song dynasty, proclaim that I am betrothed to Tassia Raven, strategist-in-training, of the Wheat Sky empire. You bear witness to this — and I just may need every last one of you before long."

He dismounted and strode purposely over to her, placing the ring of his family crest on her thumb — the only place it would fit — and kissing her forehead before mounting up and continuing to ride.

"Are you serious?" she asked.

"Yes. And you said you were, too," he replied desperately, swivelling to look at her.

"I — Sam, you could have warned me," she laughed.

He let out a relieved whistle. "And give either of us the chance to come to our senses? Ha!"

"That rules out Nalea's option now, doesn't it?"

"I haven't wed you yet," he said, sighing heavily.

"All right, so if this doesn't work, then what?"

"I renounce you, accept my responsibilities and let my parents know about Nalea's offer. Either I remain the crown prince of Mountain Song or an ambassador of the court. And I tell them that Nalea wants peace and for my union to her to be the first bond between the two nations." He spoke swiftly, reciting what had been weighing on his mind for so long.

"You really want that?"

"No, but it's better than being put to death, don't you think?"

"We'd still be apart, and then I'd have to watch you with my friend. I — no, I don't want that."

"You'd rather never see me again? If they don't let me have you, then it's Nalea or nothing."

The brief moment of carefree joy following his impulsive marriage proposal had faltered in the face of the reality ahead of them. Tassia felt hollowed out.

"This is why I haven't wanted to think about my options. They're heartbreaking."

She nodded, but quickly found her resolve. "All right, we'll try it," she finally said.

Sam looked at her in shock.

"Why not? If it keeps you from being executed, then let's try it. It will bring two countries together. I've always wondered how Nalea would get around her sexual preferences. Once you gave her an heir, it would only be a marriage on paper, wouldn't it?"

"Yes. It's just a formality — two unconventional monarchs doing each other a favour. I don't know that I could stand to have you as my mistress."

"Let's hope it doesn't come to that. But it would allow me to stay in the army. I'm sure your parents don't have very high standards for mistresses, do they?"

"Not especially. Well, it's preferred that they be particularly stunning specimens, but you've got nothing to worry about there. To the best of my knowledge, my father has had no fewer than three mistresses and has perhaps a dozen bastard children."

Tassia arched her eyebrows in surprise.

"Wheat Sky doesn't treat bastard children any differently than other children, so I suppose you'd have nothing to worry about," he pointed out.

"It still feels so awful to consider," she said.

He nodded and was silent for a while. "All we can do is try. If it's too ugly to bear once we're in the thick of it — if that's what it comes to — at least we can say we tried."

"All right, so we'll try to convince your parents to let us be together outright," she recapped. "That's unlikely to work, but we'll try. If that fails, you bring up Nalea's offer, unite the two kingdoms and I become your mistress."

"Yes. And your children would be kin to Nalea's."

She let out a little laugh. "Maybe it wouldn't be so bad after all. It would be terrible at first, I think, but in time I'm sure we'd adjust."

He nodded, but grew solemn.

"There's only one other option, isn't there?" she finally asked.

"Yes, and it's the most likely."

"You really think death awaits you? You don't think they'd just reject you having any involvement with anyone from Wheat Sky, force you to take your rightful place on the throne and try to marry to you to some pretty noblewoman from your homeland?"

"They might try that, yes. But my adamant refusal would likely lead to my execution."

"Sam, be reasonable. Take anything they offer you that doesn't involve the gallows!"

Sam gave her an even look. "Tass, you saw me in court — you saw the way I get. My mouth will get ahead of my mind, and I'll talk myself right into my grave."

"Then keep your mouth shut and remember that as long as you're still alive, you have the chance to outlive them. Once you're on the throne, you can do as you please — and that includes renouncing it and naming your sister as heir, divorcing whoever they've forced you to marry and returning to Wheat Sky."

"Now you need to be reasonable! Even if I managed to outlive them and do all of that, you'd have found someone by then."

"I sincerely doubt that," she said. "I can barely picture myself with you, even after all we've said and been through. I certainly can't picture myself with someone else, now that I've had you. Especially not with the possibility that you would return."

He was horrified. "Tass, if they separate us, please promise me that you won't pine for me. I couldn't bear that."

"I won't pine for you, but I don't think I could be with anyone else. Before you, I really always envisioned myself becoming a spinster."

He sighed wearily. "We'd better find a way to stay together then."

They rode silently until dusk, when they reached the end of the long valley where the ascent into the narrow pass began. They stopped there and set up camp, wanting full light, good weather and to be well rested before they attempted the pass.

"Slivers Pass," Sam said. "That's what they call it." He dismounted and looked up the shoulder of the mountain to the path they would take. "If there's a caravan coming the other way, either our group or theirs will have to turn back. There is only room to go single file up there. We should probably send a scout across first."

"Why would anyone risk it? Surely there's another way!"

"There's a safer pass to the north, but it will still be under snow this time of year. It will be a month or more before it clears enough to be even remotely passable. There's nothing for quite some distance to the south because of a canyon far more treacherous than this pass. We would have to detour nearly a fortnight to reach the pass to the south."

Tassia began unloading their mules, but one of Sam's assigned aides rushed up to assist her.

"No, no, Tass. Tonight, you sit with His Grace and rest. We must celebrate the afternoon's news!"

"Celebrate? We haven't the supplies."

"Her Grace sent much wine with us," the girl countered. "More than we are likely to need. We can spare a few barrels. Commander Traxin has already decided, and the others have already begun to prepare."

Tassia and Sam looked on, stunned. The soldiers had been hunting small game in the valley all afternoon, and now spits full of waterfowl and rabbits were being erected over newly lit fires. Those in the convoy who had instruments were unpacking them, while barrels of wine were being rolled from where the mules had been tethered for the evening. Other soldiers were streaming back out of the forest dragging long poles of dead wood and stacking it for a monster bonfire.

Tents began to spring up while the aroma of roasted game filled the camp. The busy chatter of the rest of the convoy was merrier than usual, their conversations frequently punctuated with bursts of laughter. Tassia and Sam sat together amidst the chaos and watched their betrothal celebration come to life around them. The last of the fresh fruit and vegetables that they'd taken with them out of the city were being prepared for an extravagant dinner.

When their tent had been erected, they were led inside. One of Sam's servants helped Tassia strip off her armour and delivered them basins of fresh water before leaving them to some peace. As Sam pulled off his shirt to change into the only fresh one he had left, Tassia again noticed the lattice of scars on his back, and she carefully ran her fingers over them.

"I've just about forgotten they're even there," he said, taking her hand and stooping to steal a quick kiss.

"It looks like they've all begun to fade, even the newer ones."

He nodded, pleased. "I feel distant to what happened in that colony. It almost seems as if what Hetia did happened to another man and not me. I suppose it makes sense for the visible scars to fade along with the intangible ones."

"You're finally free of her?"

"Yes, I think so. I have you to thank for that — if not for you, I would have died there one way or another. You saved my life in more ways than one that day. When you let me embrace you — I could feel your warmth, your energy — it coursed through me and drove away the helpless cold I'd felt since the first time Hetia took me. Every time I saw you, more and more of my time there was erased."

"Then let's keep it that way," she said with a smile and pulled off her shirt, pressing her breasts against him as her lips brushed his.

One of his hands clutched her braid and the other cupped one of her breasts, while his tongue wrestled hers. He drew away only enough to peck at her earlobe and then her neck. Then his lips found hers again and got lost there for a time. He backed away from her thoughtfully, still holding her hands. Then he undid her belt and slid her riding trousers to the floor, bringing her britches down with them. Kneeling before her, he took hold of her hips and pulled her to him. She arched her back, but held her balance when he spread her open and drove his tongue inside.

She moaned pleasurably, but tilted his head away and sank to the ground with him, finding his lips again and working to remove his pants.

"You never let me," he said, sliding a finger into her to emphasize his point. She finished removing his pants and pushed his hand away from her.

"No, it's — I can't feel your whole heat that way. I want your skin on mine," she replied, straddling his hips and helping him inside her. He leaned back, bracing his arms on the ground behind him, and she began to rock slowly, wrapping her arms around his shoulders and pulling his face back to hers, her fingers clutching his hair.

He felt like she'd managed to wrap her small body around him entirely and understood what she meant. Nothing could replace the feel of her skin on his. They came quietly together, moaning softly amidst the chaos of the bustling camp, and then cleaned up in the fading light, dressing in what clean clothing they had left.

They didn't have long to wait before the feast was served. With bellies full of food and heads full of wine, they got up to dance afterward. Tassia found the wine did wonders for her ability to dance. Their comrades played music until even the moons got tired, but the chill of the mountain night finally drove everyone to their tents and their furs.

Sam and Tassia retreated to their tent, drunkenly enjoying each other one last time before sleep found them in a tangle under their many blankets.

CHAPTER 13

Sam groaned against the vertigo and leaned in his saddle so that his shoulder brushed up against the side of the mountain. He wished he'd been thinking of Slivers Pass and its treachery while he was drinking wine the night before. The pass was dangerous enough at the best of times, and he was concerned that he was still drunk.

Tassia was riding ahead of him, silent except to complain that her head was ready to explode from the pain, but she was handling the pass much better than he was, sitting erect and vigilant in her saddle. There had been a few sections of the trail where two mules could pass side by side, but otherwise Sam's description had proved wholly accurate. The climb to the pass had taken most of the morning, and they'd stopped for lunch early, knowing there would be nowhere to stop again until they reached the other side near day's end.

The drop from the side of the trail wasn't a sheer cliff face, but was close enough to vertical that Sam didn't expect anyone would be able to recover should they fall. He pulled out his canteen and drank deeply, hoping his head would stop trying to tear itself apart before it caused him to tumble to his death. If he leaned out too far, he risked the mule falling, but if he leaned too far into the side of the mountain, he was in danger of getting stuck between the mule and the rock face. Sighing, he leaned forward and clung to the beast's neck, focusing his gaze on the view of the path directly in front of him. The pungent, barn-smell of the animal made his stomach turn, and he swore he would never touch wine again.

Sam nearly wept with delight when Tassia called back to him, saying she could see the descent now. The trail would widen in a few minutes, and they would soon find themselves back in the forest. They would reach the valley floor by dusk. He called the message back to the soldier behind him and heard the message drift down the line, some people whooping happily when it reached them.

Sam didn't have the energy to whoop or he likely would have joined them. He kept focusing on the trail until it finally began to widen and the cliff face next to him eased to a gradual slope. He was able to ride alongside Tassia again, though neither of them spoke until long after they'd stopped to set up camp.

Sam ate little that night and said even less. The stars had barely begun to shine when he clawed his way back to their tent. He couldn't remember actually finding his bedroll, but awoke in it the next morning, sprawled across Tassia with his head against her breast. He smiled at her, feeling tired but better, and wondered if he had time to enjoy her before they had to break camp and head onward.

"I don't think so," she said, grinning playfully when she awoke to see his ravenous expression. She kissed him deeply and then climbed from the bed to wash and dress, while Sam stayed in the warmth of the furs and sulked.

Tassia hadn't quite finished putting on her armour when they heard the first of the cries echoing over the valley from the mountains. Shouts of alarm rose up all around them. Sam cursed, scrambling from bed to hastily dress, while Tassia dropped her armour and picked up her sword, dashing out into the midst of the camp.

She reached Traxin a moment later, and his expression was dour.

"We need to get deeper into the forest," he urged.

"What good would that do? The sight of the camp would alert them to our presence, and they will light the entire forest ablaze."

"They will devour us alive if we stay out in the open. We must hide."

Tassia pursed her lips into a pale thin line and nodded grimly. "Collect only the most basic supplies and lead everyone into the forest," she instructed.

It sounded like the dragons were coming from the west, directly ahead of them, and Tassia remained in camp with Sam solemnly at her side as they waited for the first to crest the mountains so they could see just how much trouble they faced.

When the beasts finally appeared on the horizon, Tassia collapsed in relief.

"Blue!" she cried out, spinning on her knees to face the forest and get the message to her companions. "Come back, it's the blue!"

Those who had been fleeing slowed their paces and turned, and a few faces appeared at the treeline, watching cautiously, but no one came back into the immediate camp. Blue or not, dragons were still dangerous creatures.

Tassia and Sam watched, frozen in place, as the beasts swiftly overtook their camp, blotting out the pale morning sky. The flight of dragons passed by without so much as a glance at the camp — this clan was far less interested in humans than their red counterparts — and began to disappear over the mountain behind them. But the largest of them finally broke from the diamond formation overhead and circled in a wide swoop to land at the edge of their camp, its wings seeming to span the entire width of the valley.

The massive beast lowered its head until its chin touched the ground, and Tassia knew that it was safe to approach. The blue clan could be a threat, but were more likely to aid humans than hinder them, and Nalea had worked to strengthen an allegiance with them. Tassia suspected this dragon had recognized the crest on the tents. She cast her blade aside, knowing it would do her no good anyway. She bowed before the great creature and was surprised to discover that it had stopped to deliver a message.

(Bandits.) It lifted its head to look back the way they had come. *(Two days from here. Krunleks. Be vigilant.)*

Tassia bowed her head again in thanks. With a mighty cry to its companions, who had stopped at the Sliver summit, turning the peak glacial blue in the early morning light, it rose up into the sky, the gale from its wings nearly knocking Tassia over. She had remained kneeling, knowing she'd end up back on the ground otherwise.

They all watched in amazement as the creatures disappeared over the mountain, their echoing cries finally fading away.

With the dragons gone, the rest of the convoy began trickling out of the forest to nervously break camp. Tassia returned to where Sam still stood, astonished.

"They're amazing," he finally gasped. "If I can't die peacefully in my sleep a hundred years from now, then I want death by dragon."

Tassia grinned and shook her head. She planted a kiss on his chin and then moved to start breaking camp with the others.

"What was that about, anyway?" Sam called.

"A warning. There will be trouble ahead."

"How do you know?"

"The dragons don't speak aloud. They send their thoughts to you, and that one told me there are marauding Krunleks two days from here."

"I didn't think dragons meddled in the affairs of humans."

"The blue ones will aid their allies, and Wheat Sky is an ally. The Krunleks most certainly are not."

While the servants packed everything up, Tassia conferred with Traxin, relaying the dragon's message. They decided to leave the road in a day's time and travel only in daylight, lighting no fires at night, for the three days afterward. Soldiers comprised three-quarters of the convoy, and they didn't expect to run into a group large enough to be a proper threat.

However, when they stopped again at dusk, Tassia armed Sam and went through some of her training drills with him to refresh his skills.

The attack came the next day, hours before dusk. Leaving the road hadn't done them any good after all, as the Krunleks were hunting game as well as travellers. The raiding party was a little less than half the size of their convoy, but the Krunleks had always been renowned for their brutality.

Tassia left Sam back with the servants and the supplies while she charged ahead with a contingent of soldiers, and Sam watched nervously as she disappeared into the forest after her quarry. Her plan was to drive the Krunleks away from the servants, supplies and Sam before methodically taking them apart. She intended to slay them all, not giving them a chance to retreat to find more help. She knew she had enough soldiers to handle the Krunleks, but they were unfamiliar with the territory and risked allowing some of them to escape.

Tassia hadn't had her fill of vengeance after the cursed barbarians had taken apart her brigade, and she relished in the opportunity to spill more of their blood. This raiding party was not on par with the soldiers she had faced in war — they had inferior weapons and only animal-hide clothing. They were prepared to fight travellers, not a fully armed and suited group of battle-ready soldiers.

Tassia's heart raced in anticipation, riding the high of leading her first battle, no matter how small. There was no one in front of her, no one to have to peer around or fight her way past. She issued the command for surrender — a request met with derisive laughter from her enemies.

"Then we will spill your blood," she vowed. "All of it."

She drew her sword and led them into battle, ducking under the axe of the first Krunlek to attack her and slicing his leg open, rupturing the artery. She let him fall without a second thought, knowing he would be dead before he could give anyone further grief. She continued forward, blocking a spear and trapping it under her foot just long enough jab her sword through the hollow spot at the base of her opponent's throat. She paused longer than she would have liked to retrieve her blade when the edge caught bone as she tried to pull it out.

At least there were no enchanters to worry about in this battle. The Krunleks were wary of them and often executed them for witchcraft, only resorting to using their services under dire circumstances. There were five enchanters in Tassia's company, and they were making even quicker work of their enemies than she was.

With her blade free again, she pushed on through enemy ranks. She pivoted away from one attack to gut a man. Another flew at her, axe in hand. She ducked and watched as his axe wedged into a thick root in the ground. Before he had the sense to let go of the blade, she had taken his hand cleanly off.

She had started to turn from the downed Krunlek — expecting him to retreat or at least try to free his blade with his other hand — when he lunged at her, knocking her to the ground. His momentum had carried him past her, and she had just enough time to roll onto her back and get a firm grip on her sword before he attacked again, diving at her and intending to bludgeon her with his remaining fist.

Tassia tried to get her sword up in time. She raised it far enough that when he hit her, it drove into his pelvis, catching bone and ramming the hilt into her hip, nearly breaking it. The man rolled sideways, her blade trapped in his torso, and Tassia rolled away from him, gasping and trying not to vomit from the pain. Had she been lying against anything less forgiving than the forest floor, thick and soft with the previous autumn's leaves, the bone would have been shattered. Although it certainly felt broken, she doubted it was actually damaged beyond some bruising, but the pain was blinding and she curled up, trying to stymie it.

She was relieved to hear Traxin calling her name from just above her. Through the pain, it seemed like he was leagues away, but she still responded through gritted teeth.

"I need a moment," she gasped. "Cover me."

She had her hands pressed fiercely against her hip like she was trying to hold back an explosion. Her breaths finally came slower and deeper, and she opened her eyes to re-focus on the battle around her. She clawed her way to her feet and was relieved to find that she could still stand. Adrenaline and rage quickly buried the pain, and she approached the writhing man who had impaled himself on her blade. She grabbed the hilt and braced her foot on his chest, twisting the blade and finally wiggling it free, oblivious to his howls of agony. As soon as the sword was free again, she slashed his throat open, right down to the bone.

She looked around to see that she and Traxin were alone on the other side of the line the Krunleks had formed. Still hobbling from the pain, she followed Traxin as they worked their way back to their enemies and started cutting them down from behind. Tassia took the legs out from under three of them before any of them noticed she was there.

As the Krunleks realized that their line had been broken, some of them began to retreat. Traxin gave chase, leaving Tassia on her own again. She had nearly forgotten the pain in her hip, though it hindered her ability to move. She chose to stay put and pivot on the other leg, making her enemies come to her.

Standing still made the work much harder and mitigated her usual advantage of speed. She had to meet them head on now, and it began to wear her down quickly. She was relieved when two other soldiers broke through the line of Krunleks to support her.

As more and more of her troops reached her, she began sending them the way Traxin had gone.

"Run them down!" she commanded. "We can't let any of them escape or they will chase us to the borders of Mountain Song."

As the last of the Krunleks in the vicinity were cut down, Tassia limped back to where Sam waited with the others. She was shocked to see a trail of bodies all the way back to where Sam had waited with the servants and the supplies. She was even more surprised to see Sam sitting on a fallen tree while one of the servants cleaned and dressed a gash on his cheek.

"They got through the defense you left us, and I was one of the few left who even knew how to hold a sword," Sam said when he saw her. Then he noticed her limp and brushed the servant aside, rushing to Tassia.

"You're hurt," he said.

"I'll be all right. Just bruised."

She sat heavily next to him and instructed those nearby to start scavenging the bodies of their enemies for supplies — weapons and food. When Sam told her that seven of the convoy had been lost, she sent the servants to collect the bodies as well.

"We camp here tonight. Begin building pyres for our fallen comrades. Collect their swords and bring them to me so they may be returned to their families," she insisted.

Their bad luck continued. Traxin returned to report two more deaths in their ranks. At least four Krunleks had also gotten away.

"We couldn't risk following them any further and being drawn into an ambush," Traxin said apologetically.

"We'll remain on alert through the night and make haste in the remainder of our travels," Tassia said.

"We could detour south in a week's time," Sam suggested. "It will take us farther away from Krunlek territory and into Sianshin. I understand that's a neutral territory and strong trading partner of Mountain Song. I suspect they will be willing to shield us from the Krunleks, should those brutes be foolish enough to track us that far."

As the others continued to pile mounds of wood for their fallen comrades, Tassia made a quick decision to take Sam's suggestion. It would add nearly a week to their travel time, but it would be far safer, and Tassia didn't want to needlessly risk any more lives.

"We fly for the Sianshin borders then. We pyre our comrades and leave at dawn's light. We have a bird, and I will send the message back to Nalea so that she can relay the message to both Sianshin and Mountain Song."

Tassia crawled from her bedroll, road-weary and stiff, and slowly began to wash and dress while Sam still slept. It took her far longer than she liked to get ready in the morning. They were two days into Sianshin territory, accompanied by an armed guard that doubled their numbers and would escort them to the Mountain Song borders, but Tassia's hip was still a ball of fire and she barely slept.

The bruising had faded and a healer among their new hosts had assured her that the bone was still intact, but the pain had receded very little since the battle with the Krunleks. The healer had given her a stinging balm that soothed it for a short time, but she always awoke twice in the night to reapply it and then woke early as it wore off again. Now she worked it into the skin on her hip, feeling the muscle relax slightly. The healer had also shown Sam how to massage the muscles, and it had helped significantly, but she still awoke stiff every morning. The day's riding left her in agony.

Sam finally awoke and they began to break camp, ready for another long day on the road. Since reaching Sianshin, they had been doing less talking through the day, though Tassia wasn't sure why. Their escorts were intimidating, mostly because they were strangers, and Tassia was back to being shy about expressing her feelings for Sam when others were watching.

She was relieved to stop at midday so she could massage more of the balm into her hip.

"I'm going to run out of this long before we reach Mountain Song," she said to Sam, who was using his riding cloak to shield her while she sat in a sparse patch of grass among their craggy surroundings, half disrobed, to apply the balm.

"I can have a word with the healer when we stop tonight and see if she has any more, or if she can make any," Sam offered. "I understand we'll be passing through a town in three days. It will be a good opportunity to restock a lot of our supplies."

"I could kill for a real bed," she said, only half joking.

"Yes, I think I could, too, and it hasn't been that long since I travelled much lighter than this," he admitted.

"Did you ever have to travel injured?"

"Yes. When I escaped that oppressive matriarchy — do you remember me telling you about that one?" She nodded. "I had just received quite the lashing and had open wounds on the road. I was lucky they didn't begin to fester, but I think the risk was worth it."

"Likely. I don't know how any foreigner could last in such a place."

"I suppose some people are better at being obedient," he said with a wistful grin.

"It's not going to be easy for you to go back to Mountain Song. They're going to constrain you one way or another. You'll be answering to the monarchy in some capacity, no matter what happens."

He sighed wearily and turned his face upward for a moment to feel the warm spring sun on his face. "Yes, but I knew it couldn't last forever. Another year or two certainly would have been nice. I would have eventually taken Nalea's advice and gone home of my own accord, after winning you over and marrying you properly, of course."

She gave him a sidelong look. "I don't believe you ever would have told me the truth if it hadn't ruined your plans."

He grinned but didn't reply. He liked to think he would have told her the truth on his own given the time, but he wasn't sure.

That evening the healer came straight to their tent to examine her wound again.

"Your muscles were damaged in the strike," the woman said, "and you have residual tension and damage throughout your core. Massaging it will continue to help, but it will not resolve itself until you are able to spend some time resting properly."

It was still a fortnight until they would reach Mountain Song and the roughest terrain was still to come. Tassia groaned and draped her arm across her eyes, squeezing them shut against her frustrations. The healer helped Sam adjust his technique, and Tassia gritted her teeth against the hot, tender pain, but felt much better by the time he was done.

Halfway through, the healer left, and Tassia was grateful for the privacy. Sam helped her undress completely, and then she lay on her side so he could have full access to the tensest muscles. His strong fingers skilfully worked over her hip and down her thigh, then across her back and around to her front, trying to ease as much of the tension as he could.

She ran a finger down his arm suggestively as he worked at the tight muscles in her abdomen and inner thigh. Tassia was fully moist by the time he'd done all he could for her pain, and he undressed, erect and aching for her. He rested the backs of her knees in the crook of each of his elbows, pushing her legs up on either side of him, relieving pressure on her damaged hip. She felt the least amount of pain with her leg drawn up, so she often slept curled in a ball. She could only enjoy sex if Sam braced her legs so that her knees were nearly at her shoulders.

He entered her carefully, always worried about causing her more pain now, and she braced her elbows on the ground beneath her so that she could arch her back to meet his thrusts. It still caused the fiery ache in her hip to intensify, but the pain was manageable and worth it.

When they were both spent, Sam dug his fingers into her hip once again to ease the tension their lovemaking had caused. Then she curled into a ball and he curled around her and they drifted to sleep.

CHAPTER 14

Tassia fell silent as they approached the wall across the pass. High cliffs towered on either side of the broad pathway, perfect for an ambush. She cast her gaze up to the peaks, expecting to see archers appear and rain death upon them at any moment. Sam seemed nervous as well, though for entirely different reasons. The pass marked the border of Mountain Song, and now they were a mere three days' travel from the capital and what he was certain was his doom.

"Relax, Tass," Sam finally said to break the silence. "They won't attack a neutral party. We'll be okay. Well, you guys will be okay. I half expect to find an executioner on the other side of this wall."

"You really don't think they'd give you a trial?"

He sighed. "Yes, I expect a trial, but it's been a long time so it's hard not to think the worst now that we're so close."

The commander of the Sianshin host was already at the wall, negotiating their passage, and Tassia gave a start as the massive stone gate began to slide open. She caught a glimpse of the massive gears controlled by a dammed-off river, the sluice gate agape now to let the water through and open the gate, but her attention was quickly diverted by what the open gate revealed.

There was an armed guard on the other side, standing shoulder to shoulder and lining the entire broad avenue. What looked to be a massive stone staging area directly across the border was brimming with a host from the Mountain Song army.

The Sianshin escort now took its leave, and Tassia led their convoy through the gate, riding cautiously and watching those around her, not sure what to expect. She had been alerted upon reaching Sianshin that Sam's parents were sending a host to meet them at the border and escort them the rest of the way to the capital, where her convoy was to refresh their supplies before making the return journey. They were to rest that night in a town at the bottom of the pass.

As the last of her people came through the gate, she halted them in the massive courtyard and waited expectantly. The gates slid closed again, the booming grind of stone on stone the only sound. Once the gate was fastened, a group of soldiers followed a woman mounted on horseback to where Sam waited with Tassia.

The group of elite soldiers moved in to surround Sam and Tassia once the woman halted her horse before them. She was tall and lean, with long blonde hair tied back from her small oval face, but flowing loosely down her back, nearly reaching the saddle. Her grey eyes watched them closely, and she emanated an unshakeable air of power. On closer inspection, she wasn't a woman at all but a girl with incredible poise.

"Samleni Teslerin?" she asked pointedly.

"My lady," Sam replied, dismounting and bowing. "On behalf of my hosts from the Wheat Sky empire, I thank you for assisting us in these last days of our journey."

"I have been instructed to ensure that you arrive safely to your trial," she said. Sam nodded; they had expected as much. She gave him a curious look before continuing. "You don't know me, do you?"

"I'm sorry, my lady, I have been out of these lands for far too long," he said carefully. Tassia watched, worried about what he was getting into now.

"I am Santrini Teslerin. Sam, I am your sister."

Sam's eyes widened in surprise. "And they've let you come this far on your own?"

That earned a trace of a smile. "You will find that things have changed somewhat since you left. I have earned their trust and am surrounded by their top men."

"I still find it hard to believe that they sent you."

"I insisted. They are more likely to give me what I want, seeing as they have only one heir at the moment."

"My sister, I assure you I wish it to remain that way."

"I would not say that too loudly," she warned, leaning forward and speaking softly, "or your wish may be granted, but not in the manner you seek."

"Yes, I'm sure the executioner is sharpening his blade as we speak."

"I shall not mince words, brother; you are in a very dangerous position."

"This is as I expected, but I insisted on returning, nonetheless."

She nodded, somehow pleased. "We will have the opportunity to speak further on the return journey. I chose to come here to greet you because I wanted to see you without their bias clouding my opinion. You did not exist in my life for so long, though your spectre has haunted the courts for many years, quietly shaping the decisions being made."

"I'm curious to see how things have changed."

Santrini turned to Tassia. "Thank you, madam, on behalf of the Mountain Song dynasty, for bringing my brother this far. The generosity of Queen Nalea and the Wheat Sky empire has not gone unnoticed, though my family does have some questions on how Samleni was able to exist within Nalea's court for so long, undetected."

Tassia bowed to the girl.

"Santrini—" Sam began.

"Call me San," she said, smiling. "Most do."

"San, you must know something before we get on our way." He cast a cautious glance to Tassia before continuing. "Do you know much about my circumstances in the Wheat Sky empire?"

"Only what you have put in your messages. Queen Nalea has been suspiciously vague in hers."

"And with good reason. I have not made it easy for her. She caught me in a raid on her enemies, and I was a slave in her service for a season to work off my debt. In that time, I became involved with one of her top soldiers, who happens to be a close confidante of the queen."

"How involved?" Santrini said, narrowing her eyes.

Sam looked to Tassia again and then glanced to the Teslerin crest she still wore on her thumb. Santrini followed his gaze, spotting the ring before Tassia could cover her hand. The girl gasped.

"You ridiculous fool!" she spat at her brother. "Have you married her?"

"Not yet, but we are publicly betrothed," he said, looking around sheepishly. "The convoy can confirm that."

Santrini winced. "What were you thinking? They will execute you for certain."

"Because I am betrothed? Surely that's something easy enough to break if it means avoiding the gallows."

"Possibly, but they will not take the news lightly. I do not imagine there are many high-born soldiers in Wheat Sky."

Sam's silence spoke volumes, and Tassia gave him a stony look.

"Why would you do this? When you say yourself that it can be easily broken, why bother?"

"San, can we speak of this later? It will take some time for me to explain, and I must know first what you've been told of my past."

"Very well," she said. "We are not set to leave until tomorrow morning. I will show you to your quarters and then we can talk more at length." She glanced at Tassia for a moment. "She may stay with you, if that has been your arrangement thus far."

The Wheat Sky convoy trailed the Mountain Song escort down from the pass and through the cobblestone streets of the town at the bottom, toward an estate on the outskirts. The manor itself was fairly small, but the grounds offered more than enough room for the convoy to set up camp. Santrini's aides escorted Sam and Tassia to his quarters, and Santrini joined them before long.

"We have some time before dinner is served," she commented. "Would you like to tell me what's going on?"

The room was well-furnished with soft couches and chairs that Sam and Tassia's travel-worn bodies welcomed as the height of luxury. Sam and Tassia sat on the long, soft sofa — he nervously on the edge while Tassia sank into the corner next to him with a pillow under her hip. Santrini took up a seat across from them. Her personal guard was stationed near the door, staring impassively ahead of him, looking at nothing but watching everything.

Sam cast the man a cautious look before shrugging and beginning with why he had left.

"Yes, that is every bit as ridiculous as what our parents have led me to believe," Santrini said pertly, once Sam had finished.

"Well, at least they didn't make me sound any worse than I actually am. San, you must admit that it's ridiculous not to have even the slightest choice in who you spend your life with."

"We have no choice who our parents are, and we still spend our lives with them," she countered.

"I didn't," he said gravely.

"I suppose I can see your point," she conceded reluctantly. "I have not had the constraints that it seems you did — I have been given the freedom to reject suitors. At least to a point."

"I expect you have my absence to thank for that."

"Yes, brother, I think you are correct." She leaned back comfortably and waited for him to continue.

"All right, so I got fed up and left." He leaned forward, resting his elbows on his knees and watching his sister closely. "It was foolish, and in hindsight, I might be tempted to tell my younger self to stay put. I have been through one nightmare after another, little sister. I have seen some miraculous things and met the best people our world has to offer, but I have seen demons come alive."

"He has the scars to prove it," Tassia said quietly. "I met him while slaying one of those demons."

Santrini looked at her curiously for a moment before turning her attention back to her brother.

"Until about this time last year, I would have come home defeated and told our parents that I was nothing short of a fool — I would have taken my punishment lying down and admitted to my wrongs."

"You left seeking love — storybook love," Santrini said, undertones of sarcasm in her otherwise neutral voice. "I am familiar with the kind our wet nurse — we had the same one, you know — would have filled your mind with. Is that what happened?"

"To a degree. I had begun to believe that her stories were just that — just the fiction of an old woman who spent far too much time in the company of babes."

"Ah, but then you found it, did you?" Santrini arched an eyebrow in curious amusement. "Or at least you believe you have."

"It has not been easy," Sam admitted, shaking his head and giving Tassia a fond glance. "She's as stubborn and as blind as

I am, but yes, I believe I have. I am not willing to part with her now that I've found her. She's my vindication, San. I am willing to continue to renounce my title — especially with you to carry on our family's honour. I will do anything and everything I can to stay with her."

"It will not go your way," Santrini insisted gently. "I can only assume by the way you skirt her lineage that she is low-born. Mother and Father will not have it. They will not let you continue your foolishness. They expect you to return to your duties and your place in the court, even if I continue to bypass your right as the true heir. When that happens, you will not have the option of keeping a low-born wife."

"San, are you certain? I am a poor fit to rule and I no longer belong in a royal court. Look at me — listen to me. I have become a commoner. I have lived in filth for over a decade, working menial jobs — I have been a slave more than once."

"Brother, you should do what you can to improve your countenance or you will not escape execution."

Tassia spoke up, "He has some alternatives, and my queen is poised to raise my station, to make me a minor lady in the court. Surely that will help?"

Santrini shook her head. "Your queen is our rival, and my parents will have a low opinion of anyone in her service."

"She wishes for peace," Tassia explained. "Part of the reason she sent us here as she did was for Sam to petition your parents for peace."

Santrini was thoughtful for a moment. "It may change things, but I would have to know the details."

Tassia and Sam exchanged a glance. "It can't hurt to tell her everything," Tassia said. "I believe that she is neutral, as she says."

Tassia waited while he weighed his options and tried to find the right place to start, but they were interrupted by a bell from the town centre which had begun to ring furiously. Tassia looked up alarmed, and they both looked to Santrini. She listened closely for a moment, and then her expression dropped and her colour became ashen. Her personal guard sprang into action.

"Quickly, m'lady, you must gather your belongings. We must hurry," he urged.

"Dragons," Santrini explained to the other two.

"By the moons, more dragons!" Tassia cursed.

"We've seen more dragons in these past months than I have in my life," Sam said.

Santrini gave him a curious look, but they did not have the time to speak of it further. They quickly gathered up their things and followed Santrini and her escort out of the manor to a squat building in the back courtyard that served as the entrance to the shelter. The manor was on a slope that overlooked the town, and they could see the townspeople below scrambling to get underground. The rest of the Wheat Sky convoy was streaming around the side of the house, heading their way to take cover.

They could hear people shouting that it was the red clan as they rushed through the door of the bunker. They charged down the stairs and down the long hall, entering the massive chamber first. Tassia's hip ached like it had already been set ablaze.

The others began rushing in behind them, and Tassia was impressed that this shelter had a separate room for the monarchy. It was well-supplied with comfortable furnishings, including two large beds on either side of the room.

Tassia collapsed onto the bed, grateful and relieved. Sam left her with his sister so that he could take stock of everyone coming in. When they were satisfied that they had everyone and the doors were sealed, Sam returned to the two women.

"We've got everyone. Let's hope this one doesn't last any longer than the last."

Santrini's curiosity was piqued, and they recounted the tale of the siege on Nalea's castle.

"I received a bird this morning, not long before your arrival, and it stated that there had been a similar attack on our palace just after I left. It was short-lived, nothing more than a failed assassination attempt. I suspect these are the very dragons responsible, hopefully only passing through on their return journey."

"I hope they haven't found out where you are," Sam cautioned. "You will have become more of a target than our parents, or even me, since I'm sure most people suspect that I am dead."

"Yes, Mother is beyond her childbearing years now. There are always Father's bastards — he has fifteen now — but I do not know if the court would be willing to change the laws simply to accept one of them as an heir."

"What would happen if the dragons succeeded?" Tassia asked. "What would that mean for the kingdom?"

"I do not know if there is a contingency for that. I suppose it is worth exploring, and I will ask when we arrive home."

"I'm beginning to hope, for once, that we actually make it there now."

"You said on the way here that you preferred death by dragon above all else," Tassia said playfully.

"I'm not so sure about the red clan. The blues can devour me any day."

"You encountered blue dragons as well?" Santrini asked.

"Yes. We have had more than our share of dragons. That's what makes this so unreal."

"It is unusual for them to be so involved in human politics," Santrini commented. "As you suggested, it is unlikely that they are acting of their own accord with these attacks. But who could be sending them?"

"Your council hasn't had any ideas?"

"I have not had the chance to discuss it with them."

They settled into silence for a time, and Tassia got Sam to help her with the balm again while Santrini watched on impassively. Tassia rolled her trousers away from the worst section, while Sam worked the balm as he had become accustomed to doing. He helped her get comfortable again afterward, propping some of the extra pillows around her to help ease the pressure on her hip. He kissed her cheek and stroked her long braid as she settled in to rest.

"You're right," Santrini finally admitted. "You *are* in love with her. Mother and Father have certainly grown close over the years, but he would never tend to her the way you tend to Tassia."

"She has saved my life in more ways than one."

"Well, my brother, I do believe we have some time for you to share the tale."

Sam had had some time to gather his thoughts and began telling her of the places he had been — only the worst of them — beginning with the first and ending with his time spent at Hetia's.

"That was where I met Tassia, when Nalea sent the army to clear the colony."

He described the darkness of the place and the darkness of his soul, doing his best to convey how Tassia's very presence had been able to drive it back and how her simple touch had brought warmth back to his life. He described his time in Nalea's court and how his service to her mirrored his time in the dark colony.

"That time we spent in her garden brought me back to life, and the time I spent in Wheat Sky was the freest of my life."

"The demons you have faced…" San said, shaking her head in disbelief. "And yet you still say it was worth it?"

"It wasn't a nightmare the whole time."

A servant brought dinner in to them, and while they ate, Sam began to describe some of the beauty he had seen.

"Tell her about the desert," Tassia urged.

Sam did his best, but words still failed him, so he went to his bag and retrieved the painting Tassia had given him.

"This is stunning," Santrini said. "You have such tales to tell, and I do hope that our parents see the worth in your experience."

"Do you?"

"You wish to forge peace between Nalea and our kingdom. I assume your intention is to continue that work and build allies for Mountain Song in these fantastic places we have never even heard of."

"Nothing would make me happier," he said. "As long as I could do it with Tassia by my side."

"My brother, you are a fool, but I think your ideas are worth considering."

Tassia and Sam spent the remainder of their evening telling Santrini about their time together and the plans they had begun to make in hopes of being able to stay together.

"I like my position in the court," Santrini admitted, "and I would prefer not to have to defer my status to you. They have been grooming me to lead since I was born, and it is clear that you have all but lost that ability. I think it would be in my interest as well as yours to help you achieve what you desire. And I think that if our parents will not let you have Tassia directly, they will accept your proposal to wed Nalea. They can say nothing about your mistresses. Tassia is certainly worth more than some of Father's women."

"I have not been near our parents in far too long, but you seem far more reasonable than they are — perhaps it's because you are so young, but I think it has more to do with your character."

"We both seem to have inherited a certain defiant spirit," Santrini agreed. "I have been able to push for far more freedom than most would imagine, like coming here to meet you. Some of my freedom I can thank you for, but some of it I have contrived on my own."

"It seems to me that you like your power — you wear it well — without abusing it the way our parents do."

"I would advise not suggesting that to anyone beyond this room, but they can be draconian," she said, smirking. "They are far too resistant to change, and a kingdom cannot thrive under that kind of rule."

"You'll help then?" Sam asked. His voice rang with hope.

"I shall do what I can," she promised, stifling a yawn.

Tassia awoke in the middle of the night, disoriented, exhausted and in pain, and found that Santrini was sitting by the fire. She got up and joined the girl while she applied the last of her balm to her hip.

"Why are you awake?" Tassia said to the girl.

"There are many things to think about," Santrini replied. "I am amazed you can sleep with all that we will face shortly."

"We're exhausted. We've been in the wilderness for a month and spent over a week of that time running from our enemies. Sam and I have already mulled these problems over and have come to terms with them."

"It is not going to be easy," Santrini admitted. She stood perfectly erect, wrapped in a thick night robe, and maintained a steady gaze on the dying embers.

"Why do you want to help him?"

"He wants to bring peace. He wants to be a part of the court and to benefit the kingdom. He just does not want to do it the way our parents believe he should. I am sure you can see where he gets his fool-hearted nature. Both of our parents are so stubborn, but they are blind to it. It is no wonder they clashed with Sam to the point that it drove him out. Everything he has done has elevated my station — his self-exile is quite likely the reason I exist at all."

"He has some unconventional ideas. And I *am* low-born," Tassia cautioned. "Perhaps not what some countries would consider untouchable, but certainly a far cry from nobility."

"You are still a woman of honour," Santrini said. "I can see your loyalty, and I doubt that it is limited to my brother. Your tales of battle prove your courage, and I have no doubts that you would rise within the courts of your homeland even if you were not a confidante of your queen. I am willing to make allowances, even if my parents are not. We shall see if we can convince them."

"Thank you, San. We'd begun to lose hope. This last month has been beautiful, but desperately so."

Tassia and Sam stood together outside the thick steel gates to the palace. She could feel him tremble. The imposing walls of the palace jutted out from the terraced mountainside and were made of dazzling white marble that glinted in the sun. This was the strength of the dynasty. She squeezed his hand as royal guards exited the palace and approached them. Santrini had ridden ahead of them that morning to prepare the king and queen for what to expect on Sam's return, while he remained with the slow-moving convoy. Now, she appeared, quickly overtaking the castle guards as they came to collect her brother.

"You will be shown to your quarters and remain under guard there until the court is ready to accept you," Santrini explained, watching Sam closely. "I have brought your statement to the king and queen — that you wish to maintain freedom while serving the kingdom and that you still do not covet the throne. They are considering it now and will speak with you in front of the court once they have come to a decision."

"That doesn't sound promising."

"There is still room to negotiate, and I will try to guide you in that regard." A playful smile danced across her lips. "Do not despair, my brother."

Sam embraced Tassia and gave her a quick kiss before Santrini and the guards escorted him into the palace. Tassia was led back to the estate where she and the rest of the convoy were being housed in small but comfortable quarters. She was looking forward to the rest and to a final resolution. The dragon siege at the border had been another short one, but sleeping in the comfortable space overnight had gone a long way to easing the pain in her hip. She was now under the care of her host's healer and had a new balm to help speed her recovery.

She quickly set to work, making use of the facilities to wash all of her travel clothes and scrub her armour to a gleaming shine, knowing she would have to present herself to the court before long. She was clean, although her clothing was still a little damp, when the summons came that it was time for her to testify on Sam's behalf yet again.

Tassia's escort ushered her into a handsome cab and brought her across the grand estate of the palace. Nalea's towers in the centre of the city rose mightily from the prairie in a grand display, and the grounds in Mountain Song were equally grand and dazzling in their lush greenness, but sprawled across the terraced slope of a mountain overlooking the city. Everything was richly detailed and emitted a warm glow, but it offered no comfort to Tassia as her footfalls echoed across the marble floors.

The looming doors to the court hall were pushed open, and Tassia's heart began to vibrate when she saw the theatre crowded with nobles and the king and queen seated at the far end with Sam kneeling at centre. Santrini stood to the side, near her parents. With all four Teslerins in the room, the resemblance became unmistakable. Both Teslerin children had their father's grey eyes and tall stature. Santrini was thin and blonde like the king, while Sam had inherited his mother's thick torso and dark locks.

Tassia stopped at the threshold and bowed to one knee. She stared down at her boot, not allowing herself to make eye contact, while she waited to be summoned to the proceedings by the monarchs. She breathed deeply, trying to calm herself.

"You may enter," King Dantrin said. "Rise and give your name."

"Your Grace," she obliged, finally standing. "I am Tassia Raven of Wheat Sky."

He nodded tersely. "Come forward and address the court."

She walked uncertainly to the centre of the room and knelt beside Sam, unsure of their customs. She hoped she wasn't making too much of a fool of herself.

"Rise and state your relationship to the prisoner."

She tried to contain her despair at hearing the word, realizing things had gone badly before she arrived. She gathered her courage, preparing for battle — this time, it was her wits, not her sword, that would have to save them.

"I am his betrothed." She spoke in a neutral tone and kept her gaze on the monarchs, trying to keep her posture relaxed enough that she didn't come across as defiant.

A brief murmur went through the room, but silenced quickly as the king continued his interrogation.

"How long has this been so?"

"Just over a fortnight, Your Grace. Though we have been lovers for almost a year."

More murmuring and a few shocked gasps, but the king maintained fierce control of the proceedings, barely pausing with his questions.

"How long have you known the truth of Samleni's identity?"

Tassia had been staring ahead at a space between the king and queen, but now she met the king's gaze directly.

"Your Grace, I'm quite certain I was the last person in all of Wheat Sky to learn the truth."

"Do not toy with me, girl. You are an agent of a hostile kingdom, and I will have you executed where you stand if you lie to me."

"I am not lying, Your Grace," she replied carefully, keeping her fury contained. "My queen delivered the truth only after she forced Sam to send word to you that he had been found and was returning."

"How long did your queen know who she had in her midst?"

"I—" she paused uncertainly, not wanting to complicate things with lies or the truth. Deciding it would end badly regardless, she went with the truth. "I don't know for certain, Your Grace, but I suspect she knew in the autumn. Sam met with her privately, at her command, near summer's end."

"And yet you maintain you did not discover the truth until the winter?"

"Yes, Your Grace. My best friend is an insufferable gossip, but she keeps most of it to herself if she thinks it will upset me. Sam's identity was revealed by the Teslerin crest on the ring he carried, and while the ring meant nothing to most of us, my gossipy friend brought news of it to the queen, who recognized it. The truth, however, was kept from me."

"Very well." The king leaned forward. "Tell me, girl, why do you think it took your queen so long to bring news of Samleni's whereabouts to this court?"

"I suspect Sam manipulated her somehow," Tassia said immediately, casting Sam an apologetic glance, but he remained kneeling with his head bowed and his expression concealed. "He wanted to remain with me and likely stalled her until the weather made the journey here impossible. Once the mountain passes were blocked for the winter, her hands would have been tied. I'm sure she kept his secret after that as a service to me."

"We have been told that you are a confidante of your queen. Are you truly in such favour with her?"

"We have been friends since girlhood, and I helped her win her crown."

King Dantrin nodded dismissively. "That will be all."

Tassia fell silent, but remained beside Sam as the king resumed questioning his son.

"Samleni, what do you have to say in response to your lover's remarks?" The king's tone was accusatory and laced with menace.

"What she says is true," Sam answered evenly, keeping all emotion out of his voice.

"You manipulated one of our enemies in order to stay in their midst?"

"Yes, Father. I wanted to remain with Tassia, and suspected these very charges if I was ever to return here." He had almost kept his emotions in check, but suddenly he blurted, "Can you blame me?"

"Silence, you insufferable fool!" the king barked. "You have made a mockery of this court for long enough. You renounce this woman now and take your place in this court, or the treason charges stand."

"I committed no treason," Sam said fiercely, refusing to address the rest of his father's demands.

"That is for this court to determine," Queen Kelteni said, finally speaking up. "You have weak evidence and no further witnesses, Samleni."

"Mother, if I may speak...?" Santrini requested.

"You wish to testify on your brother's behalf?"

"Yes, Your Grace." Santrini moved so that she stood before her parents, between them and Sam and Tassia.

"I refuse to believe there's no compromise possible," Santrini said, addressing her parents directly.

"Your brother made his decision, and he is a traitor to this kingdom," the king snapped.

Tassia was impressed at Santrini's graceful composure. She kept her hands folded comfortably in front of her and her expression calm in the face of her father's fury.

"Father, do you really wish to execute your only son? I have already assured you that our monarchy's bloodline is secure with me, so I ask that you consider other options."

"What would you have me do?"

"I have spoken with my wayward brother at some length. I do not believe you can convince him to return to this court, and, as foolish as they are, I respect his convictions. If you were to succeed in bringing him back, I do not believe that would be in the best interest of this monarchy."

"Explain yourself," Dantrin growled.

She gave her father a shallow bow and continued, "Sam has been out of our lands and away from the customs of the court since he was a boy, and he has become accustomed to life on his own, making decisions with only himself in mind and, to some degree, taking orders from other leaders. Whatever leadership abilities he once had, I believe he has lost. He seems to defer most of his decisions to his escort, the one he proclaims to love."

"You question his ability to lead then?"

"Yes, Father."

"You have not yet explained why I should spare him. A poor leader is no better than a traitor."

"Give him a secondary role in the courts. You have already chosen to bypass him for succession. His return does not mean that has to change; I can still be queen."

"He has forsaken this kingdom and should be punished accordingly."

"He never forsook this kingdom, only your wish that he marry whomever you chose. His lover is a high-ranking soldier in Nalea's army and is on track to become a strategist. She is also friends with her queen, and Nalea will be quick to elevate her to a noble position and make her a lady in the court."

Dantrin mulled over this information, glancing briefly at Kelteni. For a fleeting moment, Sam held out hope that Santrini had found a solution. Finally, Dantrin addressed Tassia directly.

"What is your lineage?"

Sam winced.

"I'm a soldier," she answered promptly.

"And your family? Soldiers as well?"

"Farmers," Sam said. As the word fell from his mouth, hope vanished again.

"Farmers!" The king bristled with rage. "San, what are you having at? I do not care what foolish titles the queen of a foreign land gives the woman, she is still barely removed from swine! No member of this family will mix with someone so low-born."

Santrini remained unflinching, and Sam wondered what she had left.

"Very well, let him denounce his title and his claim to your throne, and extend that to exclude any of his heirs from laying claim to this kingdom. You can keep your son, I can have a brother, and nothing has been lost — no honour risked."

"He has been in the service of another queen," Kelteni pointed out.

"Mother, Father, use that to your advantage instead of using it to condemn him. Nalea is a reasonable queen and a far better leader and potential ally than the dolt she replaced. See Sam's actions not as service under her, but as service to you as an ambassador of this kingdom. Instead of preserving enemies, use this as a chance to cultivate new allies.

"Sam left here thirteen years ago to defy you," Santrini continued, "but he remained at large to search for a reason that would justify his actions. He has found that reason in Tassia Raven and he will not relinquish her now. He will take execution before he will let you remove her from his life. Let him have her, but keep your son to help expand our kingdom's influence. Since the moment he left these borders and you discovered a second heir, there was never any doubt in your mind that he would never sit as king on this throne. Nothing has changed, except that you get your son back and perhaps gain a daughter-in-law."

"What she says is true," Sam jumped in quickly, awed by his sister's manoeuvring. "I will relinquish my right to the throne and extend that vow to all my heirs until time grinds this kingdom into dust. You will never have to worry about a challenge. San can have it all and her heirs can continue it. I would be overjoyed to serve you in the courts, to serve my sister, and Queen Nalea broached the subject of a truce before sending me here. To be able to act as an ambassador for this kingdom and help forge new allies would make me proud to have returned."

The monarchs shared another glance. This time it was Dantrin who spoke, but he addressed his comments to Tassia.

"Any fool can see your integrity, daughter of farmers or not, so tell me, girl, will your queen make you a lady in the court?"

"I can't be certain," Tassia said. "I know that she has stepped far beyond her duty in order to help Sam, to ensure his safety and to help us stay together. She has no family and considers me almost a sister. She has mentioned a minor ladyship when I complete my strategist training, and she intends to make a commander of me."

"You do not wish to be a lady in the court," Kelteni commented, gaining insight from what Tassia left unsaid.

"I—Your Grace, I *like* the rush of battle and wish to remain a soldier in some capacity, but I don't know if my queen will let me have my military position as well as such a noble title. My sincerest hope would be that she will allow both."

"You would choose the military over Sam? You would forsake a noble title even if it allowed you to be with my son?"

Tassia paused and looked to Sam, still kneeling before the whole of his kingdom's court, and made her decision once and for all.

"I would take the title whatever the consequence, Your Grace, if it means you will let us be together."

Sam bowed his head even further, trying to mask a broad grin. His parents exchanged one final glance before Dantrin delivered his decision.

"Those are the terms, then. The girl becomes a noblewoman in her homeland, and you and your heirs until eternity denounce any claim to this throne. Furthermore, you will obtain peace with Nalea for us. These are the conditions we lay before you, and if you succeed, the girl is yours and you will find a place among our ambassadors."

Sam grinned wildly as he stood.

"Your Grace, consider it done," he insisted jubilantly. "I will send a bird to Nalea immediately with your terms, and we will at once begin to negotiate peace."

Sam didn't wait for a reply and embraced Tassia, kissing her deeply. Santrini watched a glimmer of an amused smirk surface on her mother's face, one free of malice and perhaps even containing a trace of joy. Tassia and Sam wiped tears of gratitude and relief from each other's eyes, grinning madly, and shared one final, quick embrace before Tassia was escorted away again, back to the estate with the rest of her people, while Sam joined his father to finalize the terms.

Sam walked with his father to the estate's modest training grounds to meet with Tassia. It was the first time the king had come to the estate in the three days since Sam's trial had ended, and Sam was still worried that a misstep might incite the king's wrath and undo their fragile victory. A pair of guards trailed them. Sam had started to grow accustomed to their presence. He was only allowed to see Tassia during chaperoned visits, and she was continuing to be housed at the estate with her comrades until Nalea confirmed whether or not she would grant Tassia the title of lady. Dantrin wouldn't be convinced of his decision until they received word from Nalea about Tassia's status and the prospects for peace, and it would be a few days still before they would hear back. He couldn't change his mind about the matter of succession, however, as his advisors had helped him draft the decree mere hours after the decision had been made and Sam had eagerly signed it.

"Yes, I can see that you are no longer a true leader," Dantrin growled at Sam's insistence that it had been the right decision. "You were too young when you left and too long in the wild away from civilization. If not for the fact that your looks have barely changed since the day you left, I'd scarcely believe you to be my son."

"My education has been lacking, Your Grace," Sam admitted. "I was preparing to enter the university in Wheat Sky before returning. I have a keen interest in astronomy."

The king harrumphed, "Absolutely not! You will study here, and you will study politics. You will study a lot of things, for that matter. That girl of yours has better manners than you do."

That only made Sam grin, and Dantrin's scowl deepened.

"You may study what you like on your own time away from here," the king conceded, "but you will be properly trained for the job you desire before I let you beyond my realm again."

"Of course, Your Grace."

They reached the training grounds to find Tassia going through a drill with her troops. The pain in her hip had eased with rest and the comforts of a real bed, making it possible for her to train properly again. A small group of soldiers was sparring in full armour, and Tassia was at their centre. The steel shone off her helmet in the afternoon sun as she dodged, pivoted, thrust and slashed. With her braid tucked in, her stature was the only thing that gave her away.

As the practicing soldiers began to notice the king's presence, stillness spread over them like a wave. They first stopped and turned, then dropped respectfully to one knee to honour their host. The king and Sam moved through their ranks to where Tassia stood, and she removed her helmet and came toward them.

"Your Grace," she said, greeting the king with a bow. She grinned up at Sam, and he put an arm around her shoulders, pulling her into a quick kiss.

"Father has opted to join me on my visit here today. He'd like to speak with you again, so can we retreat to your quarters?"

"Yes, of course."

She walked with them inside, and Sam noticed she still limped faintly.

"You're still not quite better, I see."

"Not yet. Good enough to fight properly, at least, so that's something."

Her quarters consisted of a single room, but it was larger than the others', with a desk near the window and a set of chairs by the hearth. The pair of guards stood just inside the doors, much as Santrini's personal guard had done on the road. Sam and the king sat in the chairs while Tassia stripped off her armour and stood before them.

"I trust you find your accommodations adequate," the king said.

"Yes, of course. Your Grace is quite generous. This is much bigger than my quarters at home."

The king raised an inquisitive eyebrow, and Sam jumped in to explain.

"She's not a reserve, Father. She's in the standing army and lives in the barracks. All of the soldiers live in pairs, sharing huts about half the size of this room."

Dantrin turned in his seat to watch his son.

"Then where under the moons were you sleeping?"

"At first I had a bed in the dorms — in the slave quarters until my release — and then at the workhouse until I earned enough to rent a shack about half the size of her hut. I was a farmhand."

"And you admit this with pride?" The king was flabbergasted.

"It was better than sleeping in a ditch, and you can be certain I did plenty of that over the years."

"You would be wise to stop bragging about such vagrancy," the king warned. He finally turned his attention back to Tassia. "All right, you were not sharing a residence with him, but you've admitted to being lovers for quite some time."

"Yes, Your Grace," Tassia answered immediately, even as she felt her colour rise. "We were together infrequently at first — when my roommate was away and when Sam had that little shack of his own. It became more serious on the journey here."

"You've been sharing his bed since you left Wheat Sky, have you?"

"Yes, Your Grace," she said softly, fidgeting, but maintaining eye contact. "We did not expect to receive your blessing, no matter how tentative, and tried to make the most of the time we had."

The king nodded gravely. "It is as I feared. Girl, are you with child?"

"I—" Tassia stammered, wanting to answer but not knowing how.

"Father, please!" Sam protested. "It doesn't matter. I won't be your heir, and we'll be wed soon enough."

"We do not know that yet," the king snapped.

"What difference does it make if she is?" Sam asked. "San has said you now have more bastards than I have years of absence from the realm."

"You know the custom."

"You can't be serious," Sam balked. "If Nalea won't agree to your terms, we can just send her back to Wheat Sky and no one has to know."

"*I* will know."

"I wouldn't know how to tell," Tassia interrupted them, bringing the discussion back to the king's inquiry. "But I don't think so. And Sam and I haven't been together like that since we entered your realm. We were always sharing rooms with San."

"There," Sam said, satisfied. "She says she isn't, so let's not worry about it until after we hear from Nalea."

"She also says she does not know how to tell. I am going to send your mother to speak with her. Come along, Samleni. You can return with Kelti this evening."

"For heaven's sake, Father, just let her be!"

Dantrin was already on his feet and moving toward the door.

"I have made more than enough allowances for you. Now come along."

Tassia stopped Sam in the doorway, concerned.

"What does he mean, Sam? What custom?"

"There's this idiotic law about bastards; an unwed man is forbidden from having any. The man, of course, is not punished for it. The bastard is — and sometimes, depending on the man involved, the woman as well."

Tassia grew concerned, but Sam had become livid with a flash of insight.

"Is that why you agreed to this?" Sam accused, turning on the king. "You were hoping to use that foolish custom to do away with her before we even heard from Nalea, weren't you?"

The king said nothing and continued down the hall, his guards close at hand, leaving Sam no choice but to follow him. Tassia stood in her doorway, trembling, as she watched them go.

When Sam returned with his mother that evening, Santrini was with him as well. She was as upset as her brother when she learned of the scheme. Tassia was worried she wouldn't have the right answers. Before leaving her parents' home when she was practically still a girl, Tassia hadn't asked many questions about her womanhood and her mother hadn't offered any answers. After her sister's pregnancy had gone so poorly, the topic had become difficult to talk about in her family, so she just hadn't. While she didn't feel like anything had changed since they'd left Wheat Sky, she was quickly informed that at first, nothing would seem different.

Santrini and Sam were both relieved when Tassia's answers to the queen's questions proved that she had been right in her assumption. By determining Tassia's cycle, the queen had concluded that she hadn't been with Sam during the crucial period.

"Does this mean you'll still accept her if Nalea grants her the title?" Sam asked. "Or will Father dig up some other obsolete law to try to get rid of her?"

"I do not believe there are any others he can use against you," Kelteni replied, sounding apologetic.

"So you are sincere in accepting her and Father is not?" Santrini asked.

"I think it is less a matter of sincerity and more a matter of denial," the queen replied with a wry smile. "Now if you have any sense, do not lay a hand on the girl until after you are wed!"

Sam nodded miserably, hoping that wouldn't be too much longer.

"Your father's pride is wounded, Sam, but he will come around. I am overjoyed to have you back, and I look forward to the sound of babes bringing some warmth to this palace," the queen admitted. "Try to be careful until you are wed, but I will do what I can to dissuade Dantrin from pursuing the matter any further."

Sam and Santrini burst into the courtyard during a training drill, both calling excitedly for Tassia. Santrini's rare exuberance reminded them that she was still just a girl. Santrini held a small scroll in her hand and held it out to Tassia when they reached her. Tassia looked at the scroll and saw Nalea's seal, neatly cut to read the message, and guessed what it must be.

"She's coming here," Sam said, unable to contain his excitement. "She's bringing a convoy of advisors to work out a truce, and she's also bringing you a title!"

Tassia grinned but was too excited to speak.

"She said she would bestow you with any title that would suit our parents," Santrini added, grinning.

"And she expects both of us to return with her," Sam continued. "She will stay until a peace accord is reached and then wants you back for your strategist training. I'll come too to help deliver the accord to the court."

"And your parents? Your father — does he have any objections?"

"He's furious, but his hands are tied. He put it on paper that as long as you were elevated to a noble rank and peace is reached, then we may wed. He has no grounds to turn back now. Mother has said the chaperoned visits can end — you can join me at the palace, if you like."

Tassia grinned and embraced Sam, sharing a deep and unrestrained kiss. She hugged Santrini, profusely thanking the girl for all she had done to help them.

"Nonsense," Santrini insisted. "I agree with Mother — this costs us nothing and brings us a fuller family. Father will finally calm down once he has physical proof of your title and of the peace accord. His conditions have been — or will soon be — met."

Tassia read over the full note from Nalea, still grinning wildly, but she saw she had some work to do as well. Nalea had requested that Traxin lead the bulk of their convoy back toward Wheat Sky to meet her party and provide a heavier guard through the mountains.

"It seems I've got arrangements to make with Traxin today," Tassia said. "But meet me after dinner, and I will come back with you to the palace."

Sam and Santrini left her to her work, but both returned again in the evening to escort her back to the palace. Traxin and the convoy would head out in three days' time to meet Nalea, but they had decided that a half dozen of the convoy would stay behind to serve Tassia — equal numbers of servants and soldiers. They would relocate to the palace with her, removing the burden from their hosts of keeping her safe. They did not need to give Dantrin any further excuse to resent or persecute her.

"I've got some work ahead of me," Sam said to her as they rode back to the palace. "I've been thinking about the dragons, and I suspect there's a connection between the attacks. I'll need to seek out more information to be certain, but after speaking with my parents and their guard, I'm certain the attack here was identical to the one on Nalea."

"So the dragons were likely sent by the same person."

"It's likely, and I suspect the Krunleks."

Tassia sat alert and faced him. "Yes, they share borders with both kingdoms. Perhaps you should look into whether there have been attacks on any of the other kingdoms bordering them."

Sam nodded. "I will send birds to all of their neighbours and go to them if they confirm attacks. First, I will bring my theory to my father and Nalea once we have them both here for the truce."

"A common enemy is a good way to build an allegiance," Tassia agreed.

Tassia had been in the library studying the books for her strategist training when she received word of her queen's arrival. Nalea had to first pay her respects to the host court, and then Tassia was to meet her in her state room before that evening's welcome feast.

Tassia retreated to the apartment she shared with Sam, far too excited to work any further. She washed up and changed into her best robes, unsure if she would have time to return to her room before dinner. She had been warned that she and Sam would be guests of honour for both nations, as Nalea had suggested through her messengers that she wanted to use their union as a token of peace.

Tassia grew more nervous as she waited. Eventually she moved out into the hallway, pacing through the palace and followed closely by one of her guards. The three remaining soldiers rotated watching over her, though it was really more of a formality, since she was fully secure in the care of her hosts. King Dantrin had given up trying to drive her out, slowly warming up to the idea of her and Sam's union, though he was still prone to fits of rage over the arrangement.

She finally roamed her way to the wing of state rooms. It turned out to be easy to find Nalea's. A guard she recognized was stationed outside the room.

"Livia!" she cried out gleefully, racing to see her friend.

"Good to see you," Livia said, returning her greeting with a hug.

"Nalea never said you would be here."

"She wanted to surprise you. Butch is here, too, and a few others from the barracks. It's been slow this summer, with the commanders training new soldiers to build our unit back up. She also wanted me along as part of my strategist training. I suspect she also thought you would like to see some familiar faces when you *wed Sam*."

"Can you believe that's actually going to happen? I certainly can't."

"I can't believe you agreed to be roped in," Livia teased.

"Nalea certainly knew what she was doing when she sent me as his escort," Tassia admitted.

"I'm happy to hear that. I'm also happy that you'll be coming back with us. You can be there when Butch and I finally wed!"

"You've committed to it then, have you?"

"As soon as I complete my training in the autumn, Nalea will remove me from battle and have me with her in the war room."

"Butch will still be fighting though, won't he?"

"Yes, so we'll keep our hut for now. But you should get in there; Nalea is waiting for you."

Tassia was surprised to see that Nalea's antechamber was full of her advisors and the table scattered with documents.

"Ah, here she is!" Nalea said, smiling broadly and spreading her arms in welcome. "Come and greet the court, future Duchess of Winterberry."

Tassia's shock was unrestrained, and Nalea laughed merrily. "Duchess?"

"You are my sister, even if not by blood, and I've been instructed that it is the highest title I can give you and allow you to remain a military strategist. I have confirmed with your future in-laws that the title is sufficient."

"I—" Tassia stumbled, still shocked. "This can't be possible," she finally said.

"There is a royal estate, long disused, on the edge of Winterberry, not far from your brother's homestead, as I understand, and we will have it restored for you by the autumn. The estate profits from extensive farmland, and I have negotiated with your hosts to provide a number of hands to help work the land and the estate. I will match their numbers, and you and Sam will have a solid base in my lands. Your specific tasks will be decided once you have completed your training. I believe that will give you both plenty of time to adjust and begin to envision your future."

"I can still fight, then? You said I can still be a strategist — does that mean I'll still see battle, too?"

Nalea smiled and nodded. "I know you've still got plenty of fight left in you. With the way you handled yourself against the Krunleks, in the war and on the way here, I would be a fool to pull you from a battle position before you were ready."

Nalea moved around the large table to where she stood to embrace her and usher her to the table where all of the necessary documents were laid out.

"Read it all carefully, but you'll find that it's all as I've stated," Nalea said. "Then we sign." She gestured to the only three men in the room that Tassia didn't recognize. "These are our host's emissaries, and they will bring the copies to the Teslerins for final approval before the feast tonight. We will introduce you officially tonight as a duchess."

Tassia sat heavily at the table, shaking and nervous, nearly crying from the fear, anxiety and joy.

"Does Sam know?"

"He was present with his parents and sister when I delivered these documents. You will be wed soon, Tassia, as part of our treaty. I have convinced the king that it will be a strong gesture of commitment to the accord and move to strengthen the new bond between nations."

"Have you spoken much of peace?"

"We will be discussing the details of the accord tomorrow."

Tassia nodded and scanned through the documents, finally taking up the quill and signing herself into nobility. Nalea added her signature, and they watched as the half dozen witnesses added theirs as well — three representatives from each kingdom. The Mountain Song delegation then left to take their copies to their king. Tassia was still shaking as she watched them leave.

"It will be all right, Tass. There's a reason I insisted you both come back with me to Wheat Sky when I return," Nalea said, placing a comforting hand on Tassia's shoulder. "I wouldn't want you to end up feeling trapped here, and I chose the autumn to put you through your strategist tests so that it will be too late in the year to send you both back here. You'll get another winter together away from the direct influence of Sam's parents."

"I think that's probably best for everyone," Tassia agreed, exhaling a shaky breath. "It will give His Grace more time to adjust to this without us here."

"I suspected as much — and it will give you the better part of the summer to work in your garden."

Tassia was surprised, looking up at her confused.

"I've done as you asked and had three servants tending it for you under Livia's direction. Your hut is still empty, and if you'd like to stay there until the end of the harvest, I will grant you that. I have not failed to notice how vital that garden was in all that's going on here today."

Tassia grinned. She hadn't thought of her garden since leaving Wheat Sky, but was relieved at the thought of returning home to such normalcy. She realized how much she missed getting her hands dirty.

EPILOGUE

They had just finished setting up camp, a week away from the borders of Mountain Song, when one of the messengers brought Nalea a note. Nalea hadn't noticed the bird's arrival and was surprised to receive anything while they were en route. She smirked and looked across the fire to where Sam sat with Tassia.

"It's from Sletrini," she said. "Their convoy will be arriving shortly after we return home. Prince Tanz is very interested in exploring my proposal."

"You sent him a bird with that in it?" Sam sputtered.

"Oh, heavens no! I sent a trusted messenger after I sent a rook to his parents." She tossed the message into the flames and smiled. "You're proving to be quite useful, Samleni. I hope your father is beginning to understand that."

"He seemed impressed over my theory about the Krunleks and the dragons."

Sam was returning to Wheat Sky with a tutor and a mission. Once he'd received a little more training, he would be investigating the Krunleks' activities to see if he could link them to the dragon attacks. He had already received word from Sianshin that their monarchy had been subjected to a similar attack, and he had heard a rumour that a dragon ambush on leaders to the north of the Krunleks had been successful. Confirming a link between the attacks and the Krunleks wouldn't be necessary for all the surrounding lands, but Sam wanted to ferret out the truth. The combined efforts of the Sianshin, Mountain Song and Wheat Sky empires could defeat the Krunleks, but Sam wanted to ensure the Krunleks didn't manipulate any of their neighbours into getting involved as allies. It would be his duty in the coming year to seek the truth and build an alliance among the nations bordering Krunlek territory.

Tassia sat quietly, nestled against Sam, and listened to them talk. She was just relieved to be going home to the peace of her hut and her garden. She looked forward to the end of the harvest, when they would be moving to Winterberry. Her sisters had promised to make the journey — Varia was confident that she was finally well enough for the trip — to spend the winter solstice with them at their new estate and finally meet the newest member of their family.

Sam was still getting used to the idea of being part of a family again — not just one family, but two. Tassia had sent the news of her title and her marriage to her side before the ink had even dried on the peace accord, and she had received their jubilant replies just before leaving Mountain Song. Only Janso had met Sam, but he expressed that he was pleased that things had worked out. He looked forward to Tassia and Sam's help keeping their parents' garden going. Their estate would be close enough for Tassia to still work the land of her childhood.

Livia and Butch joined them at their fire just after dinner, and while Butch shared the latest gossip, Livia and Tassia compared notes on their strategist training. They'd been riding together with their tutor and studying while they travelled. Sam had been doing much the same, none of them wanting to waste any time growing into their new roles. Sam was only an honorary ambassador of Mountain Song until he could return in the spring to take his exams.

He was fretting over one of his books, reading by the firelight, when Livia and Butch turned in for the night. Tassia took his hand and gave him a reassuring smile.

"You've got nearly a year," she said.

He smiled and kissed her forehead, closing the book. Nalea grinned and watched them walk to their tent hand in hand, as they had every night since their union had sealed peace between their kingdoms.

ACKNOWLEDGEMENTS

I must give thanks to the What-If Fairy, my garden, soil under my nails, and Smaug for getting the idea going. I want to thank the Editors' Association of Canada and Ryerson's publishing program for making me an editor, which had the desired side effect of making me a better writer. Many thanks to NaNoWriMo for helping me maintain the ability to turn off my internal editor at will and for providing me with time to write this book and many others.

I want to thank my husband for giving me the space to create, my daughter for being adorably hilarious and my dogs for keeping me company through the long days.

On the more technical side of putting this book together, I want to thank Marg Gilks of Scripta Word Services for helping me fill in the gaps and making the story more exciting; Greg Ioannou at Iguana for taking another chance on me; Amanda Plyley, Kate Unrau and Meghan Behse, also of Iguana fame, for keeping everything on track and coming up with great cover art; and Kathryn Willms, my talented copy editor, for bringing out the best in my words. Second thanks to Amanda, for doubling as proofreader and being the book's last line of defense against typos. And many thanks to Bev Bambury for helping take the ick factor out of promotion. You guys are all kinds of awesome with a side order of brilliant.

Finally, thank you to everyone on the Contributors page for supporting the book's fundraising campaign, and a special thank you to every proud owner of a copy of my first book, *Dragon Whisperer*. Your encouragement keeps me going.

CONTRIBUTORS

Janice Allen
Danielle Arbuckle
Matthew Bin
Al Bleeck
Ivy Courtney
Jessica Cowan
Marg Gilks
Anne Godlewski
Rosa Harrington
Maxine Henry
Rachel Kiernan
Cat London
Patricia MacDonald
Jeanne McKane
Susan Parkes
Rhonda Parrish
Giuseppina "nonna" Ricci
Louie Ricci
Susanne Ricci
Olivia Riccia
Jo Rogers
Gael Spivak
Ben Stoddard
Jack & Charlotte Thode
Janice Thode
Mike & Sofia Thode
Sharilynn Wardrop

Iguana Books
iguanabooks.com

If you enjoyed *After the Dragon Raid*...
Look for other books coming soon from Iguana Books! Subscribe to our blog for updates as they happen.

iguanabooks.com/blog/

You can also learn more about Vanessa Ricci-Thode and her upcoming work on her blog.

thodestool.com/blog/

If you're a writer ...
Iguana Books is always looking for great new writers, in every genre. We produce primarily ebooks but, as you can see, we do the occasional print book as well. Visit us at iguanabooks.com to see what Iguana Books has to offer both emerging and established authors.

iguanabooks.com/publishing-with-iguana/

If you're looking for another good book ...
All Iguana Books books are available on our website. We pride ourselves on making sure that every Iguana book is a great read.

iguanabooks.com/bookstore/

Visit our bookstore today and support your favourite author.

CPSIA information can be obtained at www.ICGtesting.com
Printed in the USA
LVOW12s2031171014

409330LV00004B/11/P